The world can't get enough of Miss Seeton

"A **most beguiling** protagonist!"
New York Times

"Miss Seeton gets into wild drama with fine touches of farce . . . This is a **lovely mixture of the funny and the exciting**."
San Francisco Chronicle

"This is not so much black comedy as black-currant comedy . . . **You can't stop reading. Or laughing**."
The Sun

"**Depth of description and lively characters** bring this English village to life."
Publishers Weekly

"Fun to be had with a **full cast of endearingly zany villagers** . . . and the ever gently intuitive Miss Seeton."
Kirkus Reviews

"Miss Seeton is the **most delight**
since Miss N
Ogden N

Miss Seeton

Quilts the Village

A MISS SEETON MYSTERY

Hamilton Crane

First published in 2017 by Farrago,
an imprint of Prelude Books Ltd
13 Carrington Road, Richmond, TW10 5AA, United Kingdom

www.farragobooks.com

ISBN: 978-1-911440-74-1

Have you read them all?

Treat yourself again to the first Miss Seeton novels—

Picture Miss Seeton
A night at the opera strikes a chord of danger when
Miss Seeton witnesses a murder . . . and paints a portrait
of the killer.

Miss Seeton Draws the Line
Miss Seeton is enlisted by Scotland Yard when her paintings
of a little girl turn the young subject into a model for murder.

Witch Miss Seeton
Double, double, toil and trouble sweep through the village
when Miss Seeton goes undercover . . . to investigate a local
witches' coven!

Turn to the end of this book for a full list of the series,
plus—on the last page—**exclusive access to
the Miss Seeton short story** that started it all.

Chapter One

"Welcome back, Miss Seeton!" Lady Colveden, emerging from the post office, sounded pleased and slightly relieved at the same time. Several weeks had passed since her ladyship's son and his bride had been handkerchief-fluttered on their honeymoon way by family and friends. Many guests had gone straight home after the wedding; Miss Seeton was one of those who had elected to make further visits in the north before returning to Kent. "Were the Highlands as spectacular as ever? And did you enjoy the Lake District? But of course you did, or you'd have come home sooner. I hope your friend—Miss Walkham, isn't it?—was well when you left."

Miss Seeton beamed. "Dear Anne, such a treat to see her again and spend a few days catching up, rather than relying on letters, and in so lovely a part of the country. And famous of course for *Swallows and Amazons*, which I had never read as a child—I was at art school when it first appeared—but so many people spoke of it in glowing terms that in the end I had to read it to find out why, especially as the second edition was illustrated by the author himself—and it was excellent."

Lady Colveden smiled. "Yes, the books were excellent, though I always found his technique for drawing people a touch bizarre. Julia didn't much care for the way you seldom saw more than the backs of their heads, and when Nigel was very young he used to talk of the children not having proper faces, and wondering if that was because they lived in the olden days, and he was glad he didn't."

"Dear Nigel." Again Miss Seeton beamed. "He and Louise looked so very happy. Have you heard from them? Are they well?"

"One postcard," said Nigel's fond mother, "and he forgot to put a stamp on so it took ages to arrive. But nothing dreadful seems to have happened to them." She smiled again. "Or to you, in the Lake District. Arthur Ransome captured the idea of the scenery very well, don't you think? And the sailing pictures have a good deal of atmosphere."

Miss Seeton, retired teacher of art, could not disagree. "I believe he never cared for faces because he found them difficult—but he does indeed capture atmosphere very well. We visited several places thought to be his original inspiration for the lake, and in more than one I felt I knew where I was almost before I was. There, I mean. Anne is a most careful driver, and very sensible about not letting herself become distracted, which a guided tour of the local sights might very well do. Pointing things out, that is, while still on the move rather than stopping in a convenient place to do so."

She chuckled. "Until she was told about the heron, I should add. After the telephone call I fear that on our unexpected journey to Blackpool she drove rather faster than her usual cautious speed."

"Heron?" Lady Colveden tried to look as if she understood. "Telephone call?"

"*Nyctanassa violacea.*" Miss Seeton was rather proud of not stumbling over the Latin. "Dear Anne promised—she is an enthusiastic bird-watcher—there would be much of interest, and to be sure to pack my binoculars, which of course I did.

And there was—quite as much as in Scotland. Many birds one does not see in these parts, and then a friend called to let her know that a yellow-crowned night heron had suddenly appeared on the beach just north of Blackpool. All the way from America. Caught up in high winds in the Gulf of Mexico, I understand, and the poor thing was blown on the deck of a cargo ship heading for England."

"I remember now." Her ladyship wrinkled her forehead. "Yes, the television news, one of those snippets at the end meant to leave you feeling more cheerful than the previous half hour ever does. Didn't the crew take care of it all the way across the Atlantic, only before they could hand it over to a bird sanctuary to be properly looked after, it escaped?"

"To be properly, or rather thoroughly, looked *at* rather than looked *after*." Miss Seeton smiled. "So fortunate that, by the time we arrived, the authorities had taken control of what had seemed, at first, likely to become a somewhat disorderly situation. Serious bird-watchers, I understand, often descend in their hundreds upon even the most distant locations should a sufficiently rare bird be spotted. There were people directing the traffic in a one-way system, and telling one where to park, and making everybody form a queue to approach the area where the bird was feeding, and letting no one stay for more than ten minutes."

Lady Colveden blinked. "When you'd dropped everything to drive all that way? I must say, that sounds rather unfair."

Miss Seeton gently shook her head. "One was allowed to start to queue again at the back, as many times as one wished. Every day—though suitable accommodation was a little difficult with so many people. But the organisation was excellent. We ourselves made three attempts before we achieved a sighting. Dear Anne is blessed with great patience and enthusiasm, as well as knowledge, and of course there was much more to see in the area beside the unfortunate bird. Some persons queued half a dozen times even when they already had—seen it, I mean. A night heron is apparently unknown in this country. One was tempted to move everywhere on tiptoe, and certainly to keep as quiet as possible."

So engrossed were the two ladies that they failed to notice the approach—almost an encroach—of two other ladies heading for the post office. One was tall and thin, with a face many would say reminded them of a horse. Her companion was shorter, and stout—many would call her dumpy—with snapping black eyes. On the post office threshold, their ears still flapping, the new arrivals paused to exchange speaking glances. Those who knew the Nuts (as equine Erica Nuttel and solid Norah Blaine are known in Plummergen) would have waited with impatience to learn what those glances were saying...

The post office is one of three general stores in Plummergen, and the largest. While Mr. Takeley the grocer and Mr. Welsted the draper stock many of the same items, with enough variety to keep all three establishments in business, there is no doubt as to which is the hub of village rumour and surmise. Mr. Stillman, the postmaster, has more floor space. He also has prime position in the main street—The Street—near the bus stop, so that anyone buying books, bacon, tinned goods or even stamps will have, should she (almost always she) wish, an excellent view of the comings, goings, and general doings of her fellow villagers.

The Street—wide, tree-lined, with no street lighting—runs in a gentle curve from north to south. Anyone who pops outside the post office (sometimes so crowded) for a breath of air has an excellent view along The Street, whether up or down, and of the movements of any stranger who might arrive on the bus. She will already know, or at least be able to guess, where a non-stranger is going. Usually she is making for the post office,

10

either to ascertain what might have happened during her absence, or else to dispense what gossip she has picked up in Brettenden, a small town six miles to the north where Plummergen shops when it cannot find what it requires at home. The Brettenden bus (or buses) these days will make the trip just three times a week. One journey has been authorised by the council; the other two are covered by the public-spirited courtesy of Crabbe's Garage, next to the post office and close to the bus stop, and perhaps these days the bus stop's *raison d'être*.

Those with a turn for pedantry sometimes wonder if Crabbe's Garage's apostrophe should be moved to indicate that these days more than one family member is involved in the business. Old Crabbe, in his youth, came to Plummergen from foreign parts—anywhere further than twenty miles distant is viewed by the village with suspicion—at the request of his blacksmith cousin Eggleden. The new-fangled motorcars beginning to appear, and to break down, in the Kent countryside were beyond the smith's understanding. Cousin Crabbe, a younger man with modern ideas, had understanding to spare, as well as time to study the workings, repair, and maintenance of the internal combustion engine. Dan Eggleden, the current blacksmith and farrier, continues with his cousins to share, and to solve, such transport problems as the locals have, whether involving horses—Dan has learned how to make bridles as well as bits—tractors, or cars. Old Crabbe's son, Young Crabbe, died in the war. His son, Very Young Crabbe, is father to Jack, who drives the bus to nearby Brettenden twice a week.

A local-by-adoption is postman Bert—red-headed, obliging, efficient and popular despite his foreign origins: a true Cockney, he was born within the sound of Bow bells, far more than twenty miles from Plummergen. Bert lives in Brettenden, but his heart is in the right place. He plays for the village's cricket team, as well as emptying its letterboxes and collecting bulky hessian sacks twice daily from Mr. Stillman's post office.

Now on the post office threshold Miss Nuttel and Mrs. Blaine exchanged their speaking glances, but said nothing. From the relative positions of Lady Colveden and Miss Seeton they guessed it was the latter who was about to enter Mr. Stillman's shop, as her ladyship had just left it. The Nuts resolved to take extra care in the selection of vegetarian meatballs (the Nuts refuse to touch, taste or ingest animal products) so that Miss Seeton might be ushered to the front of the queue, could complete her business, and would then depart, leaving the floor free for speculation.

After accepting an invitation to tea at Rytham Hall, Miss Seeton said goodbye to Lady Colveden and went into the shop to greet acquaintances with a nod and a smile.

"Back home at last, Miss Seeton?" said Mrs. Skinner.

"You'll have some catching-up to do, being away so long," said Mrs. Henderson. It irked her to be in even slight agreement with Mrs. Skinner—there had been a quarrel over the church flower rota some years ago—but sometimes you had to put up with things. Like Mrs. Skinner, Mrs. Henderson had seen the promising gleam in the eyes of Miss Nuttel and Mrs. Blaine, but knew nothing could be said until Miss Seeton was out of the way. "Martha Bloomer can't shop for more than herself and Stan, not beyond what you might call the basics, not for other people. You go right ahead with your shopping, Miss Seeton—I'm sure nobody minds waiting, do they?"

A general chorus that nobody minded. Plummergen thrives on gossip, and can always depend on Miss Seeton to provide good value. As Nigel Colveden remarked after her first adventure—when, accidental witness to a fatal stabbing, she had been pursued by its aftermath from bustling Covent Garden to rural Kent—the village had become involved in murder, suicide, drowning, gas, shooting, car crashes, abduction and embezzlement. The village could never make up its mind about Miss Seeton. Her supporters knew the police found her assistance invaluable. Her detractors said such official interest only went to prove her general untrustworthiness. You always had to keep an eye on her…just in case.

A glow of pleasure warmed Miss Seeton as she moved to the general counter. So very kind of everyone. At last she was home in her own dear village. East or west—though in this particular instance perhaps it should be north and farther north—but home was, without question, best. Naturally, she had enjoyed her week with the MacSporrans after Nigel's wedding, and her visit to the Lake District had been a joy, even if the unexpected arrival of so rare a visitor as the yellow-crowned night heron had of necessity somewhat prolonged her stay, but…

Elsie Stillman coughed impatiently. "How can I help you, Miss Seeton?"

Miss Seeton blushed. "Oh, I'm so sorry. I fear I may still be a touch abstracted—yesterday's journey, rather more tiring than I had supposed. The train itself is a wonderfully comfortable mode of travel, but I had forgotten, after the peace and quiet of the north, how very *busy* London can be, even if one takes a taxi rather than try to struggle with a suitcase on the Tube."

Mrs. Stillman nodded. She and her husband seldom went farther than Ashford, fifteen miles away. "At least you didn't even think of the bus, Miss Seeton. In a taxi there's none of this hopping on and off changing, you just sit and watch the world go by. And now you're safely home again. So what can I get you?"

Martha Bloomer, who cooked and cleaned and generally "did" for Miss Seeton two days a week, and who had readjusted for the umpteenth time her village rota when her employer telephoned to say that she really would be back the next day, had already laid in ample stock of almost everything Miss Seeton might require. One item, however, Miss Seeton had not thought to request. She knew there were different sorts—modern manufacturing, so innovative—and wanted to make sure by asking someone who sold them all the time.

"I need new batteries for my flashlight, please," said Miss Seeton, producing it from her capacious handbag.

Miss Nuttel looked at Mrs. Blaine. Mrs. Blaine looked back at Miss Nuttel. Mrs. Blaine sighed and pursed her lips; Miss Nuttel sighed and shook her head. Only Miss Seeton failed to observe these promising signs. Everyone else brightened. So the old girl was up to her tricks again, and not back five minutes from foreign parts! The crowd of shoppers began to drift away from various shelves and display stands to be in at the very start of whatever speculation might in due course begin.

Both Mr. and Mrs. Stillman liked Miss Seeton. Elsie Stillman had noted the looks, the sighs, and the drifting. While not wishing to annoy her customers by saying anything, she must make it clear she did not approve. "Of course," she said promptly. "Always pleased to oblige, Miss Seeton. I know you buy the Ever Ready, and they're very good or we wouldn't sell them, but now we're trying out these new Duracells, even though they're more expensive. They last a lot longer." She produced two packets and laid them side by side on the counter. One set of batteries was a rich blue, with red and white lettering; the other was of a striking black and coppery gold design that appealed at once to Miss Seeton's artistic eye.

"I think I might try this new sort, with autumn on the way and the days growing shorter. Twilight is so much later in the north. One loses track. And fresh batteries now will avert any risk of their going flat—the old ones, that is—at some critical moment out of doors…"

They made sure that Miss Seeton, having paid for her purchases, was safely out of earshot before they began.

Miss Nuttel bowled the opening ball. "Bunny, have I got it wrong? Thought the clocks didn't change for a month or more."

Mrs. Blaine—Bunny to her friend, the Hot Cross Bun to the village—tittered. "So did I, Eric, but with the Common Market perhaps it has to be European time now. You know how they even drive on the wrong side of the road—though I'd like to see them try anything of *that* sort here—and it would cost far too much to change all the signposts and things, anyway. Everybody's taxes would have to go up, you can be sure, if they made us do it—but clocks would be easier, wouldn't they? We must have missed it in the news."

"That you didn't, Mrs. Blaine," said Mrs. Skinner. "October they change, I forget exactly when, but nothing so early as this week. The kiddies have only just gone back to school."

Mrs. Henderson remembered the Girl Guides. "Be Prepared, I should say," she chipped in as Mrs. Skinner drew breath. "Very sensible, if her old ones might run out any moment. Best to be on the safe side."

"But she said twilight lasted much longer in the north," said Mrs. Blaine. "And it's true. The sunset lasts for positively ages, doesn't it, Eric?" The Nuts, before deciding on Plummergen, had years ago taken a variety of coach tours to look at scenery as well as likely locations for their retirement. Scotland had been their final sortie. Their tour had taken them encouragingly close to Balmoral with its royal connections, but in the end, defeated by the accent, the midges, and the weather, they settled for the south of England and descended upon an unsuspecting Kent.

"It does," agreed Miss Nuttel. "But she's been staying up late and creeping about in the dark, remember. Easy to flatten a battery without noticing."

"Tiptoeing in the night, Eric, I think she said."

"Same thing." Erica Nuttel shrugged. "Not something I'd do myself, nor would you—"

"I should think not!"

"—but," persisted Miss Nuttel, "no accounting for taste. Just strikes me as an odd way to behave, at her age."

"And to encourage Lady Colveden as well," said Mrs. Blaine. "Tiptoeing in the dark!"

"Ah," interposed Mrs. Flax, the local wise woman. "Not so very far off All Hallows' Eve, is it, which ain't all turnip lanterns and bobbing for apples—not for them as knows the old ways." Her audience shifted uneasily. "But for them as don't know 'em so thorough as others there'll be preparations to make, rituals to learn afore they can hope to see the spirits of the dead. You can't rush matters o' that sort—that'll be why she's starting so early."

"Halloween's more than a month away," objected young Mrs. Scillicough. Mrs. Scillicough was one of the few locals sometimes able to voice opinions contrary to those of the witch. Mrs. Scillicough and her Kevin were the parents of triplets whose frightfulness was a Plummergen byword. Threats against them, should they fail to mend their ways, were legion. Pointed remarks about the Royal Military Canal at the bottom of The Street were made. Mrs. Scillicough had asked Mrs. Flax for advice and nostrums. None of these worked. The contrast between the young Scillicoughs and their Newport cousins (four under five, every one angelic) was so marked that Mrs. Scillicough sometimes felt almost sick with envy of her sister.

A sister who now joined in, with an observation so pertinent that honour all round was satisfied, and the shoppers could return to their shopping.

"When it's Miss Seeton," said young Mrs. Newport, "you never can tell what might happen next!"

Chapter Two

Some weeks earlier, in an office on the umpteenth floor of New Scotland Yard, five men met in conference. One, the youngest and much the largest, made shorthand notes in silence, contributing nothing unless directly addressed. Detective Sergeant Bob Ranger knew his place. He knew too that most persons of his humble rank would never have been permitted to hear, let alone record, details of the matter under discussion. He recognised that he owed such privilege to the insistence of Detective Chief Superintendent Delphick, whose sidekick he had been for some years; but as he concentrated on his pencilled loops, hooks and curlicues he wondered if this time the chief superintendent, the Yard's legendary Oracle, might have been dragged—and might have dragged him—into something a bit too rich for their liking.

"...the People's Republic of Stentoria," groaned Morley Fenn, Deputy Assistant Commissioner, Special Branch. "These Iron Curtain countries stick together. What one knows the rest know, very often before the people who've had the information stolen, leaked, whatever you call it, know themselves."

"I would remind everyone of the need for extreme caution," said Duncan Oblon, voice of the Foreign Office. "We have no desire to become embroiled, even remotely, in any situation that might hold the slightest risk of a diplomatic incident. Stentoria is one of Soviet Russia's most loyal satellites."

"I've been there," said a man introduced as "a colleague from the Ministry" and given no name. "Once—and that was quite enough for me. Just as grey and grim and blank-faced as any Marxist could want. You could use the place as a pattern and stamp them out in dozens. You can be sure Moscow has been licking its lips over what's been leaked ever since the leak began."

There was a pause.

"Is it still going on?" enquired Delphick.

Fenn groaned again. "We don't know and we can't tell. Stentoria is not about to trumpet what they've got at full volume, are they? Even to rub our noses in it. If Gabriel Crassweller hadn't written himself off by driving into that tree we might not have found out for—well, far too long for our liking."

There was another pause.

"High-ranking British officials," went on Fenn, "do not customarily have dealings with the National Bank of Stentoria. Finding that photocopied counterfoil in his wallet was…"

"A very nasty shock," supplied Oblon. "A deposit of so large an amount suggests several unpleasant possibilities."

There was yet another pause while these things were considered.

"If we upset Stentoria," said Oblon, "we could be looking at very serious long-term—at the worst, maybe even short-term—consequences, harmful consequences, in our relations with the whole communist bloc. And these are delicate enough at the best of times."

"Which is why investigation of the most discreet nature is required," emphasised the nameless third man Delphick privately dubbed Greene, or perhaps Welles—maybe even Lime. The Oracle couldn't decide, but he recognised the type. Greene (or Welles, or Lime) shot a pointed glance at the chief superintendent, and a sideways frown at the pot-hooking Sergeant Ranger. He knew the two made a good team, but in theory this sort of talk should have been kept from the young giant's ears. His youth was the problem. Discretion must be assimilated slowly, thoroughly absorbed until it became second nature. Few were born with it. Those who were had usually been talent-spotted by the relevant authorities almost in the cradle. Ranger, he knew, had not. Why, should the current situation escalate, somebody somewhere might press the ultimate button. If the detective sergeant—a mere sergeant—let anything slip…

"I agree," said Fenn. "We must keep the lid well down on this. But we can't investigate the leak, or leaks, ourselves. We cannot let Stentoria know we know they know—and if we started poking about they would soon find out." He sighed. "Besides, they probably already know more about the Special Branch and, ah, so forth than we do ourselves. Files on each of us and photos by the dozen, I dare say."

"I take it," said Delphick drily, "that the same will apply in reverse."

Greene (or Welles) frowned. "That is hardly part of your remit, Chief Superintendent."

"Merely an observation, sir." The Oracle's tone remained dry. "But—this may sound immodest, I know—but what leads you gentlemen to suppose that they don't already know who I am?"

"They're bound to," agreed Fenn. He brightened. "Nobody could have missed the publicity over your most recent case."

Oblon nodded. "Yes, indeed. It was most fortunate for our purposes that the newspaper photographs were of such poor quality your own mother wouldn't have recognised you—"

"My wife certainly didn't."

"—and none of the television news programmes broadcast a good likeness of you."

Yet another pause.

"I've been set up," said Delphick at last. "You want me because I am currently viewed by the world as one who not only understands the tortuous machinations of the brewing industry, but who at the same time has an instinct for the more dubious forms of road traffic accident. And you have deliberately withheld, or distorted, any accurate public likeness of myself so that I will not be recognised as I begin to investigate...whatever it is for which I have been selected."

Fenn looked smug, Greene frowned, and Oblon gave a discreet but sympathetic nod.

"Friends in Fleet Street," said Delphick heavily. He harboured brief, resentful thoughts against Amelita Forby, crime correspondent of the *Daily Negative*, and her sparring partner, colleague and cohabitee, Thrudd Banner, of World Wide Press. They'd all known each other for years. One of them could have tipped him the wink. Neither had.

Then he softened. Someone, a high-up someone, must have waved the Official Secrets Act under editorial noses. He contemplated Mr. Greene. Mel and Thrudd wouldn't normally be deterred from following a good story. Whatever it was he was about to become involved in must be a good deal more serious than he supposed. Because his last case, newly concluded, had been a big one...

It hadn't even started as a case for the Yard. Bungall & Tappitt owned a small West Country brewery not noted for the fine quality of its beer—but it was hardly a crime to sell cloudy beer. If Devonshire drinkers disliked the stuff they could drink something else, as most of them did. The apple orchards and cider-presses of the district flourished, while Bungall & Tappitt survived through the undiscriminating taste of unwary tourists, and a sufficient number of impoverished locals who could afford nothing better.

Then someone died. Over-pickled liver and a deep road-side ditch on a dark and stormy night were at first blamed, but an enthusiastic young police surgeon performed a textbook investigation, made copious notes, and took samples that he tested in his newly appointed laboratory. He stayed late at work, pored over his Petri dishes, and cultured sinister gelatinous messes at various temperatures to show how the rate of cell duplication might be affected. He drew lines on charts; consulted calendars. He advised the authorities that the premises of Bungall & Tappitt should be subject to the most thorough investigation for certain bacterial and microbial irregularities that could be a hazard to public health.

The affair snowballed. The enthusiastic young police surgeon reported that someone had tampered with the steering of his car. His house was burgled. HM Customs and Excise promptly commandeered his files, notes, and cultures, but couldn't understand them and took the young doctor into protective custody to explain them at his leisure. This was the best thing they could have done, for there soon came rumours of similar escapades in other parts of the country. Scotland Yard was called in when what had originally seemed another case of faulty steering, in an elderly car belonging to an elderly police surgeon, turned out to have been unquestionable, deliberate tampering...

"*He Saved British Beer.*" The chief superintendent quoted just one of the headlines that had upset him, and couldn't bring himself even to think of the others. "No need to note that down, Sergeant Ranger," he added as Bob in his scribbling corner smothered a cough. "And my name blazoned in the press as an expert in the controlled hygiene of fermentation. With a wintry look he turned to the Foreign Office representative. "No doubt you were even then…preparing for eventualities?"

Oblon looked at Fenn. Both looked at Greene. The latter frowned.

"We knew it would need a biggish sort of gun," said Fenn quickly. "Everyone else of suitable rank or experience was tied up with investigations that wouldn't be easy to interrupt or delay or hand over to anyone else. Your own investigation was drawing to a close—a gratifyingly successful close—" Delphick failed to look gratified "—and so your name was put forward and approved, after checks at the highest level."

"*Your* name," interposed Greene. He directed one of his frowns towards Detective Sergeant Ranger, who was underlining *the highest level* and missed this one as well.

"Sergeant Ranger is a trustworthy colleague of many years' standing," said Delphick. "He is as trustworthy as myself. Trust me, and you trust him. We work together, or I don't work at all—on this particular case, that is to say."

Fenn looked at Oblon, then at Greene. "I told you so," he said.

Greene sighed. "Very well. In the unexpectedly prolonged absence of the Assistant Commissioner, Crime, we cannot insist. We must rely on you. Both of you."

"As I'm sure Sir Hubert would have told you, had he been in the country, you may safely do so," said Delphick. "Rely on our discretion, that is. As to whether you can rely on us to achieve results, it would be of the greatest possible assistance if we had at least some small idea of what you three gentlemen want us to do."

Oblon looked at Fenn. Both looked at Greene. "Isn't that obvious?" he snapped.

In his corner, the busy pot-hooker coughed as he studied his notes.

"Sergeant Ranger and I," said Delphick, a warning note in his voice, "are equally perplexed. It is not obvious. Perhaps, Mr. Greene—" the man blinked, but said nothing "—you would care to make it obvious. We can understand words of more than one syllable. Can we not, Sergeant Ranger?"

"Er—yes, sir."

"We want you to find out," said Greene. "Everything. Why Gabriel Crassweller killed himself, who his contacts were—theirs and ours, if any—we want you to go backwards and forwards. Turn the man inside out. What made him turn traitor? We'd have said he was as patriotic and loyal as anyone in this room. It can't have been blackmail. Homosexuality has been legal between consenting adults for years now. Check his bank account—bank accounts, even."

"You'll get nothing from the Swiss, though," warned Oblon, who had more than once tried to penetrate the financial fastnesses of Zurich and Geneva.

Greene was silent. Fenn took over. "Look for connections that don't seem to add up. Just…find out. Is his death the end of the leaks—or are secrets still slipping through the system?"

"In the manner of a delayed-action bomb," Delphick suggested.

Greene frowned, Oblon sighed, Fenn shuddered. "That's what we need to know," he said. "Did the man set up a whole series of security booby-traps? Or might it on the other hand be safe for us to try turning the leaks to our advantage, rather than trying to plug them, once we've found out what and where they are."

"Misinformation," said Delphick. "You flatter me, gentle-men. I am a humble detective, not a whitewash expert or a double-thinker."

"There's nobody else," said Fenn, "as we explained—and we don't want to wait until Sir Hubert is safely home to pull rank on you. We need to know yesterday."

"If not sooner," said Greene, but Delphick had pounced on one careless word.

"Safely?" He directed his attention to the Foreign Office man. "Where is he? I had thought...Is there any serious threat to the assistant commissioner? Surely he has diplo-matic immunity, even in a country currently—and so unex-pectedly—embroiled in revolution."

"He went there for a holiday," replied Oblon, "not an official visit. He will naturally have paid a courtesy call on the—ah—then ruler of the country, accompanied by his wife to emphasise the purely private nature of their presence in Costaguana. It seems that Lady Everleigh collects Geor-gian silver coffee-pots and had a fancy to see the mines from which the—ah—basics were obtained. As there is restricted access to these areas, permission for foreigners to visit would have had to be granted at the highest level."

"Which, when Sir Hubert and her ladyship first arrived in Costaguana, would have been El Dancairo, without doubt," said Fenn. "Nobody bargained for a military coup." He shot an accusing glance at the Foreign Office representative. "No-body even suspected!"

"These Latin American countries..." Oblon waved a wea-ry hand. "Sooner or later one can expect their dictators to be overthrown, sometimes on so regular a basis you feel the presidential palace should be fitted with revolving doors. Highly excitable—and the climate can't help. Naturally, we're doing our best to get the Everleighs out, but their permits were issued by the previous regime, most of whom fled the country as the army approached the presidential compound. Negotiations are at a delicate stage and I can say nothing more at present."

"Then," said Delphick, "I will ask you, all of you, nothing more at present. Sergeant Ranger and I will begin our investigation into Crassweller's death just as soon as we have studied the relevant files."

After Fenn, Oblon and the anonymous ministry's Mr. Greene had taken their leave, the chief superintendent sat back in his chair, and sighed deeply.

"I am not pleased, Bob,' he told Sergeant Ranger. 'I am a policeman, not a paper-pusher—or rather, I push no more paper than seems necessary. An over-egged pudding makes a sickly sweet."

"I feel a bit sick too, sir. To hear those three talk you'd think that if we got things wrong, which we easily might, the Third World War could break out."

Delphick smiled bleakly. "Then let us address ourselves to the files, which I have no doubt are even now on their way to us, with great energy. How about tea and buns while we wait? We need to keep up our strength."

In Plummergen, after his day's teaching, headmaster Martin C. Jessyp locked himself away and set about enlarging and printing the final batch of photographs from Nigel Colveden's wedding. This took care, and much time. Mr. Jessyp, a perfectionist, knew that black-and-white photos showed every detail, every flaw, more than colour ever could. Had Sir George Colveden (his son being absent on honeymoon) not been so busy, Mr. Jessyp might have allowed the bridegroom's father to help him in the darkroom. Sir George from time to time was a keen amateur photographer, and Mr. Jessyp was not selfish. He was, however, a sensible man, and knew he must not disturb a short-handed farmer.

He was also sensible enough to accept that, skilled though he might be in the taking and developing of black-and-white stills, colour photos and cine films were another matter. A Brettenden chemist had been entrusted with his other precious mementos of the handsome Nigel's wedding to the delightful brunette Louise, formerly Mademoiselle de Balivernes, daughter of an old wartime comrade of Sir George.

With the new school term upon him, Mr. Jessyp had been slow to develop and print his films. The first few days were always interrupted by parents complaining to him about matters over which he had little control. If a child squinted at the blackboard, was it his job to take said child to the optician? All he could do was sit the child at the front and issue stern reminders of the need to pay attention. He listened to the parents grumble about the expense of public transport and the government's duty to pay, when it was all for the good of the kiddies. The headmaster did not feel the complaints should be left to his second-in-command, Miss Maynard, and indeed she would rarely have heard them because everyone knew it was his job, and Alice Maynard just a girl, still a bit flighty and what did she know anyway, teaching the Tiddlers as she did, not the Bigguns where it mattered a lot more.

The colour photos and cine film were ready within a few days. A showing of the film at the village hall for all who had not travelled to Scotland for the wedding was arranged. There had been debate as to whether an entrance fee should be charged, proceeds to the church roof fund. The general feeling was that they'd already clubbed together for Mr. Jessyp and his cameras to attend the ceremony, and they didn't think it fair they should be asked to pay any more. A compromise was reached whereby a modest collection box stood by the door of the hall for voluntary offerings. Most of those who sniffed and handkerchiefed their way from the film show—a lovely girl, such a beautiful dress, Nigel so good-looking, eyes only for each other, written in the stars— slipped a surreptitious coin or two into the box, although when the money was counted very few bank-notes were discovered.

Plummergen also felt strongly that the wedding presents should go on public display. They'd bought some of them, hadn't they? Or at least most of 'em contributed a few bob, and they wanted to know everyone'd had their money's worth. By rights it did ought to be in the home of the bridegroom, the bride being from across the Channel, even if her poor dead mother's family was Scotch…

"No," said Major-General Sir George Colveden, Baronet, KCB, DSO, JP.

"But George," protested Lady Colveden, "it's understandable they're interested."

"No," reiterated her spouse. "Just an excuse to snoop. You'd find heaven-knows-who popping out of cupboards and coming down the stairs trying to make believe they'd lost their way while they'd been digging through the wardrobes and opening drawers and probably checking in the bathroom, too."

"We could hang decorative cords across the stairs—" began his wife.

"No, Meg! Some years ago now, but the same sort of thing—remember that woman with her confounded axe?"

"Oh, my goodness." Lady Colveden, until this grim reminder, had deliberately driven from her memory the occasion when her husband found their nearest neighbour, a widow in her sixties, swinging an amateur axe at a cypress in his grounds. Harried from the property (Sir George only returning the axe he had seized from the trespasser once she was back on the Queen's highway) the neighbour complained to Brettenden Rural Council, and insisted to the district surveyor that, if he looked through her late husband's binoculars, he would see that the growing cypress now blocked her view of the bedroom windows at Rytham Hall. Lady Colveden spent some uneasy days thereafter glancing nervously upwards on the watch for privately hired helicopters, or even a hot air balloon.

Thwarted, the widow decamped in the end to Dungeness, where no trees more than a few feet high could grow because of the paucity of the salty, windswept soil. She professed a sudden interest in birdlife, and bought a very large telescope.

Lady Colveden grimaced. "Oh, yes, I remember. Then what should we do?"

"Interest is understandable, said so yourself—the village has known Nigel a long time. But they'd want 'em on display for more than an afternoon or two. Takes time to cart the stuff anywhere and lay it out neatly, and we're busy enough as it is, with the boy away. Nobody to spare for the heavy work. And once he and Louise are living here with us, while the builders get on with renovating the house, there'd be no room to do the thing in proper style." He stroked his toothbrush moustache, and winked. "Good enough, m'dear?"

Her ladyship smiled. "How clever of you, George. We can move things a few boxes at a time to the village hall, and everyone can look at them when Mr. Jessyp shows his film. How lucky we haven't unpacked them since they arrived from Scotland."

But Sir George shook his head. "Sticky fingers, in the dark. Too great a temptation for some. Entrapment," said the magistrate knowledgeably. "Or breakages—just as bad.

After the film show, that's when we'll start shifting things up there. Warn Potter to keep his eye on the place—next door to the police house, after all. Good man, Ned Potter."

"And nobody knows we haven't unpacked any of the boxes yet," said Lady Colveden. "Only Martha, bless her, and she'd never breathe a word. You think of everything, George." She blew him a kiss as she began to stack plates and tidy cutlery. "She'll be here soon to help me finish the spare bedroom." A wistful note entered her voice. "Won't it feel strange, when Summerset cottage is finished and it really is just the two of us here."

"Take in lodgers, if you're lonely," suggested Sir George. He hated to see his wife's face even slightly downcast. He chuckled. "Could always look up Daphne Carstairs."

"Daphne Carstairs will enter this house over my dead body," said Lady Colveden. Her own soft wavy brown hair had always been a sad (in her mind at least) contrast with the luscious fair locks of her husband's old flame.

"Black always looks good on blondes," said Sir George. "Wait six months, of course."

Lady Colveden, a sudden glint in her eye, set down the plates and drew a deep breath.

Smiling to himself, Sir George stroked his moustache.

Chapter Three

Nigel and Louise Colveden returned triumphant to Plummergen in the little red MG that had taken them to France to meet those of her family who had not travelled to Scotland for the wedding, and back via the Isle of Wight for their proper, private honeymoon.

"Only for a few days," Nigel warned, "because of the farm. It's close enough for me to get home in an emergency. They can always leave a message at the hotel—though I hope they don't."

Louise smiled, and patted his hand. "You must not worry your pretty little head about a thing. Have I that correctly?" The slight lisp of the French difficulty with "th" was enchantment to Nigel. "If they require you, of course they will say and we must go, but your papa was very sure they would not."

"I would rather like to see the model village again. We came once when we were kids, me and Julia—Mother brought us—and it's bigger now. Not the models, the village itself, there's more of it, I mean."

Louise enjoyed watching him relive his childhood treat quite as much as she enjoyed the whole excursion. "Godshill is where they ended up in *The Day of the Triffids*," he said, and having to struggle with translation was even more enjoyable as he acted out the threat of an eight-foot walking plant with a venomous lashing sting. They laughed and joked. Louise saw something sinister lurking in the undergrowth and Nigel had to hold her close, in case it came to get her.

He was bursting with pride and happiness as they neared his own, full-sized village, and he drove very slowly down The Street so that everyone could see them. Behind windows, lace curtains twitched. Honest goggle-awpers (more translation needed for his wife) came outside and waved. Nigel's heart was full.

The young couple were received ecstatically by Lady Colveden, with a bashful grin and a nod by Sir George, who turned pink as Louise kissed his cheek, and shook Nigel firmly by the hand in case he'd picked up foreign habits while abroad.

Nigel was full of questions about the farm. While his mother whisked his wife away to inspect the spare bedroom he pestered his father with demands to know what had been done, who had done it, and how they had all coped while he was away.

"Thank goodness we tied the knot in Scotland," he said. "If Louise and her father had insisted on France I'd have eloped with her. Six weeks' residence requirement is far too long for a working farmer to kick his heels in idleness. And talking of the farm…"

"Relax, m'boy, and stop worrying. Won't say you weren't missed, because you were, but I promised we'd manage and we did. You've trained young Hosigg well. He worked like ten men, much later at night than I really liked, but then he used to drive those long-distance lorries. Said odd hours wouldn't bother him, if we didn't make it a regular thing. Your mother had Lily and the baby here a couple of times so that Len wouldn't worry and they wouldn't be lonely. Ah." Sir George blushed. "Your mother. Yes."

"We haven't been married five minutes," protested Nigel.

His pink-faced father turned purple. "She's bound to ask," he muttered. "Given her ideas, little Dulcie on the spot. Just thought I'd warn you."

"Well, thanks, but if she wants to dote on grandchildren she can visit Janie in London and dote on her." Nigel grinned. "And what's all this about the presents going on show?"

Plummergen had agreed that the official opening of the wedding-present display at the village hall should be carried out by the young couple on their return. After all, the presents had been given to them and they ought to have a say in the matter.

"Gave Jessyp time to do a good job on the photographs," said Sir George. "Enlarged them as far as he can without losing too much definition. Got 'em with the colour prints in order round the walls, with your bits and pieces on tables underneath."

"Do we have to cut a ribbon, or make speeches? Or do we just say 'Hello, everyone, come along in for a snoop'?" Nigel enquired. His father supposed that a few words of welcome from the groom, some smiles and waves from the bride, and a ceremonial cutting of Martha Bloomer's cake would probably do the trick.

"I'll borrow your ceremonial sword," said Nigel, and practised a ceremonial wave.

Some days after the Crassweller investigation had begun, in an office on the umpteenth floor of New Scotland Yard, in a paper-laden atmosphere of concentration, two tired men simultaneously set down their pens, closed their notebooks, and yawned. Around tottering heaps of documents befrilled with cross-reference slips, they peered at each other thoughtfully.

It was Delphick who finally spoke. "Of course, we don't talk the same language as the cloak-and-dagger merchants, and I accept that a degree of obfuscation must remain, in the national interest, essential, but one has to ask if all this—" he swept a cautious but expressive arm around the crowded room "—is indeed all of it? In the context of our investigation it hardly makes much sense, if it is."

"We know a lot more about all sorts of stuff we didn't know before," said Bob. "If the Special Branch were happy to sponsor him through university, it makes him an unlikely villain. They're pretty thorough in their vetting procedures, aren't they?"

Delphick smiled. "He appears to have supplied them with not a few likely prospects in the student radical stakes on whom, no doubt, the eyes of the security forces will have kept more than passing watch through the years. Some of those names, indeed, are familiar today as pillars of society. Yes, we know far more than we did."

"Trouble is," said Bob, "most of it doesn't exactly point in any particular direction, does it, sir?"

"So it would appear." The chief superintendent emphasised the final word. "As an exercise in widening our intellectual horizons, these past days have been…enlightening, but as to their true importance in the greater scheme of British security I wouldn't care to hazard an opinion. According to such evidence as we have studied, when we've been able to make sense of it, Gabriel Crassweller does indeed appear to have been as loyal and trustworthy as everyone always thought he was."

Bob looked at him. "So *you* think the Foreign Office and… that other chap's anonymous ministry are holding something back too, sir?"

"The possibility has certainly crossed my mind." Delphick frowned. "You know, Bob, I can't help wondering whether..."

Sergeant Ranger waited. The Oracle wasn't usually so... hesitant. Granted, this was hardly the usual sort of case, but after spending as much time as they both had looking into things, he generally had some sort of theory.

"Oblon admitted I'd been set up over the news coverage," said Delphick at last. "After so many days with these labour-intensive files, it occurs to me that I might also have been set up in other respects."

Bob gaped. "Wh-what for?" was all he could manage.

"And there you hit the nail on the head. I can think of no reason anyone should wish to nobble me on this case. Can you?" Bob could only shake his head. "If they hope, by embroiling me in this particular investigation, to deflect me from some future investigation of dark importance about which as yet I know nothing, their methods are more than convoluted, they're impenetrable. They move in their mysterious ways—yes?"

Sergeant Ranger suddenly jumped. A thought had occurred. He found his voice. "Talk about impenetrable, sir, it's only just dawned—the computer." Delphick sat up. "Well, sir, none of this looks anything like that line-printed paper with holes down the side. What we've got here is all carbon copies and fading type, the way it's always been. Our mechanical monster in the basement churns out reams of the striped stuff the minute you press the appropriate buttons. I can't believe the security bods don't have a computer of their own. Sir."

It was Delphick's turn to be struck mute.

"So we're not seeing everything, though they assured us we should," he said at last. "An interesting thought. This could put an entirely different perspective on the case, if case indeed it is. Now, I wonder."

Bob coughed. "Talking of perspective, sir—seeing things a different way, I mean—"

"No," said his chief at once. He saw Bob's expression, and mellowed. "She's still away, quite apart from any other considerations there might be."

His sergeant accepted this mild rebuke with a grin. "You've already checked, sir?"

"Miss Seeton," Delphick informed him sternly, "has been visiting friends in the north. Even an art consultant retained by Scotland Yard is entitled to take a holiday." Miss Emily Dorothea Seeton, seeing herself as a private and conventional English gentlewoman, would have found highly distasteful any suggestion that she might be psychic. Over the years she had convinced herself that it was for what she regarded as "IdentiKit sketches" that she was paid so handsome an annual retainer, and she could never grasp that her lightning-swift, instinctive drawings were of value to the police because they so often held the key to cases that had baffled more conventional investigation.

Bob nodded. "Yes, after Nigel's wedding she went to spend a week with the MacSporrans—Lord and Lady Glenclachan and young Marguerite—then she was off to stay with a bird-fancying friend in the Lake District. But I imagine you already know this from Superintendent Brinton, sir."

The Oracle gave him an oracular look. "It may have come up in the course of a friendly telephone chat, yes."

"You didn't tell me, sir."

"You didn't ask. And it could have been viewed as a mere idle speculation, with no definite aim. To learn of Miss Seeton's absence was hardly a cause for dismay because, should I ask her to come to the Yard to produce one of her special drawings for us, I'd have to know what to ask her to draw. Being unable to get any particular sort of handle on the case, I wouldn't really know where to start."

Bob thought about this. "It's odd Crassweller's body hasn't been released for burial. They've fudged it nicely by saying they can't find his next of kin, but we know that's not true." He tapped a bulging folder. "So it's…odd."

"Another angle on the possible setting-up of Yours Truly, perhaps? Hmm." Once more Delphick favoured his sergeant with an oracular look. "Your adopted aunt, as I recall, has no objection to viewing dead bodies. Those visits to the hospital in her student days, as well as surviving London through the Blitz, must have hardened her for the sight of most corpses—yet I'm reluctant to show her Crassweller's. The tree around which he wrapped himself in his car had a particularly unpleasing effect."

"Aunt Em wouldn't turn a hair, sir, you know she wouldn't—especially if it was put to her that it was her duty to look at him. They could tidy him up a bit—somehow—couldn't they?"

"You've seen the photographs."

Bob shuddered. "Yes, well—and there you are, sir. Tell her it's too grisly in real life, I mean death, which it certainly is, but that we need a decent likeness for—oh, some reason or other. Show her the pic from his personnel file, tell her it's hush-hush and unsuitable for public use, but we could do with something better that doesn't give away any state secrets. She'd believe that, sir, you know she would."

"Particularly," agreed Delphick, "when it happens, more or less, to be true. Thank you, Bob. I suppose you've had no news of her? No idea when she's coming back?"

Neither he nor Bob had the least idea that, in Plummergen, Lady Colveden had for some days past been asking exactly the same question.

Nigel uttered words of welcome. He and Louise smiled and waved and thanked everybody for coming, and Mr. Jessyp for the photographs, and all those who had sent presents which they could see were most tastefully arranged. Sir George had refused the loan of his sword, but Lady Colveden had polished the horn-handled carving knife. The young couple cut Martha's cake with a flourish as more photographs were taken, Nigel muttering that honest English baking beat piles of French profiteroles any day.

He muttered again as he eyed the locks and window-bolts of the hall. Police Constable Potter took him to one side and murmured that he wasn't to worry, there'd be a watch kept on the place until it was all over, but to say nothing in case it put ideas into people's heads, seeing as how there were some strange folk in town.

"When were there ever not?" said Nigel.

"Foreigners." Potter tapped the side of his nose. "Real ones—but you've no need to concern yourself, you and your good lady," he added in a normal voice, bringing Louise into the conversation. "Right glad we are to see you here for good, Mrs. Colveden!"

She was still in the proud, blushing stage of matrimony, and turned a delicate shade of rose. "Thank you, Ned—it is Ned, is it not? We have met before."

"Ah, it's the uniform that folk tend to remember, but Ned indeed it is, miss—that's to say mamzelle, I mean, Mrs. Nigel."

"Louise," said Nigel, before his wife had quite disentangled the policeman's accent. Cricket (both men played in the village team) is a great social leveller. "Come and meet Mabel and young Amelia—though not Tibs, I hope."

"Rabbiting down by the canal," grinned Ned. There were few in the village not made uneasy by his Amelia's fearsome feline companion, a tabby of generous proportions who ter-rorised any living creature on four legs, and many (if not most) on two.

Nigel returned the grin, dramatically mopped his brow, and ushered his bride into the thick of the chattering crowd. Introductions were made, and promises to drop in for tea and a proper chat once things had calmed down a little.

The Colvedens had discussed the wisdom of leaving present-givers' cards with their presents, but knew Plummergen would think they'd got it wrong whatever they did. They left the cards. If the village chose to compare and contrast personal generosity, and squabbles ensued—well, this was no more than what happened most of the time anyway. On tables ranged around the hall, therefore, beneath Mr. Jessyp's photographic mural (the arrangement of which had involved a spirit-level, and a new brand of polish for the drawing-pins) three electric toasters stood guard over four shining toast racks. Two sets of coffee mugs flanked a yellow percolator that matched neither. A fondue dish in bright enamel was accompanied by a selection of cookery books. The ironing board stood loaded with sheets and pillowcases, gleaming in cellophane; blankets and an eiderdown, likewise embraced in shiny wrap, were on the next table.

The patchwork quilt had a table of its own, where it draped in full and colourful glory, admired by all. The loving hexa-gons, in medallion pattern, had been exquisitely hand-work-ed over paper shapes and many years by a Scottish great-aunt for Louise's marriage-kist, the large box or chest which in England would be her bottom drawer. The two central me-dallions Aunt Christine had prudently left blank, for the ad-dition of dates and initials when the time should come. This new addition she had deputed to her younger sister, Janet, whose fingers were not so stiff as hers now were.

Aunt Janet was a noted needlewoman. Her own wedding gift was a detailed cross-stitch likeness of the bride's long-dead mother's family home, one of those small granite castles with stepped grey gables, circular turrets and narrow windows for which the Scots are famous.

"It may not be a chateau," said Aunt Janet, "but there's history and breeding on both sides of your family, Louise, as you must never forget."

Louise had promised she wouldn't. Nigel asked later if perhaps the picture might be a suitable adornment to the walls of their spare room. Louise had quietly smiled.

Now she was admiring the photographs rather than any of the presents, including Aunt Janet's cross-stitch, and Nigel could only hope for the best.

"But these are splendid!" she cried. "Monsieur Jessyp—where is he? We must thank him at once for such a—a kind compliment. To have worked so hard!"

"They look grand, don't they? It must have taken ages to put 'em all out like that." Nigel looked over people's heads for the schoolmaster, but couldn't see him in the crowd. He was glad Louise was genuinely pleased. Martin C. had gone to a lot of trouble, and Nigel didn't like to disappoint a friend by ingratitude. He smiled on his wife for her delighted spontaneity, and in a spirit of reciprocity nodded at the cross-stitch castle.

"And does it remind you of your history?"

"Oh, poof!" Louise dismissed her heritage with an airy giggle. "For the spare room, maybe yes, but my history begins now, with you, Nigel, here in my new home. Of course..." Again she contemplated the photographs. "As to history, does not this arrangement have something of the tapestry of Bayeux? The story of one historic day, in pictures."

"Hmm…" Nigel was not only modest, he was still looking for the schoolmaster. "Oh—there he is. We'll squeeze through the ravening hordes," and he took her by the hand to lead the way.

"Well!" said Mrs. Henderson. "Well, I really don't know."

"As if we haven't history of our own," protested Mrs. Spice.

"She's foreign, don't forget," said Mrs. Skinner, grudgingly feeling that Mrs. Henderson had expressed what everyone thought.

"She's young," said Mrs. Welsted, the draper's wife. Mrs. Welsted and her daughter Margery had studied the patchwork quilt and the cross-stitch picture closely, and with envy. They wondered how long it must have all taken—far longer than Mr. Jessyp and his drawing-pins, that was for sure. "Still…Bayeux Tapestry…that's another matter altogether."

"Gloating," said Mrs. Henderson. "Or so I should call it, with her father a count and most likely descended straight from one of them knights of the Conker."

Nobody spoke. Among the general hubbub, this remarkable silence went unremarked.

"The Frogs burnt the whole of Plummergen to ashes, *and* tumbled the castle to ruins," Mrs. Spice reminded everyone at last.

"And much later than the Battle of Hastings," said Mrs. Skinner.

"But nowhere near as bad as the Danes," said Mrs. Henderson quickly.

"When Murreystone never come to help," said Mrs. Spice darkly. To this day, Plummergen cannot forget the Viking invasion of AD 892 and still bears a grudge, ignoring the fact that against two hundred and fifty longships and several thousand beweaponed warriors the men of a neighbouring village that was far smaller could have offered very little in the way of practical assistance.

"And Queen Anne arriving in her barge to drink a glass of water from the well," said Mrs. Skinner. "You're right, Mrs. Spice. We've history of our own, sure as eggs."

And again nobody spoke as they contemplated the array of presents on the tables, and Mr. Jessyp's photos round the walls.

Next morning, breakfast at Rytham Hall was a thoughtful and unprecedented affair. Nigel sat in his usual place, Louise beside him. Sir George at the end of the table cast longing glances in the direction of *Farmers Weekly*, but could in deference to his daughter-in-law's presence not bring himself to read it. He ate eggs and bacon in an unhappy silence, and kept rearranging the salt and pepper pieces in front of him.

Lady Colveden offered coffee. Louise smiled, and said she was growing accustomed to tea, of which as an Englishwoman she must learn to drink as much as she could, as often as possible.

Lady Colveden looked sharply at her. So she *had* overheard…she'd hoped the accent would have dulled Louise's comprehension. She took the bull by the horns.

"They meant nothing personal towards you, my dear," she said. "Honestly, it isn't anything to do with your being French so much as—well, the village is rather proud of its history. Just because we've never exactly been the size of a town…Why, some of the families go back as far as Domesday."

"Come off it, Mother," said Nigel.

"Well, back to the start of the parish register. Four centuries, at least—and you've only got to look at the names on the tombstones. Not that I believe there ever was a castle here," she added. "Dr. Braxted from Brettenden Museum told me all about earthwork ramparts when she was digging up our Roman temple a few years ago."

"Even more history," said Nigel cheerfully. He and his mother then told his wife how an unexpected Second World War grenade had blown itself up, revealing traces of a long-buried mosaic and a hoard of Romano-British silverware.

"We'll pop across to Brettenden one afternoon and I'll show you." It had been agreed that for the first few weeks Nigel's hours on the farm should be flexible. Sightseeing, and the paying of courtesy calls, must take priority before the clocks changed and the nights began to draw in. "Is that okay with you, Dad?"

"What's that? Oh, yes," said the baronet, collecting his thoughts as he crunched toast. *Farmers Weekly* would have to wait; nothing to be done about it. It meant he'd be out of doors so much the sooner, he supposed. More time to catch up and give the boy less to worry about. With resolution he pushed back his chair. "My dear," he said to Louise, and bowed, and was gone.

"Poor George." Lady Colveden smiled at her husband's hurrying back. "Don't worry, Louise, he was no different when Julia was first married. I can't remember how long it took him to relax with Toby around, but he did in the end, honestly."

"As honest as Louise being French?" Nigel grinned re-assuringly at his bride. "Don't worry, Louise. They'll get used to it—but they really love a good moan and if there's nothing legitimate, so to speak, they'll invent something."

"Nigel." But his mother's protest was faint.

"Oh, this does not trouble me, *Belle-Mère*," Louise assured her mother-in-law. "I understand. It is with much the same spirit that we in France…moan, yes? of *Albion Perfide*. This is no more than custom, such moaning. In the same way *les Anglais* they call us Frogs, because of history."

"Napoleon," said Lady Colveden. "Not that he came here any more than Hitler did, thank goodness."

"The Royal Military Canal wouldn't have stopped either of the blighters," said Nigel the realist. "A few strong planks, Bailey bridges or what have you, and they'd have been over in a flash."

"But the canal wasn't just to *stop* him," said his mother. "Or even delay him, as of course it would have done." Nigel smiled, but said nothing. "Either of them. It was for gun emplacements, and transport—guns, and munitions, and food supplies and—oh, everything armies need. They'd have marched along the Military Road in double-quick time with horses pulling barges, and sentries on the alert."

"Well, thank goodness we'll never know," said Nigel. "As you said."

"Mm." She looked at Louise. "But you do seem to have started something, my dear. Everyone's been talking about it. Phyllis Armitage phoned last night to tell me I'd be roped in—as will you, because you started it—and Molly Treeves, that's the vicar's sister who keeps house for him, is getting up a committee. If I didn't dislike sewing so much, I should say it might be rather fun."

Nigel spluttered at the thought of his mother sewing anything beyond a button, but his wife was all polite interest.

"What is it I started into which I am to be roped? Will it indeed be fun?"

"Plummergen," said Lady Colveden, "wants its own Bayeux Tapestry!"

Chapter Four

Nigel choked. "And they want you to make it? Shouldn't you finish that fire-screen first?"

"Really, Nigel." His exasperated mother smiled at his wife. "A silly practical joke your husband played on me one Christmas. No, of course not. Just one panel of sewing, and Louise can help, unless she embroiders or does cross-stitch or patchwork as beautifully as her aunts and would like to make her own."

Louise looked startled, smiled nervously, and shook her head.

"Then we'll suffer together and encourage each other," said Lady Colveden. "They're saying a map of the village, or something historical. I suppose some sort of picture of the Hall, seeing how we've been here for ages and so has it."

"Two birds with one stone," gurgled Nigel. They both ignored him.

"Appliqué," said Louise, half to herself. "The stitching for the edges so that it does not unravel, as with blankets or buttonholes—this I can do, a little. And also with paper. One traces shapes from a photograph, and cuts pieces of cloth in colours to match…"

Lady Colveden brightened. "That's how they made the Overlord Embroidery, Miss Armitage said." Explanations of the commemorative needlework in honour of D-Day then followed. "Longer than Bayeux—which Phyllis says isn't a tapestry, because it isn't woven, it's embroidered, only different—but we haven't the time for anything so elaborate as either. Phyllis said it took twenty women five years to complete the Overlord."

"If seven maids with seven mops—" began Nigel.

"I hope," said his mother, "it won't take half a year for the builders to finish at Summerset Cottage. I'd forgotten you could be living there soon. Of course you'd prefer to have your own home in the tapestry—or embroidery, or quilt or whatever they call it—rather than work twice as hard to help make ours too. But before you move in you could give me lessons—"

Nigel laughed. "Mother! When did builders ever complete a job on time? And never, ever before. There's weeks, probably months, of work ahead to bring that place into the twentieth century."

Her ladyship sighed. "It did sound bad, when your father had the surveyors' report. It's not that the house is exactly falling down—"

"—apart from the leaking roof," interposed Nigel, "and the damp getting into the plaster, and the plumbing pretty much the original Tudor, and the kitchen even older—"

"Nigel. Pay no attention, Louise, it's mid-to-late Victorian—certainly not Tudor, even if the house itself is. You know—King Henry VIII?" Louise nodded. "And I agree it's sadly neglected. George tries to be a conscientious landlord, but when the tenants were paying only a peppercorn rent and it was a gentlemen's agreement anyway…" More explanations. "And he's rather shy in some ways. You may have noticed." Louise smiled. "Once their father was dead he didn't care for visiting them and left it to me, and of course they paid no attention to what *I* said, even when they let me inside, which they haven't done for years."

"Three far from fair maidens, and all mad as hatters," said Nigel. "That's what he used to call them when he thought we couldn't hear. When Julia and I were kids we thought they must be the witches in *Macbeth*—three weird sisters, you see."

Lady Colveden seized on his final word. "You can't see much of a house when you're kept on the doorstep. If I'd been the sort of person who left visiting cards that's what I'd have done—" again Nigel choked "—but your father seemed to feel someone should go there and try to keep an eye on things, so I did the best I could…"

There had been three sisters: Hilda, Gertrude, and Griselda Saxon. Their widowed father, the colonel, bought Rytham Hall during the agricultural slump of the 1920s, convinced he could make it pay. He was mistaken. Had he listened to even half-expert advice, had he been able to keep his temper, he might have done better; but Colonel Saxon always thought he had the right of it, always pulled rank, and imbued his daughters with the same spirit. None of the girls ever married: nobody they met came up to their high standards. While for historic reasons Plummergen has never had a resident squire, the Hall has been where the absentee Lords of the Manor tended to house their bailiffs, and for centuries the village has looked there for civic leadership.

The colonel sub-let parts of the farm, but kept interfering. Not a single lease was renewed by a single tenant. The colonel's blood pressure began to trouble him. During the war the Hall was requisitioned, for purposes of which even thirty years later nobody knew any details—or if (like Sir

46

George) they possibly did, they said nothing. Colonel Saxon, dispossessed of his home, most of his servants rushing to join the armed forces or take other patriotic employment, took his daughters to live in Summerset Cottage. The misnamed cottage—a small half-timbered house—was part of the Rytham Hall Estate, situated towards the end of a lane near the church so obscure that, driving south down The Street, it could easily be missed and usually was. The Saxons grew more aloof and exclusive as the war progressed. On D-Day the colonel had a seizure. On VE Day he had a stroke, after which nobody saw him about the village again. His daughters likewise began to disappear from public view. When Sir George Colveden—newly demobbed, eager to turn his six-years' exhausted sword into a productive ploughshare—became the first post-war tenant of Rytham Hall, the colonel was persuaded to an outright sale, given that the purchaser was another military man and one, moreover, who outranked him.

As Lady Colveden explained to Louise, only a nominal sum was paid in rent by the Saxons. It was the security of a secluded home the family craved. When the colonel died of apoplexy (Plummergen attributing his death to blood pressure and bad temper) Sir George agreed to keep the same arrangement for the orphaned daughters as he had for their father. Thus, over the years, as nobody saw them, and the two married servants who stayed with them throughout had mostly shopped in Brettenden, the three weird sisters faded into village oblivion. What was the fun in even the most mischievous of speculation when it could never be possible to find out what the truth—however dull—might be?

Speculation in Plummergen centred on the modern 1970s rather than the 1940s, historic and worthy of stitchcraft immortality as the latter period undoubtedly was.

"…near as a touch ran into Bert's van," Mrs. Skinner was telling the post office. "What would we have done if they'd hit him and set the van on fire?"

"All our letters and parcels gone up in smoke," said Mrs. Scillicough, whose triplets—to village amazement—had survived another year and were soon to have a birthday.

"And Bert along with them," said Mrs. Henderson reproachfully. A general chorus was quick to sympathise with the popular postman's narrow escape.

"Driving on the wrong side of the road," enlarged Mrs. Newport. "Coming down from Mrs. Venning's place, not paying proper attention."

"The driver got out to apologise," said Mrs. Scillicough, who with her sister had witnessed the near miss at the end of the council house road. "Course, being foreign he didn't say much, but he bowed, and smiled, and said he was sorry."

Mrs. Newport nodded. "We yelled at them, but it was all so quick and they couldn't hear—air conditioning or summat, I suppose. That big black Bentley—it must of cost a lot. Mrs. Venning could fare worse, for tenants."

"She'll be needing somebody who can pay her fees for that nursing home," agreed Mrs. Skinner. "Switzerland's expensive if anywhere is."

"She's not writing any more, but those books of hers still seem to sell," said Mrs. Henderson. "Always more kiddies coming along to read about Jack the Rabbit." She looked at Mrs. Newport, who seemed to be putting on a little weight around the middle.

"Authors don't make that much money, do they?" said Mrs. Newport, twirling the circular stand on which such volumes as *Master Metaphysics in 30 Minutes* were displayed. *Master Needlecraft* and its patchwork, cross-stitch, quilting and embroidery companions in recent days had become bestsellers.

Mr. Stillman was reordering. "I mean—they can't, can they? Or they wouldn't need to keep writing."

The bell above the door tinkled as someone—some two— came in.

"People go on buying the books, even when the author's dead," said Mrs. Skinner.

"Somebody dead?" Miss Nuttel and Mrs. Blaine bustled into the conversation. "Surely not Bert? There was an accident, you know, but we haven't seen an ambulance."

"Yet," Miss Nuttel amended. "Nearest hospital's a few miles away, though. Takes time. Start ringing the bell as they come nearer."

"But we've heard nothing," said Mrs. Blaine, "beyond the squeal of brakes, and people shouting—" she and Miss Nuttel had listened hard, long, and hopefully "—and of course we don't like to interfere." This remark had everyone agape. "So we didn't go to look and risk getting in everyone's way, and maybe doing quite the wrong thing. Neither of us knows any first aid, and then poor Eric…"

"Blood," muttered Miss Nuttel. "Can't say I care for it."

"What we *did* see," persisted Mrs. Blaine, "was the red of the post office van all tangled up with that huge Rolls or whatever it is those people at Mrs. Venning's drive. Much too big for the lanes around here, of course." The fact that The Street is remarkably wide for the size of its village was conveniently ignored. "If they're planning to stay here long they ought to shop on foot, or catch the bus like everyone else."

"Wouldn't have killed Bert if they'd been walking," agreed Miss Nuttel.

"But they didn't," said several people in regretful chorus.

The Nuts exchanged disappointed looks, and for once could find nothing to say.

"He grumbled a bit and got back on his rounds," said young Mrs. Newport.

"And they said sorry again and drove on down towards the bridge," said young Mrs. Scillicough. "Didn't you see them go past?"

The Nuts, their gaze and hearing fine-tuned for the ambulance, admitted they had not.

"Going to Romney, most like," suggested Mrs. Skinner, whereupon Mrs. Henderson, the church flower rota ever in mind, said it was more probable they'd have turned off for Rye.

"So there's nobody dead," concluded Mrs. Spice with relish. She and Mrs. Flax had been keen but unusually silent auditors of the past few minutes' chatter.

"Not even Mrs. Venning," said Mrs. Flax. "Otherways, her house would be up for sale, which as all here must know, it ain't."

"Which is why she's rented it to rich foreigners instead," said Mrs. Skinner.

"On account of authors not making enough money for nursing homes," chimed in Mrs. Newport. "When they're not writing any more, that is."

Miss Nuttel felt that the honour of Lilikot, the plate-glass observatory she shared with Mrs. Blaine, was at stake. "Manville Henty still sells," she pointed out.

"And he's been dead for years," said Mrs. Blaine.

This was true. Manville Henty, a son of the village who early in his career adopted a convenient pseudonym, made his name in the days of Victoria as a writer of robust adventures that appealed to grown men and schoolboys alike. They sold as well as any popular author of the time, illustrated with vigour and lavishly bound in gold-lettered cloth. Fine first editions by this author were rare, his books having been read and re-read until most fell apart. Collectors from time to time arrived in Plummergen on hopeful coach tours, asking Mrs. Duncan at Quill Cottage if by any chance she had any of his books, refusing to believe that her complete set was in paperback, and departing reluctantly after dropping hints and taking photographs.

"*Night-Runners of the Marsh*," said Mrs. Newport, twirling Mr. Stillman's circular stand until she found the appropriate volume. The paperback bore a large sticker declaring it to be "By A Local Author". The shelf on which his other titles stood had a notice, even larger.

"Ah," said Miss Nuttel, who hadn't read Henty's first bestseller.

"Oh," cried Mrs. Blaine, who in the throes of what she said was influenza—even if the heartless Dr. Knight told her she had caught the cold that was going around—had.

"Smugglers." It was all Miss Nuttel could remember of what Bunny had told her.

"Like *Dr. Syn*," said Mrs. Spice. "I always reckon that writer must of took his ideas from Manville Henty." This was unfair to Russell Thorndike, creator of the smuggling pirate priest, but as Mr. Thorndike had died two or three years before, this aspect of her comment was allowed to pass.

"Who said writing folk need to get any ideas from aught but real life?" demanded Mrs. Flax. "Smuggling on the Marsh there's always been, ah, and who's to say not with us still? And more." She looked round as people shuffled their feet and lowered their gaze. Even Mrs. Scillicough seemed uneasy. "Ah," said Mrs. Flax again. "True life there always is—and truth beyond imagining. Whitgift blood runs in my veins, and the gift of seeing what no normal mortal can see—as writing folk have allus told, knowing Marsh folk breed true through the generations." Everyone tried to recall what was known of the wise woman's genealogy, which was uncomfortably nebulous. Mrs. Flax looked gratified by the general shudder, but judged it advisable to press the point no further, in case awkward questions should be asked about Rudyard Kipling.

"As for smugglers," she went on, "known to all, at times—and known to be true. Who could make up such a tale, or have need, as of that bold lad who fought with the excise men bearing four tubs of gin on his back, and then carried his injured friend all the way to safety? These writers, they take what they find and twist it to their advantage. Who's to know just how much truth there may be in the stories people tell?"

And answer came there none.

On the door of an office on the umpteenth floor of New Scotland Yard someone tapped, but did not wait for an invitation. The door opened and a head looked in, followed by the rest of a stately individual who nodded amiably to Delphick and his sergeant.

"Good God!" The Oracle pushed back his chair, and rose. The equally startled Bob followed suit.

"A trinity, certainly," replied the Assistant Commissioner, Crime. He waved his two subordinates back to their seats and carefully closed the door.

"We thought you were still in Costaguana, sir," explained Delphick as Sir Hubert Everleigh—behind his back, Sir Heavily—settled himself in the visitor's chair.

"Only just got back." Sir Hubert essayed a smile. His face was lined and pale. "All four of us—my wife, and the trinity to which you have already referred: I, myself, and me." He coughed. "As the three of us, I'm here in no official capacity, you understand. In fact, I'm not here at all, but having

52

now been debriefed at the Foreign Office I didn't want to go straight home until…"

Such hesitation was unusual, for the assistant commissioner. "You'll have read the papers, no doubt," he said at last. "There were even a few hardy television reporters around the place…"

"News coverage was very limited for the first few days, sir. We were all very concerned for your safety," Delphick said. "A most unsettling time for everyone. We had almost no idea of what was actually happening."

"Censorship by the military junta," said Sir Hubert. "Only to be expected, of course. The first thing you do in a coup is publicise the justice of your cause as widely as possible, while you stabilise your hold on the country and tell the world you're now the ones in charge. And why."

"We certainly received apparently verbatim reports of harangues regarding unbridled corruption and economic mismanagement having led to unprecedented levels of poverty," Delphick told him.

"And about some chap throwing huge envelopes full of cash and banknotes over some convent wall," added Bob as Sir Hubert glanced at him in silent but clear encouragement to make his own contribution.

The assistant commissioner's smile returned. "Has anything been said yet about the hippos? I thought not. When the presidential palace was stormed, the walls were breached in several places and many of El Dancairo's private zoo animals escaped. Most of them have been rounded up, but it is feared that a dozen or more hippopotami managed to reach the river. Ah—hippos of both sexes, you understand."

"Dear me." Delphick was tempted to launch into a chorus of "Mud, Mud, Glorious Mud", but though this was a surprisingly friendly chat with one of exalted rank he decided against it. From Bob's desk came a sudden muted guffaw that showed he, too, had felt the same temptation.

"Flanders and Swann," said Sir Hubert with—great heavens—a definite twinkle, "would have felt very much at home in Costaguana during the past few days. The hippos, you see, have no natural predators in the country, and the climate is favourable. In a few years' time there will probably be a score or more of them paddling about the place."

"Dear me," said Delphick again.

After another pause, Sir Hubert shook his head. "All I did was play a round of golf with El Dancairo. I felt it was the least I could do, in the circumstances—my wife having been granted the almost unique concession to tour a silver mine, and with a small ingot thrown in—which, by the way, we have declared to Customs—and, I might add, had we realised in time how appalling general conditions were in Costaguana we would never have gone there at all, but hindsight is a curse, and it was too late. And as for the wretched man's stomach, there was nothing whatever I could do about that."

"His…stomach," echoed the Oracle, not daring to meet the eyes of his sergeant. Bob was turning scarlet.

"He complained that its increasing bulk interfered with his swing," said the exasperated assistant commissioner. "In a country where half the population, we discovered far later than we should have done, lives at starvation level. Small wonder that Captain Morales saw this remark as the straw that broke the camel's back."

Bob could be heard choking. Delphick knew that one or other of them was bound to suggest that Sir Heavily had meant to say "hippo" instead. He sent up a silent prayer.

Whoever heard it paid attention. "Captain—a lowly rank to take the lead in so drastic an undertaking," Sir Hubert hurried on. "And yet there is no doubting the man's efficiency, drive, and general popularity. He treated both my wife and myself with all due consideration, but…" He sighed.

"There was an ugly mood about the place," he went on at last. "Captain Morales set guards over us, but they struck me as all too closely resembling the desperadoes who had been so eager to dispose of us for having consorted with the dictator. And yet we were only trying to be polite, as Her Majesty's Government would expect."

"Did you feel you were in real danger at any time?" Delphick asked, the gravity of the question suppressing much of the urge to laugh. The look on Sir Hubert's face suppressed it completely.

"Yes," said Sir Hubert. "For the first few days we did, especially after we learned that the president had bolted. We were very uncertain how things might end." He sat forward. "And this is why I wanted to talk to you, Delphick—to both of you. I want to know that you two at least won't assume the stress of recent events has sent me off my head…"

"Oh, you don't seem at all barmy to me, sir."

Bob goggled. Slang, to a superior officer? *Reassuring* slang, he realised, as Sir Hubert smiled. "Not even," the assistant commissioner said gently, "when I tell you that it was only when my wife was given El Dancairo's personal umbrella—an extravagant, bejewelled thing with a solid silver handle—against the rain as we were being transferred from one holding-place to another, that I…felt confident of our ultimate survival?"

There was a prolonged pause. Across the inward eye of all three men drifted an image of the umbrella-carrying little art consultant who, Miss Seeton to her friends and the Battling Brolly to the press, produced those remarkable drawings that had solved so many a baffling case. "He said she could keep it," Sir Hubert said. "Not that we brought it away with us, of course, but it somehow—comforted…I was fearful we might be being escorted from the palace to a prison cell, or even to stand before a firing squad, but…Captain Morales could have had no idea…"

"But the very thought of an umbrella acted upon you as any good omen must do," said the Oracle. "You're not barmy, sir. And here you are safe, as living proof."

Sir Hubert sighed with relief. "There was nobody else I could tell. You two have known Miss Seeton for years. I hoped you would believe me."

"We did, and do," Delphick assured him. "Whether Miss Seeton herself would approve of such—forgive me, sir—superstition I rather doubt, but I know she would be glad to have been of assistance, even in absentia."

Bob was still struggling with himself, and could only nod when Sir Hubert looked at him. Aunt Em and her umbrella—by association, any umbrella—a good luck charm? Would Sir Heavily, like so many of her admirers, add to her collection and commission a new brolly for Christmas? With a silver handle, to complement the Oracle's black silk, gold model from her first case all those years ago?

"…happy to confirm him as leader of the military junta," Sir Hubert was telling Delphick when Bob finally collected his wits. "Nor did he immediately promote himself to general, as so many might have done, which only reinforces my opinion that the captain has more than his share of common sense."

"Who knows," said Delphick, "he may have started a fashion. Perhaps in a few years there will come a naval overthrow of some island power led by an able-seaman, or a flight lieutenant from a landlocked country will become its supreme leader."

"An unlikely prospect," said Sir Hubert, "although stranger things do happen." He again looked towards Bob. "Do tell me, Sergeant—how is the little woman keeping?"

Bob went purple. "Doing well, sir, thank you, and the baby too, after the initial fuss and bother. They're with her parents just now, me being so busy on this Crassweller business and—oh. Sorry, sir." Sir Hubert had for a moment looked startled. "Sorry, sir, misunderstanding. You meant Miss Seeton, of course."

"I did, but I gather than congratulations are in order and I gladly offer them. Are you the proud father of a boy or a girl?"

"Boy, sir, ten pounds—that was the problem, Anne being so small—but no name as yet. We thought we'd decided in good time, but now he's safely here he—well, he doesn't seem to look like any of the names on our list."

"Miss Seeton," interposed Delphick, "is on holiday up north, sir. I have suggested that the sergeant postpone all thought of registering the birth until her return. His adopted aunt's uncanny knack for seeing to the heart of things may well come in useful."

"Except," said Bob, "we have no idea where she is—or when she's coming back."

Chapter Five

Miss Seeton, back in her own dear village, visiting the familiar shops, had been surprised on the post office threshold by the warmth of Lady Colveden's welcome. One might almost say her relief. How absurd. What could there be to trouble her? The wedding had been delightful. It did not rain. The bride was beautiful, the groom handsome. Miss Seeton sighed happily as she put away the block of annotated pencil sketches she would, in due course, turn into coloured pictures. Maybe an extra present, to hang in the newlyweds' new home? Something in pastel, blurring the soft tones of heather and moor and the castle in the background to contrast with the brilliant white of the bride's tartan-trimmed dress, the grey of Nigel's morning suit...

"Poor Sir George," she said next day, taking tea at Rytham Hall while everyone except her ladyship was off about his or her affairs. "He looked so woebegone in his top hat."

"But simply bursting with pride," said Lady Colveden. "And once he'd managed to mislay the wretched thing—I suspect Jean-Louis of a helping hand in that—there was no stopping him, was there?"

They reminisced and revelled for a while, but Miss Seeton could tell that something was on the mind of her old friend. One knew, of course, that the courteous guest does not pry.

"Tell me, my dear," said the experienced teacher. "What is troubling you?"

Lady Colveden laughed. "Oh dear, I was trying not to be too obvious. I thought we could at least have our gossip out in full before I explained."

Miss Seeton waited politely. Lady Colveden sighed.

"I'm afraid I may have accidentally committed you to a lot of work, Miss Seeton. You see…" She explained about the exhibition of wedding presents, and how it had somehow led to a Plummergen Bayeux Tapestry proposal to commemorate one hundred years since Manville Henty's first book was published, as well as the rest of the village history.

Miss Seeton was interested in this proposal, and said so.

"Ye-es," her ladyship said doubtfully. "But there's a good deal more history than I'd bargained for, as well as stories that *ought* to be history—to be true—but probably aren't. And of course everyone has their favourite."

"Like the Loch Ness Monster," said Miss Seeton, recent tourist in the Scottish Highlands. "One's rational side accepts that the existence of so strange a creature is unlikely—yet the romance of the legend cannot help but appeal."

"You've hit the nail exactly on the head. But that's how the trouble started, and you know Plummergen…" Lady Colveden saw her friend's puzzled expression. Of course she knew dear Plummergen! Had she not lived here since she retired? Lady Colveden stifled a sigh. It was clear that the numerous feuds that seethed around the village much of the time went unrecognised by her elderly friend. If (mused Lady Colveden) that was the state of mind to which yoga could bring you—Miss Seeton seldom spoke of it, but her private regime was known to her close acquaintance—then perhaps she, and Miss Treeves, and Miss Armitage should take it up at once.

"There was," temporised her ladyship, "a lot of discussion about it all. Rather too—too intense, sometimes. The legends lot insist it's all true about the smuggler with the four kegs of gin carrying his friend at the same time, and the historical people say if it hasn't been recorded somewhere, preferably with witnesses—like those three men who had rather too merry a Christmas and cracked the church bells—it doesn't count." She smiled. "And there are others who say the only history is what you can actually see…"

The art consultant, retained by Scotland Yard for the unique insight her swift sketches can often provide into even the most complex cases, nodded and blushed. Miss Seeton has always been a little embarrassed by those intuitive "flashes" for which she is paid, in her modest opinion, rather more than she deserves. When still teaching, she had always tried to persuade her pupils to draw only what was in front of them. Once they had mastered such truth they were then free to experiment beyond, into the realms of imagination and creativity. For herself, she found such exploration—especially when it came as if by chance from her unconscious mind—distracting. If not unnerving.

"And of course what they can see best," said Lady Colveden, "is their houses, so we're definitely going to have a map of The Street—it lends itself so well to going along a wall, doesn't it?—and everyone who wants to depict her house can easily put it in the right place. Louise knows two different ways to appliqué, and she'll help me do the Hall."

"So there is no likelihood of their moving soon to Summerset Cottage? Such a disappointment for them, though no doubt you and dear Sir George will be pleased to have them with you. But perhaps—in time for Christmas?"

There was further chat regarding the well-known firm of Grimes & Salisbury, building contractors of Brettenden, and their thorough but dilatory ways. The two friends laughed together over the manner in which Admiral Leighton, newly come to Plummergen, had dealt with Grimes & Salisbury, loudly threatening courts-martial and the lash. He had gone down in village history as the only man who ever made them finish a job on time.

"They're very *good*," said Lady Colveden, "and honest, but so *slow*. George, of course, is useless for chivvying purposes just now because he's so busy on the farm, with Nigel still taking afternoons off to show Louise the sights—they both send their love, by the way—and even when Fred does let me in, I might as well be still dealing with Miss Saxon and her servants because he keeps me in the hall, only now it's on account of sawdust and planks and sacks of cement everywhere, and he's worried I'll trip and break my neck."

Miss Seeton frowned. "I have had very few dealings with builders," she said warily. "My London flat was rented, and of course dear Stan looks after me now."

Lady Colveden gasped. She had a vision of Miss Seeton, chivvying with the ferrule of her umbrella the nether regions of Fred, conscientious but unhurried supervisor of the work in what would in due course of time become her son and daughter-in-law's first home. "Oh, no! I mean—no, my request was nothing to do with the builders. It's the other quilt—not the map, because everyone could agree on that, thank goodness. It's to be called the Plummergen Mural, not the Tapestry, because it will be different styles of sewing according to choice—needlepoint, embroidery, cross-stitch…" An airily ignorant hand waved through the air. "People are already hard at work to finish it in time for Manville Henty's centenary.

"No, it's the Legends and History Quilt that is the problem, and where I hope you can help. But first, Miss Seeton, you must be sworn to secrecy."

Miss Seeton, her eyes twinkling for her ladyship's solemn tone, promised she would keep any secret entrusted to her.

"Too many people wanted to sew the same stories," said Lady Colveden. "You wouldn't believe the squabbles. Far worse than children." Miss Seeton, retired schoolmistress, could well believe. "So to keep the peace we decided in the end that everyone can sew what she wants, even if we end up with a dozen Viking raids, as long as the committee knows what it is in advance for the design of the finished layout—and that's where we need your help."

Miss Seeton looked doubtful. "I fear my sewing is of a very basic nature. Practical, but hardly inspired—and I would have no idea how to begin designing a patchwork quilt."

"Miss Armitage is dealing with that side of things. Phyllis has really come into her own—she's always been so quiet, none of us had any idea she was a quilter. But she knows all about it, and apparently buys special squared paper and rulers from a shop in London." Lady Colveden frowned. "Not that I know what they're for, but Phyllis Armitage does—only she needs something to work *from*, you see, and nobody will show her what they're doing in case anyone else doing the same thing finds out and steals some of the—the inspiration."

"A certain amount of jealousy is surely understandable, among creative people—and, of course, an unwillingness to tempt fate. I believe that if you ask an author about his or her work in progress, some can be most reluctant to answer in more than very general terms, while others may be almost brusque."

Lady Colveden mentally applied *brusque* to some of the recent quilt discussions. Miss Seeton's gift for understatement had seldom amused her more. "Because she's the vicar's sister they're just about prepared to trust Molly Treeves, and she has managed to persuade everyone intending to stitch either a historical subject or a local legend to give her an idea of how they intend to portray it. But neither Molly nor Miss Armitage can turn those ideas into something on paper that can be used for the basic design. Proportion, or do I mean balance? Imagine trying to arrange five Queen Annes drinking water in the same quilt as a dozen Jack Cades leading revolting peasants. It would look ghastly, without careful planning in advance."

Miss Seeton agreed that one group would certainly overwhelm the other if proper care was not taken. It did not do to rush things. But with a deadline to meet, if both the map and the quilt were to be ready for the centenary, she would do what she could to assist—provided that she was not asked to sew. "My cousin Flora was a most delicate worker with a needle, but I possess no such gift. I fear I take after my dear mother in being barely adequate at sewing."

Lady Colveden could sympathise, though she hid it well. "Well, we do hope you'll manage a picture of Sweetbriars—" Miss Seeton gasped "—but what we would really like is that if we gave you the list of ideas, perhaps you could sketch them, fairly detailed if you didn't mind, so that Miss Armitage can lay them out—oh, dear." She giggled. "That reminds me of Mrs. Flax—" the witch attended the deathbeds of many villagers "—and how she seems to have adopted *Puck of Pook's Hill* and is claiming half the stories as her own family experience."

"The Flax name appears on several stones in the churchyard," said Miss Seeton.

"Well, yes…and talking of stories, the other reason for all the secrecy is that everyone is worried Murreystone might try to poach in our preserves. They're only a few miles away, and legends don't have boundaries as such, do they?"

Miss Seeton agreed that, generally speaking, they did not. One often encountered the same, or very similar, stories in different parts of the country, such as the hare shot one night with a silver bullet, and the limping old woman next day.

"Oddly enough, we don't seem to have that one in these parts." Lady Colveden smiled. "And if we did I'm sure Murreystone would say it happened there, too. It would be just like them to start making a quilt because we're making one, and nobody wants that—though if they did, at least it would stop the squabbling."

"United against the common foe," said Miss Seeton, and both ladies laughed.

Next morning was one of Martha Bloomer's days. As she had once "done" for old Mrs. Bannet, so Martha now "did" for Mrs. Bannet's goddaughter, relative and heir, Miss Emily Seeton. But Miss Seeton inherited far more than her cottage and its contents from Cousin Flora; she inherited the devoted friendship and willing service of Plummergen's domestic goddess Martha, as well as the cheerful arrangement her cousin had established with Martha's husband, Stan. Mrs. Bannet provided the wherewithal; Stan built a hen house. She paid for the feed; he did all the feeding, watering, mucking-out and egg collecting. What eggs the two households did not require he sold for profit in the village. This arrangement worked so well that over the years his trade had come to include flowers, fruit, and vegetables from the cottage's large rear garden that ran gently down towards the canal.

While Miss Seeton was permitted only to weed at the front, Stan was less strict about the back, and within certain limits let her potter as she pleased, under his distant and jealous supervision. She was even sometimes allowed to experiment with seeds and bulbs about which she had read in

Greenfinger Points the Way. Stan disagreed on principle with the advice given by Greenfinger, a book-learning type with no soil on his townified boots, but he accepted that it was, all said and done, Miss Seeton's own garden. So long as she didn't do nothing to give him (him as everyone knew did her garden as well as her fowls) a bad name, he supposed it might not reflect on him too poorly.

But this morning Miss Seeton had no thought of gardens. She and Martha, whose busy mop for once stood idle as the two friends drank tea together, were studying the cherry-wood sewing box inlaid with mother-of-pearl that Mrs. Bannet always kept on top of her treadle sewing machine in its veneered oak cabinet.

"These must be bone, rather than ivory," said Miss Seeton hopefully. She thought of the sad fate of too many elephants in bygone, less enlightened days, and stifled a sigh as she picked up the delicate creamy-white spools of thread. "And the silk has hardly faded at all, not that I would dream of using it in my humble efforts. It would be such a waste."

"Sweet little pin-cushion," said Martha, touching the plump red velvet back of a small, prick-eared dog cast in black metal. "Wonder what kind it is? A Pom, maybe."

A similar dog, sturdy and tailless like the first, was enamelled on the top of a circular box in which a spring-coiled tape measure was concealed. The tab was in the shape of a small silver bone. "The mechanism might be too delicate, after so long," said Miss Seeton, resisting the temptation to pull on the bone and measure something.

"Now you could use this thimble, dear. A good rub with Bluebell and it'll come up shiny as new."

With some regret Miss Seeton shook her head. "I think I prefer to keep the contents of the box together. After all, I have been accustomed for many years to darn and stitch for myself, in a modest way, and have all the basic requirements in an old biscuit tin—scissors, and needles, and pins and so on."

"Does this hold needles?" Martha was carefully unscrewing a slim tortoiseshell cylinder that rattled. Miss Seeton sighed again, for the tortoises this time, and picked up a pair of scissors with long sharp points, the handles curved in a stork's head and neck. Or perhaps it was a crane of some sort? Whichever it was, the feathers of its gold-plated body gleamed in pleasing contrast against the shining steel (she supposed, for it had not tarnished as had the silver thimble) of its beak.

There were other treasures to be lovingly examined, and both ladies enjoyed themselves very much, but in the end Miss Seeton shook her head again, preparing to close the velvet-padded lid and lock the contents safely away once more. "No, it would not be advisable for me to use any of these things. They were Cousin Flora's dear possessions—I recall her telling me the box was given to her mother as a bride—and quite apart from the risk that I might inadvertently do some damage, Cousin Flora is, I fear, too much to live up to."

They both contemplated the faded, but still exquisite, sampler in its neat wooden frame, hanging on one wall of the sitting room. *Flora Winifred Colyton wrought this in the ninth year of her age*, it announced in curlicued lettering at the bottom of a display of different alphabets and rows of numbers, stitched in fine wool on what must be linen. This central block lay between peacocks and other exotic birds most beautifully embroidered in silk, while across the top marched a row of elephants—Miss Seeton smiled—linked trunk and tail as they progressed.

"Far too much to live up to," said Miss Seeton. "Only eight when she started! Yet one can almost hear those elephants trumpeting. I also have my doubts about her sewing machine. Sewing machines seem to go so fast. Although my dear mother bought one, and we both did our best, somehow having to turn the handle and keep the fabric steady at the same time was never something that either of us found easy."

"You'd find it easier now, dear, seeing how that yoga of yours has limbered you up something amazing," suggested Martha, but Miss Seeton shook her head, reminding her that when she had left her London flat for Sweetbriars she disposed of such of the contents as did not belong to her landlord.

"Apart from my personal belongings, that is, which because we had seldom used it did not seem to apply to the sewing machine, and as Mrs. Benn mentioned that the needlework mistress was searching for a simple model on which the younger girls could learn, I naturally gave it to the school."

"Then you did really ought to try Mrs. Bannet's treadle," said Martha. "Riding your bike the way you do I'm sure you'd pick it up quick enough—and both hands free all the time, which nobody sensible does on a bike, in case of accidents."

"I suppose I could think about it…"

"And talking of accidents," said the loyal servitor as she prepared to resume work, "did you hear about Bert the other day? Right by the council houses, it was. Those foreigners who've taken Mrs. Venning's place—oh, no, you were still away when they came—anyway, they're *real* foreign, not just from farther afield than Ashford," sniffed London-born Martha, Plummergen only by marriage, "but Italian or similar, and everybody knows how the likes of them always drive on the wrong side of the road—and they did."

Miss Seeton looked dismayed. "Was poor Bert badly injured? Surely they cannot have been driving too fast, within the village limits."

Martha sniffed again. "They wouldn't understand what it means, thirty miles an hour, being metric as they are—but luckily he wasn't badly hurt. Bert stopped just in time and was about to give the other chap a right earful when he got out and apologised like a proper gent, Bert says, except that not knowing much English it was the same over and over again. But it was obvious what he meant. He takes that Mercedes—funny, I always think of a car, but that's what he calls her—to the shops and they've always got a phrasebook. Give them their due, they're shopping local as well as taking trips in that posh car, not that I've seen them around apart from at a distance, but so long as they don't upset people and do their best to fit in and don't drive too fast, I should think they'd enjoy their holiday right enough."

Miss Seeton smiled. "They will certainly feel at home with the weather." It was a fine September day. The sky was a clear, pale blue with few clouds, and the sun, warm and welcoming, shone bright on still-green trees that, this early in the season, were as yet only dappled with the gold of approaching death and dry rustles underfoot, of bonfires and bare branches that in time would be white with snow.

"I really should start work on sketching the list," said Miss Seeton. "I promised Lady Colveden—but it is such a beautiful day, and one hates to waste the sunshine, except that there is a need for haste because of the centenary. If Manville Henty's first success is to be commemorated properly, those who live in his village must play the best part they can. As my part in this project is to sketch, I suppose I should begin…"

"Stan tried reading one of his books once. In bed with the mumps. Old-fashioned, he said. Give him Jeffrey Farnol any day—if he had to read anything at all, he said. My Stan don't really hold with books."

Miss Seeton, thinking of Stan's views on Greenfinger, smiled.

She left Martha to those domestic duties she had abandoned when a cup of tea and some chocolate biscuits had occupied the sort of happy and companionable half-hour both ladies had missed during Miss Seeton's absence. Martha herself had returned from Scotland soon after the wedding. Stan could not long be spared from the farm; and Mrs. Bloomer harboured doubts about such substitute hygienas as the ladies for whom she "did" might have found for themselves—or (perhaps an even greater crime) might not have bothered to find. Built-up dust and catch-up cleaning she did not fear: it was the fear that her ladies might have tried to do for themselves what Martha knew herself to do far better—might have used (or misused) the tools and appliances she knew only she could wield with an expert hand—that had made her hurry home after kissing Nigel and his bride a tearful goodbye, and wishing them even half as happy a married life as she and Stan enjoyed together.

Miss Seeton likewise mused on Nigel and Louise as she prepared to draw her first quilt sketch. The secret list entrusted to her by Lady Colveden included several claims to the Cracked Church Bells story. Odd, that one had never closely studied the church tower. One saw it, and heard the chimes of the clock every day and the peal of the bells every Sunday, but as to how the bells were hung, and how easy it would be to crack one by mistaken pulling, she did not know. She was grateful that one panel of the quilt was going to show three cracked bells and no ringers, which should be easy to draw, but the other pictures seemed likely to prove very elaborate indeed.

Miss Seeton knew only too well how time-consuming detailed sewing could be. As she took her sketchbook from the bureau, she ruefully contemplated the neat cloth cylinder, tied with tape, where her pencils lay in individual slim compartments to protect their points. Practical, but dull. In an old book of Cousin Flora's—one of those serendipitous bound volumes of six months' or a year's run of some long-defunct journal—she had discovered the pattern for a Ladies' Jewellery Roll In Soft Velvet and realised it could be adapted, in some less exotic fabric and without the decorative feather-stitching and lace the designer seemed to feel essential, for paint-brushes, or pencils. So much easier to pop in one's bag or coat pocket than a tin. And far less likely to rattle.

Her pencil points were safe. Her stitching was neat and strong, her handiwork practical—but uninspired. Miss Seeton sighed. Like her artistic abilities. Perhaps a different choice of fabric for the brush holder—ribbon rather than tape, and in a contrasting shade—but Welsted's stock of haberdashery was likewise uninspired. She did not ask for velvets, for silk or satin or gossamer net—for the storage of artistic materials that would be absurd—but her sense of colour and texture, of light and shade and tone, demanded rather more for the brushes from whose bristles she hoped, one day, some truly worthwhile picture might come. And, should she decide to attempt a portrait of Sweetbriars in appliqué, as Lady Colveden had explained dear Louise was to show her how to achieve with the Hall, she might go into Brettenden to see what could be found there…

All this, though, was for the future. First, she must really begin sketching out the quilt panel ideas. But it was such a lovely day; she need not start at once. She would study the church tower and the bells, then stroll along Nowhere Lane to take a quick likeness of Summerset Cottage. It might make a house-warming present for Nigel and Louise, should the builders ever finish the job. Lady Colveden, over the teacups, had been most eloquent on the topic of Grimes & Salisbury.

Nowhere Lane. Miss Seeton smiled. Plummergen—always so fond of a joke...

"Miss Seeton, how splendid to see you! How are you?" Once again an old friend had greeted her return with what sounded like relief. The vicar's sister was on her way to the shops, having given her brother the early lunch she had organised so that he might the sooner be despatched on his home visit duties. "And be sure not to forget little Anne Knight—Ranger, I mean—and her baby now she's staying with her parents at the nursing home," she had warned as the vicar searched for the hat he was sure he'd left on the hall chest.

The Reverend Arthur Treeves had stared. "Nursing?" He was alarmed by visions of milky embarrassment. "I had no idea—that is to say, is she—is it—he—are they ill?" He ran an unhappy finger round the inside of his clerical collar.

Molly Treeves sighed. "Arthur, you know that it was difficult, but even you can hardly call her ill. Childbirth is a perfectly natural experience and Anne has been a nurse. Both she and the baby are doing very well now. They're only staying with her parents because Bob is apparently snowed under at work—some very important case—and it seemed better for her to be out of his way somewhere she can be sure of regular care, rather than the odd hours they sometimes work at Scotland Yard, and Bob is never there when she needs him."

The Reverend Arthur caught at her final words. "Bob Ranger? He's not there? But they were married only a short while ago. I performed the ceremony myself, and thought them ideally suited. If he has indeed left her, so soon, and with a small baby, this is very sad news. I will be sure to visit and commiserate with her, although—"

"Nonsense, Arthur! Bob is a working policeman. His wife and baby simply need some cosseting—and what *he* needs is not to worry." Molly saw his unhappy look, and softened as she handed him his hat from the peg behind the door. "You might like to ask about the christening, although I gather they haven't yet made up their minds, so you mustn't be too disappointed. The legal period for registering a birth is six weeks, so they can wait a little longer before anything has to be arranged…"

Bumping into Miss Seeton had come as a welcome change from her brother's muddled conversation. Molly Treeves was delighted to see her. "And I see you've been sketching—Lady Colveden phoned and told me you'd agreed. We are most grateful. May I look?"

"I haven't exactly begun yet, I fear. Such a lovely day—I thought the church bells first, but then I planned to take a look at Summerset Cottage, having heard so much about it from Lady Colveden."

Molly nodded. "Which comes as no surprise—but there, it's an ill wind. While Louise continues at the Hall, there's no excuse not to have a Colveden panel for the map. And she can teach the technique to others—yourself, perhaps, to make a representation of Sweetbriars." Miss Seeton looked startled. Molly ignored her. "She is such an obliging girl, like Miss Maynard, who has worked so hard to organise the children. Mr. Jessyp used a whole block of squared paper to work it all out before they began to paint it."

Miss Seeton smiled. "Lady Colveden told me that Nigel offered some of the farm tarpaulins for the base, if that is the correct term, but Miss Armitage insisted on linen."

"A special order from Welsted's," said Miss Treeves. "Mixed media, Miss Armitage called it. Once the foundation has been painted, we will start to sew on the houses as they are finished. But if you don't have the time to sew, with all your sketching—which is very kind of you—then I know Miss

Wicks would oblige. She has almost completed her cottage, and is working on her history panel at the same time."

"There is so much history," said Miss Seeton. "And some, so dramatic. Viking raids, the Peasants' Revolt, the great storm in the thirteenth century that changed the course of the river…" Out of deference to Louise she ignored the French burning in 1380 of the whole of Plummergen, and much of its church, dramatic though this had been. Not for nothing did Miss Seeton belong to the local library, and that noted historian Martin Jessyp was always happy to lend further reading, should she ask. Miss Seeton could be trusted to keep her hands clean and never to break the spines of his books, or turn down the corners of the pages to mark her place. Since becoming resident in Plummergen she had learned much about her new home, and was always happy to learn more when she could.

"Some silly people," said Miss Treeves, "take it amiss that others are so much more skilled with a needle than they are." She knew Miss Seeton had far too much sense to be of this number. "They're afraid the better ones will sew their houses for them without asking, and that we'll agree. We've tried to explain it's for everyone. With Miss Maynard painting with the children that ought to prove it's a project for the whole village rather than a select few, but you know what they can be like…"

But of course, as Molly Treeves recognised, this was what Miss Seeton did not know. Miss Seeton, as a true English gentlewoman, did not interfere with, or become too closely involved in, the doings of her neighbours and even—perhaps, especially—of her friends. As she valued her own privacy, so must they (she was sure) value theirs.

Miss Treeves rather envied Miss Seeton.

Chapter Six

Nowhere Lane was Plummergen's little joke. Before the Royal Military Canal was dug in 1804, the lane had been the main road from the village across the Marsh to Romney. The Corsican Tyrant never came, but the canal proved of undoubted benefit to the area, helping to drain the low-lying land nearby where mosquitoes had flourished, bringing the dreaded three-day ague Kipling called the Bailiff of the Marshes, who "rode up and down as free as the fog" for many centuries. When the new canal blocked the old way, the road dwindled into a lane that led nowhere in particular except a farm or two tucked away beyond the churchyard and a few quiet houses, Summerset Cottage being one.

Hardly quiet now. Miss Seeton had said goodbye to Miss Treeves, and set off with her sketchbook along Nowhere Lane. In the distance she heard a thudding, low-pitched grumble Miss Treeves had warned was the petrol generator used by the builders because Mr. Hickbody the electrician told Grimes & Salisbury that the wiring wasn't safe.

"Griselda Saxon," said Miss Treeves, "never let anyone in there, not even Lady Colveden, and the Brattles had to do as they were told or face the sack. They had nothing but oil-lamps and candles by the end, poor things."

"Picturesque," said Miss Seeton doubtfully, "but hazardous, one would have thought, for elderly persons."

Miss Treeves, eloquently, said nothing. Miss Seeton thanked her for the warning, and headed to Summerset Cottage. The sky was blue, the sun was bright. Had she only worn earplugs, she thought as the generator grew louder, it would have been a perfect setting. Except that now she could feel vibrations pulsing up through the soles of her shoes. She wondered how far they travelled. Did they reach as far as the vicarage? She supposed they must, or Miss Treeves would not have sounded so…frippy.

In the lane she hesitated. Her hearing was excellent, and she wished it to remain so. The smell of petrol did not disturb her unduly: to one accustomed to oil paints, for which the brushes must be thoroughly cleaned, such fumes were tolerable even if one personally disliked them. But this unpleasant noise…Perhaps she should come back another—

The generator shuddered, emitting a shower of sparks and a very loud bang. Miss Seeton, clapping her hands to her ears, dropped her sketchbook and umbrella. From inside the cottage came another bang. The generator stopped generating—dust and smoke and curses erupted from the open windows—and Miss Seeton, her head in a whirl and her ears ringing with such intensity she missed every blasphemous syllable, decided that another day would simply have to do.

She wondered what had caused this tumult and shouting. A gentlewoman does not display undue curiosity. Something mechanical, no doubt; she herself possessed no mechanical expertise. Quickly realising that the curses—if curses they were—continued with fluency but no accompanying screams or cries for help, she stooped—yoga, such a help to one's balance when one's ears still rang—and gathered up her scattered belongings, then headed back down the lane.

In her sitting room, she hesitated. She supposed she should really start work on her sketches from the Legends and History List, but...There would be other sunny days when she could return to Summerset Cottage. Or she might try what she could do from memory. The trained eye of an artist, even so mediocre an artist as herself, ought surely to be able to summon an image of what she had seen only a few minutes earlier...

Miss Seeton sat quietly, eyes half-closed, hands resting lightly on the table in front of her. She concentrated.

Miss Seeton sat up, opened her eyes, seized her pencil and opened her sketchbook. Her fingers flew.

Miss Seeton gasped. There before her was Summerset Cottage—recognisably Summerset Cottage—but the house was dwarfed beneath a swirl of thick black cloud that filled and overshadowed the rest of the page. Jagged flashes and showers of sparks pierced the cloud, and they came from—Miss Seeton gasped again—they surrounded and glorified the unmistakeable figure of...of his satanic majesty. The devil.

"Oh, no," said Miss Seeton. One was not, of course, superstitious in serious matters. The tossing over one's shoulder of a spilled pinch of salt, a greeting to the first magpie of the day: harmless practices, even amusing. But this. One did not lightly concern oneself with...Satan. As with witchcraft—that nonsense a few years ago, when she and young Mr. Foxon spent the night together in a ruined church so that she might draw one of the IdentiKit pictures for which the police paid her such a generous retainer—yes, as with witchcraft, it was nonsense.

But most distasteful nonsense. Even to herself, she did not care to think of her sketch as an omen. Certainly it could not be used as she had intended. Nigel and Louise must have no cloud, even an imaginary one, over the start of married life in their new home. She would return another day and try again. With one firm movement she tore the sketch from her book, and was about to crumple it when she paused. Thinking of Mr. Foxon reminded her of Superintendent Brinton, then of Chief Superintendent Delphick who had first recruited her—if that was the correct term…who had seen to it that she was paid that generous retainer for any sketch she might make, should it be required of her.

Carefully, and with reluctance, Miss Seeton slipped the stormcloud sketch into a folder in the bureau's bottom drawer, and could relax only once the drawer was shut.

She no longer felt in the mood for sketching from the quilt's secret List. She packed away pencils, eraser, sketchbook. She fidgeted a little, then remembered Cousin Flora's sewing machine. Might now be the time to examine it for possible use? Dear Martha had talked of quilting, and an even safer case for the pencils so carefully sharpened to points with the little folding knife she had, when at school, kept well away from the children.

Miss Seeton removed the sewing box from the top, and opened out on its hinges the heavy oak lid that revealed the sewing machine down in its cabinet. She seemed to recall that one simply pulled, and the machine—counterbalance? counterweight?—rose to the same level as the open lid and locked itself in position. She pulled. It did. Smiling, she bent to open the little doors near the floor. She fetched a chair of the appropriate height and sat down. Cautiously, she put two neatly shod feet on the black metal fretwork rocker—she thought of Daniel Eggleden and his smithy—and rocked.

Instead of the up-and-down rhythm of a clattering needle, there came a strange sound that was part whirr, part whispery, scraping hiss.

Miss Seeton treadled harder. The needle stayed still, the hiss grew more scratchy. It came from the right-hand side of the oak cabinet. She bent down and opened a narrow wooden door.

The leather belt meant to turn the wheel and power the machine was rigid to the touch, and flaking. Something like powder clung to Miss Seeton's fingers as she ran them along the part that was visible.

"Oh, bother," said Miss Seeton.

This year a fine crop of dandelions bloomed along the banks of the canal. Miss Nuttel and Mrs. Blaine favoured these for making wine because of the lead traces sure to linger in any weeds—wild flowers—growing by the roadside. Few Plummergen gardeners would admit to dandelions in their gardens, and public opinion had quickly suppressed the only attempt of the Nuts to cultivate a patch of their own. The wind, said Plummergen, blew everywhere. No need to go looking for more trouble when there were already plenty and to spare of the dratted things down by the canal, free for the asking.

Miss Seeton, deep in conversation with Dan Eggleden outside the smithy, paid no heed to the ladies from Lilikot as they made their way down The Street towards the canal bridge. Near the blacksmith's shop they paused to bicker over which of them should return home for a string bag for the bread (a sudden whim) from the bakery on their way home from filling their hessian tote-bags with nature's golden bounty. They did not raise their voices in the squabble— they were discreet—and they didn't see why others in the open air could not likewise moderate their tones. They really couldn't help overhearing what was being said.

"Easy. Treat it like part of a harness," said the smith, twiddling at the long narrow band Miss Seeton had given him.

"Unusual, these days, most folk using electric—but while Len Hosigg's a likelier bet if you fancy it in canvas, you can't beat leather for quality. I can whip you something up in no time…"

The squabble faded. The Nuts gazed at each other. They hurried away.

"That would be most kind," said Miss Seeton. "I never thought of canvas, but they are so busy on the farm—and this, of course, is leather. It does seem wise to keep as close as possible to the original, and if it should require more than one layer for strength, it might not fit. You can see how slim this is, and canvas must always be more bulky."

"You could always chop up one o' your old paintings, and use that instead."

Miss Seeton twinkled at him. "Now, that is something else that never occurred—but the metal footrest, and the sparks when the generator blew up, made me think of you, rather than Len, although he is a helpful young man and I'm sure would do his best if asked. Only with dear Nigel not yet fully back at work, I wouldn't really care to. Ask, that is, although I know belts of varying size may be used in all manner of farm machinery."

"Not many so small as this, Miss Seeton. You leave it to me. I'll pop across later to measure the wheel, but it looks a straightforward job…"

The Nuts had abandoned all thought of dandelions. Mrs. Blaine's plump cheeks were pale. Miss Nuttel seemed in shock. They staggered as far as the bakery, struggled into the tearoom, and sat down.

Mrs. Wyght was surprised to see them. Mrs. Blaine liked to make her own bread, when in the right mood, and both Nuts spoke of sugar with disdain. Icing and buttercream rotted the teeth and hardened the arteries, they told anyone who would listen.

"Two teas, please," Miss Nuttel brought out with visible effort. "Sugar—brown sugar." Mrs. Blaine grimaced. "For shock, Bunny," said Miss Nuttel.

"Summat upset Mrs. Blaine?" Mrs. Wyght knew it didn't take much to upset either of these unwonted visitors, and was prepared to hear of a low-flying magpie, or a sudden mouse scuttling from a hedge.

"Incitement to violence," said Miss Nuttel.

"In our peaceful village," moaned Mrs. Blaine.

Mrs. Wyght took a cautious step backwards.

"Bold as brass," said Miss Nuttel. "Right outside the blacksmith's—encouraging him to join in, what's more."

"And when you consider the difference in age, it's disgraceful," said Mrs. Blaine.

"Heard them yourself, Bunny—beating, whipping, leather—saw the whip, too. Brazen. She'll be off buying jackboots next thing we know."

"Electricity," shuddered Mrs. Blaine. "Torture—oh, Eric, it's simply too dreadful."

"Jackboots and canvas uniforms," concluded Miss Nuttel. "Proves it!"

Mrs. Wyght thought it proved only that the Nuts had somehow stirred a few, surely confusing, facts into a broth of wild conjecture. She had no intention of supping said broth. She would give no encouragement to whatever nonsense they were hatching about Dan Eggleden, son of the village, and someone at whose identity she could guess. Mrs. Wyght liked Miss Seeton. As a neighbour she was quiet. As a customer she shared her custom fairly round the local shops. Always polite to the bakery cats when she met them, she differed greatly from the Nuts, who muttered about murder and innocent birds...

80

Mrs. Wyght frowned. "Two sugared teas, then—or would you rather have a whole pot?"

So shaken were the Nuts that they agreed, without argument, to the pot.

At Rytham Hall four Colvedens sat over a late breakfast, discussing the sensational news delivered yesterday afternoon by Grimes & Salisbury's foreman regarding a discovery made in Summerset Cottage. They hadn't at first been able to take in what Fred was saying.

"Eyes? Staring? On the wall?"

"More like glaring, your ladyship." Fred ran his thumbs behind the shoulder straps of his dungarees, and shifted on his feet. "Angry eyes, scowling down."

"From the wall?"

"From the wood under the plaster, your ladyship, where it was all shook off when the generator played up."

His gaze took in Sir George, summoned from the farm, and Nigel and Louise, returned from sightseeing. Fred didn't mean to be rude, but men understood better about machinery than any amount of women, especially young and pretty foreign women. "The vibration, see, and the plaster being so old."

"And in poor condition," supplied Sir George, who had winced when the surveyor's report first came in and poured himself a double double whisky-and-soda before he read it in detail. It had taken another double double before he could explain to his wife that he didn't blame her, of course he didn't, but he did rather wish she'd insisted on going inside when she paid her weekly visit to the Saxons.

"I told you all along they never took any notice of me," his helpmeet reminded him. "I told you all along that you should have gone instead, and you wouldn't. And here we are."

Sir George, now catching her ladyship's warning eye, did no more than harrumph and say that well, he supposed, as it was all water under the bridge—

"Plaster all over the floor," interposed Nigel.

—there was nothing to be done except go and look at the damage and try to guess how much extra it was likely to cost to sort out.

"Bound to be a lot," said Sir George. "Always is. Right, Fred?"

"Right," said Fred, and led the procession.

All four Colvedens contemplated the eyes. Lady Colveden was prepared to accept that they glared rather than stared; and they were definitely angry. Nigel was reminded of one of the most choleric masters at his prep school. Louise ventured that they had the look of a pig, puffed round with fat and, if it was the word, scowling.

"Pigs are friendly creatures," objected Sir George. "But those eyes…"

"…belong to nobody friendly," finished Nigel.

"No," said Sir George. He looked at the foreman. "Any ideas?"

"They're old," said Fred. He looked sadly at his employer. "Could be historical."

"Oh dear," said her ladyship.

"Right," said Fred.

Louise turned to Nigel. "This history—it is bad?"

"Not in the sense of evil," said Nigel. "No witches or satanic spells, although there were always rumours—"

"In Plummergen," interposed his mother before he could repeat any of these, "they'll say anything about anyone if they feel like it. As you should know by now. Just because they were three sisters living together, and nobody ever saw them—"

"Or married them." Sir George shuddered. "Damned lucky escape."

"For the men," agreed Nigel. "They were just…batty old women." He dismissed the Saxons with a grin. "But not bad, as such." Lots of people had right-wing sympathies—it was all a long time ago—and anyway they were dead. "It's the historical bit that could be a problem. It'll mean notifying the museum and hordes of archaeologists examining the place for months while they decide if we'll ever be allowed to move in. Right, Fred?"

"Right," said Fred.

The breakfast discussion was lengthy, but the conclusion had been obvious from the start. "Shall you telephone Dr. Braxted, George, or do you want me to?" asked Lady Colveden. "After all, I've always been the one most involved with the place."

Sir George looked sheepish. His wistful gaze fell upon the newspaper, but now his conscience was even more firmly against reading at the table. He buttered more toast. Louise passed him the marmalade.

Lady Colveden was not a cruel woman. "Euphemia Braxted is our local historian," she told Louise. "Very keen, very knowledgeable."

Louise looked puzzled. "More so than Monsieur Jessyp? Is he, after all, no historian? From the talk I have heard around the village, I had supposed…"

She smiled her perplexity, and Lady Colveden smiled back. "I'm sorry, it wasn't mean to confuse you, my dear. Dr. Braxted is from the Brettenden museum. Martin Jessyp knows a lot about local matters, but he's not—not paid to know it, as she is."

"Rather like Gentlemen and Players," supplied Nigel. There followed a lively discussion on the good old days of cricket, which cheered Sir George until he caught his wife's eye, and subsided.

"She'll be thrilled, I'm sure." Her ladyship sighed. "I suppose we must be thrilled, too, if Fred is right, and it's historic and unusual and in all his born days he's never come across anything like it…"

"Like it?" echoed Nigel. "I don't like it. Who wants to live in a house with little piggy eyes scowling at them? Not me! I won't ask Louise what she thinks. I think it's creepy." He did not enlarge on the village view that the area might be haunted. A small triangular piece of land known as the Kettle Wedge, now forming part of the churchyard, was said in earlier days to have belonged to Summerset Cottage. Nigel did not believe in ghosts or manifestations, but he felt strongly that if those ill-tempered eyes were those of the original owner of the house, who looked like the sort of man who'd need to bargain for his salvation—well, he wanted them gone before he went to live there.

"Euphemia can knock off the rest of the plaster and take down the boards and shove them in her museum," he said. "Perhaps she'll know where we can get other old planks to match—even if they're foreign, no disrespect to you, Louise."

"He means from farther afield than Brettenden or Romney or Rye," said Lady Colveden to her daughter-in-law, who smiled.

"This has been explained," she said. "But when there are true foreigners in the village, perhaps a few planks for an inside wall may go unnoticed?"

"Oh, you've met them too," said Lady Colveden. "They're very good about local shops, aren't they? And so polite about doors and things, even if they don't say much. Italians, somebody said, although somebody else said they don't sound much like the prisoners of war on the farms here years back."

Louise hesitated. Nigel prompted her. "She doesn't bite if you disagree," he said.

Louise smiled. "My languages are not so good," she ventured. "My English, of course, because of my mother, but others, no, for Papa would never let me learn German and what I was taught of Italian I have mostly forgotten, but I would have said Spanish, perhaps, though it is an accent I do not recognise."

Sir George, still subdued, buttered more toast.

"Italian, Spanish, does it matter?" said his wife. "If we needed to know we could always look at their phrasebook, but they have beautiful manners, and use local shops, so as long as they take care how they drive, I hope they enjoy their holiday."

Sir George helped himself in silence to marmalade.

Miss Armitage had meant to be helpful, Miss Seeton was sure. Meeting her friend coming from the smithy with the new leather belt, Miss Armitage, formerly so quiet, on hearing why a new belt was required invited herself to tea, and took so delighted an interest in Cousin Flora's sewing machine that Miss Seeton asked if she would like to try it.

"And of course you'd like me to fit the belt." Miss Armitage twinkled gaily at Miss Seeton, who turned pink, and smiled.

An old pillowcase destined by Martha for dusters was sacrificed to Miss Armitage's enthusiasm. She threaded and re-threaded the machine and made Miss Seeton thread it, too. She wound bobbins, and explained how they had to fit into the neat metal pocket under the stitch plate, and how the thread must be pulled up to begin sewing. She treadled with energy and speed, spoke of bicycles, and made Miss Seeton treadle quite as fast before she would let her stop. Miss Seeton took a sketchpad and, in her rare moments of freedom, made detailed notes and diagrams.

It was strange how, even using two hands, it was not easy to keep the edge straight.

"Sticky tape," Miss Armitage prescribed, unable to watch Miss Seeton's struggle and not interfere. "Lots of people use it to guide the edge. Fold one long edge under to make it more visible—thicker—and once you've had enough practice you might not need it anyway." She rose to her feet, suppressing the urge to show how it should be done. "Practice makes perfect—and remember what I told you about unthreading the machine."

"Snip it at the top and pull the whole length through," recited Miss Seeton dutifully. "It must never be pulled backwards because of…tension. And fluff."

"Good girl." Miss Armitage patted her on the shoulder. "You've got it. Don't waste your thread on practice sewing until you can manage a straight line. And then—the world's your oyster! We'll see something splendid from you for the mural map, I'm sure."

"Or perhaps even the quilt," suggested Miss Seeton, her spirits lightening as her friend—so competent, but making one feel so inadequate—made her farewells.

Left alone, Miss Seeton sighed when the pillowcase drifted yet again to one side of the stitch plate and the row of holes described a gentle curve. "Sticky tape," Miss Seeton told herself, and hurried to the bureau.

Miss Seeton always felt that, clever as it was, sticky tape of whatever brand she bought was undeniably quick and easy to do, and almost impossible to undo. But this was no parcel to be wrapped: it was a flat metal plate to be marked. She fetched her ruler and measured five-eighths of an inch. She marked it. She fetched scissors, cut the tape, folded, stuck. She settled back in the chair and held the pillowcase as steady as she could.

Perhaps (she decided) the fabric was too large for a novice. It was now full of holes, no use probably even as a duster now. Cutting it in half could not hurt. She cut a straight edge and settled down again to treadle.

Good. Things were definitely improving. That line of empty stitching might almost be straight, if you ignored the beginning and the end. Miss Seeton cut it off, and treadled again. Yes, that was better. One could always use the cut strips for tying plants back. She made a third attempt. The sticky tape unstuck, and curled back on itself.

"Bother," said Miss Seeton. "Just when it seemed to be working." She measured another length of tape, stuck it down, and threw the first piece, no longer sticky and dusted with tiny particles of fabric fluff, into the bin.

Definitely an improvement, she decided after the creation of a large bundle of garden ties and the exhaustion of several feet of sticky tape. How clever of Mr. Eggleden to make her a new belt for her machine! How kind of Miss Armitage to spare the time to help!

And then she looked more closely at the stitch plate, and the black enamel of the main body of the machine. She had been so closely focused on the fabric and the needle that everything else had seemed unimportant.

"Oh," said Miss Seeton. "Oh, dear."

Chapter Seven

Miss Seeton, anxious to repair domestic damage before Martha noticed, hurried next morning to the post office. People stared as she entered. The Nuts, snubbed yesterday by Mrs. Wyght, had drunk their tea and, stimulated by sugar and indignation, hurried to spread the news of Miss Seeton's latest infamy. As nobody saw her after hearing the news, speculation persisted into the next day. Some said it was nonsense, others that they wouldn't put anything past her—no arguing with facts—and Dan Eggleden did really ought to know better than to encourage her in her madness. Whips! Straitjackets! (This, extrapolated from the mis-overheard mention of canvas.) Bondage!

Emmy Putts at the grocery counter was intrigued. Her friend Maureen from the George sometimes confessed to having a Thing about black leather, this being what had first drawn her to her Kawasaki-riding Wayne. Emmy wondered if there might be something in it. Maureen had a steady boyfriend; Emmy did not. But if old folks like Dan Eggleden and Miss Seeton enjoyed it, did that mean young lively folk would not?

"Stop your daydreaming, Emmeline Putts," said Mrs. Stillman. "You'll be mincing your fingers into the bacon if you aren't careful. That's far more than Mrs. Spice wanted."

Emmy mumbled inaudibly. As the postmaster's wife spoke again, the bell over the door jangled and Miss Seeton walked in.

"No, no, you go first," everyone invited. Was she about to ask for a coil of rope, rubber boots, or (a general thrill) even more electric batteries?

Miss Seeton smiled thanks to all, and approached the general counter. "I should like a small bottle of vodka, please," she said. "And a packet of cotton wool."

Sensation, muted until she completed her purchases, erupting as the door jangled shut behind her. With everybody trying to talk at once it was a while before a general consensus could be reached, but in the end it seemed the Nuts might have had the right of it after all. Cotton wool— that'd be for the chloroform, once she'd got 'em drunk on vodka, that having no taste. Easy to slip it in someone's drink and catch 'em unawares. Half a bottle'd be more than enough for them not used to it.

"You be warned, Emmeline Putts," said Mrs. Spice. "If Miss Seeton asks you in for a cup of tea or an orange squash, you say no!"

In Sweetbriars Miss Seeton poured vodka into a saucer and, tearing off a small piece of cotton wool, dabbled it damp and gently began rubbing at the sticky residue on her sewing machine. How fortunate that it came off with so little effort, despite having had all night to dry out. The newspaper was right. Vodka had no unpleasant smell, and restrained by the cotton wool did not drip, stain, or smear. Far more acceptable for this cherished item than any of Martha's patent cleaners, which for general scrubbing and scouring did very well, but for enamel decorated with flowered garlands seemed too great a risk. As for Cousin Flora's mother's 1876 *Enquire Within Upon Everything*—where should Emily Seeton, a

century later, obtain such ingredients as roche alum, powdered whiting, or rottenstone?

She packed her cleaning things away, and lowered the re-
furbished machine into its counterweighted hollow. It had all
worked out splendidly, even if she must not allow it to happen
again. But Martha need never know—and the sun was coming out. Miss Seeton closed the lid of the cabinet, replaced the
cherry-wood box, and assembled her sketching gear. Today
she would do better at Summerset Cottage. It would be so
much quieter, the builders having been sent to other jobs...

She was therefore surprised to be greeted, as she drew the
first outlines, by a loud cry that was almost a shriek. "Miss
Seeton!" An exuberant head poked from a downstairs window. An arm waved a frantic *Come in!* gesture. "Miss Seeton!"

Miss Seeton recognised both the head, and the exuber-
ance. She had first met Dr. Euphemia Braxted of Brettenden
Museum during the excavation of the small Roman temple
at Rytham Hall. Dr. Braxted, given to flinging her arms
about for emphasis, had this time settled for one quick wave
and several cries, the window being hardly large enough for
more. "Miss Seeton! Do hurry!"

Miss Seeton slipped the sketchbook into her capacious
handbag. With her umbrella to balance her as she picked
her way along the crumbling path, she hurried to meet her
friend. It was clear from Euphemia's demeanour that more
than a casual welcome had been intended, and like all good
teachers Miss Seeton approved of enthusiasm. She hoped it
wasn't for something historical she wouldn't understand.

"Lovely to see you—come through here!" Dr. Braxted
grabbed her visitor by the arm and tugged her across the panelled hall into a small but stately reception room. Miss Seeton sidestepped chunks of plaster, and tried not to breathe
in puffs of dust.

"There!" cried Euphemia, dropping Miss Seeton's arm and flinging both hers wide. "You're an artist. What do you make of that?"

Miss Seeton stared. On the wall opposite, surrounded by remnants of plaster, peering into the room and glaring—at her—was the unmistakeable face of Henry VIII.

"Good gracious," was all she could find to say.

Dr. Braxted clapped her hands. "Splendid, isn't it? I've only just cleared the face—you can tell from the position there's more to come—but it looks as if we might have a full-panel portrait of Elizabeth I's father!" As a young woman Euphemia had been a redhead, though the fire had faded now to pale copper.

"It's—it's remarkable," said Miss Seeton uneasily.

"Makes you uneasy?" Dr. Braxted chuckled. "Me, too. Never my favourite character. When he was young and glamorous, before he started putting on weight and throwing wives away like a bored child with its toys, I suppose he had something going for him—but those beady little eyes do remind me of a child plotting more than ordinary mischief."

"From what I recall of various portraits it is an accurate likeness," said Miss Seeton, with reluctance. She stepped back a few paces and considered the face again. "Which makes it all the more remarkable—that anyone should be willing to marry him, that is. Except that of course his marriages were mostly political, I believe."

"Until lust got the better of him—but if he hadn't chased after Anne Boleyn we would never have had our Gloriana." Dr. Braxted shuddered. "Imagine! The country ruled by that sickly Protestant fanatic Edward—or that neurotic Roman fanatic Mary—why, it doesn't bear thinking about. No Raleigh, no Drake—no speech at Tilbury—no Shakespeare…"

Miss Seeton tried to imagine it. She sighed. Euphemia ignored her.

"The Colvedens won't like it, but they'll have to lump it. This painting could be unique. The rest of it must be uncovered with great care, and it will take a long time. With limited funding, and so few assistants…I might rustle up a couple of students, but that'll be the lot. This is priceless, Miss Seeton. There will be photographs to take, measurements to be made, sketches…You were starting to sketch outside in the lane—that's when I spotted you. This house isn't going to run away. There's always tomorrow—but for all I know, now it's been uncovered to the air, the paint might dry out and flake off overnight. I've brought my camera, of course—I wish the museum could afford a Polaroid—but things can go wrong, so would you mind jotting down what we have so far?"

Miss Seeton opened her bag, and prepared to sketch the scowling face of Henry VIII. Would she ever complete her picture of Summerset Cottage? "And I wonder why," she murmured to herself.

"Why here in Plummergen? Goodness knows. There'll be some digging through the archives on this project—but I'm no expert. First thing I'll do once I'm back in Brettenden is telephone my sister."

Miss Seeton had met Dr. Eugenia Braxted, Euphemia's identical twin, who much preferred the less strenuous and less muddy aspects of history and worked at the British Museum in an office crammed with papers, parchments, and dusty vellum rolls.

"Yes, of course," Miss Seeton said absently, still sketching, "but what I really meant was—why is the house called 'Summerset Cottage'? It is, after all, in Kent, not Somerset. One could understand had Sussex been the name—Sussex being our neighbouring county, and boundaries can change—but so far as I know it has always been assumed that the volatility of spelling in past centuries is the reason for the Summerset misspelling. But it has never been clear *why*." Again she glanced at Henry, and returned to her work wishing she had brought coloured pencils as well as graphite. She jotted notes about shades and tones. "Was not one of Henry's numerous brothers-in-law called Somerset?"

"Edward Seymour," said Euphemia, "brother of Queen Jane, was the first Duke of Somerset. He was also the Lord Protector who egged on that pious little squirt Edward after Henry died, had his brother executed for treason, and got his own head chopped off not so long after."

Miss Seeton stayed her note taking. "Those were different times, of course, but would you have said a suitable candidate for commemoration in Plummergen?"

"I wouldn't have thought so, but that's where Genie comes into her own. My sister really enjoys digging through records and unearthing obscure facts. This place might have been a hunting lodge for the Duke—somewhere to get away from it all."

"Which in Tudor times would have been a very wise idea." Miss Seeton doodled the semblance of a heavy crown where the top of the head merged into the unbroken plaster. "Or somewhere to keep a mistress. Another Fair Rosamond, perhaps—though no maze. Remarkable. And…uncomfortable."

Dr. Braxted peered over her shoulder. "Splendid," she said. "Thank you, Miss Seeton. Now, if the paint flakes off when there's nobody here and my photos go wrong, we'll have some sort of record. Belt and braces. Oh…I don't suppose Mr. Jessyp would oblige?"

"The children are back at school, Dr. Braxted."

Euphemia chuckled. "It was worth a try. And by the time you've been able to develop your notes into a reasonable likeness, I'll have been up to the Hall and broken the bad news and gone back to the museum to start phoning. This could make history in every learned journal ever published!"

Miss Seeton left Dr. Braxted to her jubilation, suspecting that it might be a while before the Colvedens learned of her discovery. Such enthusiasm and energy. Miss Seeton smiled, making straight for home while that uncomfortable image was still clear in her mind and her notes would make the best possible sense. The word "exorcism" was over-dramatic and inappropriate, if not blasphemous, but she felt—so foolish of her—that if she could draw Henry's face with sufficient clarity to please Euphemia, she could then dismiss those mean little eyes, that grey-gold beard, those jowls, completely from her thoughts. No wonder the workmen had been startled. No wonder Nigel had said the painting could be—must be—offered to the museum! Lady Colveden, who had told her friend all about it, hadn't then seen the whole face. She hadn't, then, *understood*.

"...yelling at her to hurry up inside!" Mrs. Newport had been approaching the entrance to Nowhere Lane as Miss Seeton turned into it. Mrs. Newport wondered why, when there was so little down there of interest. Mrs. Newport duly pursued Miss Seeton along the lane, and heard the cries of Dr. Braxted.

"All excited," said Mrs. Newport now, "and straightway in trots Miss Seeton."

"Maybe that history woman *found something*," suggested Mrs. Skinner.

"Like what?" challenged Mrs. Henderson. "The furniture and stuff was all sold. "

Mrs. Skinner rose to the challenge. "A place like that could hold a load of secrets...beyond what we already know about."

The younger element among the post office gossips looked puzzled. "I don't know nothing," said Mrs. Newport.

"Nor me," said Mrs. Scillicough. "Mum's never said a word to us about that house." It occurred to neither sister that a woman spending much of her time looking after a frenzy of grandchildren was unlikely to waste any of that time on village history. While nothing definite had ever been proved, and because the village believed in ghosts, the original story told by Jacob Chickney, Plummergen's disgraced and unpopular mole-catcher, had at the time of telling been accepted rather than questioned.

Three decades on, questions were surfacing from a younger, less credulous generation. "So what's there to know?" said Mrs. Newport. "Old Griselda was off her head for years, we all know that."

"You're too young to remember the war," Mrs. Henderson began. Both sisters said together that they knew this very well. "D-Day, it was. Sixth of June 1944, and a full moon—and Jacob Chickney on the prowl down by the Kettle Wedge."

"Said the spinney was haunted," enlarged Mrs. Skinner, for once in agreement with her rival. "Said he saw lights through the trees, and *shapes* moving about—"

"And pushed off sharpish." Mrs. Henderson regained the narrative. "He said he went back later and looked, but with the ground so wet he couldn't find nothing, so much rain as there'd been."

"He *said* he didn't find nothing," countered Mrs. Skinner. "But you can be sure he'd have looked good and hard, the wicked old man."

"But he didn't go back straight away," said Mrs. Henderson, "on account of their father being seizured that self-same day. As near to death as makes no difference, and Jacob Chickney fearing he might have been witness to a foreboding of what was to come. Stirring things up, he said. So he let them lie for a while."

Mrs. Spice, that practiced fence-sitter, at last joined in. "Mebbe he found something after all," she offered. "Could well of been their uniforms, as was suggested by some at the time."

"Whose uniforms?" came a further chorus from Mrs. Newport and Mrs. Scillicough.

The older members of the party looked at one another. Mrs. Henderson won.

"Them Saxons," she said. "There was allus talk about how the family could of been in the pay of Hitler for years, just biding their time till he came, and uniforms all ready to show their support when he arrived—that's whose."

"So maybe that's what Dr. Braxted found and wanted to tell Miss Seeton," concluded Mrs. Skinner.

"And yet," said Mrs. Henderson slowly, "what call would Dr. Braxted have to dig for uniforms in the churchyard when it's them eyes in the house she's meant to be exploring? If Jacob Chickney couldn't find them—"

"He might of done," said Mrs. Skinner.

"So he might," agreed Mrs. Spice. "And blackmail, after, if he dug up the uniforms and told the Saxons they'd do well to let him have a share of Hitler's gold he paid them over the years…" The tabloid press would have been gratified at its influence in Plummergen. "They couldn't of spent it all, intended as it was for bribery and corruption after he came, which o' course he never did."

"Could explain why the Saxons never had much money," said Mrs. Henderson.

"Never seemed to," said Mrs. Skinner. "But Jacob Chickney never had none, either."

There was a contemplative pause.

"So—what *were* they burying, then?" demanded Mrs. Scillicough at last, reluctant to accept ghostly forebodings. "Uniforms? Box full of Nazi gold?"

Mrs. Henderson looked at Mrs. Newport. "She was in the house, you said? And called Miss Seeton inside?"

"And told her to hurry up," nodded Mrs. Newport.

"Then what was buried in the Wedge could still be there, and whatever she's just found, it's in the house." Even Mrs. Skinner could not fault this logic. "And whatever it is, she wanted Miss Seeton to know of it afore anyone else."

"Whatever it is," Mrs. Scillicough echoed wistfully. "That box of gold, maybe..."

"Well, when it's a matter of Miss Seeton," Mrs. Newport reminded everyone, "you never can tell, can you?"

Miss Seeton, walking home, found her thoughts turning from Henry VIII to the music-hall song of Harry Champion. Miss Seeton's voice was neither tuneful nor strong, but she enjoyed herself. "I'm her eighth old man named Henery—I'm Henery the Eighth I am!"

The Reverend Arthur Treeves swept off his hat, and to her surprise—he was normally so shy—began to reprise the chorus in a pleasing baritone. "I'm Henery the Eighth I am, Henery the Eighth I am, I am—I got married to the widow next door, She's been married seven times before—Every one was a Henery, She wouldn't have a Willie or a Sam..."

Miss Seeton joined him in the final couplet, forgetting self-consciousness. The dear vicar seemed to be enjoying himself so much. "I'm her eighth old man named Henery—I'm Henery the Eighth I am!"

"Bravo, Miss Seeton," applauded the Reverend Arthur. "The old songs are undoubtedly the best." He recalled that when he was a curate...but that was many years ago. "Perhaps a duet at the Christmas concert? Or maybe," he temporised; she was, after all, unmarried and it might be misunderstood, "my sister Molly could make it a trio."

"But then who would play the piano?" Miss Seeton smiled kindly at him. He had been carried away by the song of his youth, and now wished to be relieved of his embarrassment. "Miss Treeves, I know, has many talents, but singing is so much more comfortable standing up, whereas playing the piano is not. Perhaps we might think of something else."

With a smile and a nod she walked on, leaving him trying to remember why he was on the corner of Nowhere Lane going…he could not remember where. Molly had told him, as he left the vicarage, that he must be sure to visit someone he had forgotten to visit the previous day. He had better go back to ask, even though she had reminded him only a few minutes ago. She was sure to know—unless, of course, she had already become engrossed in her piano practice…

Back at home, Miss Seeton made a cup of tea and settled with her notes and coloured pencils to the sketch of Henry VIII. Relaxed now, she concentrated. Into her mind drifted once more the cheerful Harry Champion song, and once more with pleasure she warbled the chorus. She hardly noticed that her fingers, unbidden, had picked up a pencil and begun to draw…

"Oh." In place of the bloated, pig-faced Henry she expected, she saw three elderly women—long of hair, bright of eye—in floor-length dresses advancing down a flight of stairs, their robes held well clear of their booted feet. Their eyes were the most vivid part of the drawing; their expressions, like their hair and their apparel, identical. Glaring. Intense. Were they angry? Challenging? Fearful? Three of Henry's unfortunate wives? All six had undoubted cause to fear, for much of the time. But surely he had always—apart from the fortunate Katherine Parr, who outlived him—chosen youthful wives of child-bearing age? Which these three females clearly were not.

The Fates, perhaps? Spinning, weaving, cutting the fabric of life…Miss Seeton smiled ruefully towards the cabinet of the sewing machine. Perhaps she had been over-optimistic in her needlecraft intentions, after all.

"Oh, bother," said Miss Seeton. Despite her detailed note taking, Henry's colourful image had somehow been completely swamped by those three weird sisters. "Sisters," said Miss Seeton. The vicar's mention of a trio must have confused her. Quickly she checked the clock. Dr. Braxted had said she would go to Rytham Hall to break the news, then to Brettenden Museum to start her telephoning. Miss Seeton knew Euphemia. She would almost certainly still be chipping plaster from the walls of Summerset Cottage. The door would not yet be locked.

Miss Seeton slipped her tin of coloured pencils—they rattled; yes, she would teach herself to quilt, and make a proper carrying-case—into her bag. She chose a fresh sketchbook, shutting the other on the troublesome Fates, putting it and them in the bureau.

In the hall she arranged her hat—perhaps that grosgrain trim was a touch too lively; she might unpick one crest—popped on her jacket, and unclipped an umbrella from the rack. As she trotted down the front path, she found herself humming yet again the song that had first helped to drive from her thoughts that uncomfortable image of Henry VIII.

She frowned, and shook her head. This would never do. Dr. Braxted had asked her to draw the painting—should it be called a fresco?—as an aid to her research. Amusing as the song was, she must concentrate on forgetting it. She did not, in her concentration, notice the vicar emerge for the second time from the vicarage. He raised his hat, saw that she did not see him, and was at once overcome with guilt for his earlier presumption, and the offence he must so unwittingly have caused.

So troubled was the Reverend Arthur by Miss Seeton's obvious snub that he could not now remember where he was supposed to be going. Molly would know, of course, but his sister had been a little…restive when he apologised for disturbing her piano practice a few moments earlier.

Miss Seeton smiled as she drew close to Summerset Cottage. The sounds of someone hard at work with some sort of tool—she thought of sculpture, and her student days—came clearly through the open window, together with puffs of dull white dust. She walked warily up the path and coughed, not altogether because of the dust.

A cough answered her from inside. Yes, undoubtedly Dr. Braxted. Miss Seeton called her name.

"Is that you, Miss Seeton? Come on through!" Euphemia, on a stepladder, turned with a wide, square-bladed knife in her hand. "The builders didn't take all their tools, and I knew they wouldn't mind if I borrowed a few bits and bobs for today. Tomorrow we'll have the proper equipment, but for the moment…"

She tapped the plaster with energy and a knife-blade corner. Miss Seeton, smiling, noted that there was a good deal less of the plaster on the wall than there had been, and many more chunks of it on the floor.

"You have managed to uncover a considerable—" she began, and then: "Oh!"

From the point where Euphemia had tapped, cracks began to radiate like some swift-moving spider's web in every direction, widening all the time and with increasing speed. "Oh, Dr. Braxted, do take care!"

Miss Seeton stepped back, opening her umbrella as a sudden hail of fragments fell from the wall. They shattered and crumbled as they fell, they bounced off the brolly and the floor, they crumbled further as they spread like a thick, dry fog throughout the room.

Miss Seeton began coughing again. Up her ladder Euphemia coughed so much it looked as if she might fall. "Do take care," called Miss Seeton, peering round the umbrella. She coughed. "It seems to have stopped…"

Dr. Braxted climbed down the steps. "Outside, to let it clear," she croaked, and both ladies picked their way through the litter out on to the path.

They gave it ten minutes in theory, but Miss Seeton was not surprised when Dr. Braxted called time after about seven. "With luck that little mishap has done the rest of the work for me. Shouldn't have been so careless, of course. Hardly the behaviour I'd like to see in any of my students, but if we keep it our little secret…Gosh!"

They were back in the parlour, staring at the imposing fresco revealed by that one sharp tap from Euphemia's knife. "Oh, my goodness!"

"Yes, indeed," was all Miss Seeton could say.

"Oh, gosh," breathed Euphemia. "I've never seen anything like it!"

It was Henry VIII, enthroned in scarlet robes of a richly patterned fabric edged with a curving of dark fur, fastened at the throat by an elaborate brooch of gold and jewels. He sat with his knees apart, square and dominating with his body as well as his expression. In one plump hand on an enormous knee he held a sceptre; with the other he clutched a large orb surmounted by a long-stemmed cross. A crown sat heavily above his huge, pale face, overshadowing his features so that even his eyes seemed less oppressive. The colours were a little faded, but the drapes and folds of the cloth—embroidered velvet, perhaps a luxurious brocade—were very clear, if muted by the passage of time.

"It—it's magnificent," said Euphemia. "It's amazing!"

Miss Seeton could only fall back on her original comment. "Remarkable," she said.

"The hours of work!" Euphemia flung out her arms. "The detail! See the writing in those side panels? Looks to me like biblical texts of some sort."

She sprang forward, or tried to, but her toe clipped a chunk of plaster and she clutched at Miss Seeton's arm. Miss Seeton, who after careful shaking outside had closed and furled her umbrella, now dropped it. Dr. Braxted's forward motion was interrupted. Arms akimbo, legs likewise, Euphemia tripped over Miss Seeton's umbrella, staggered, spun round, and fell with a crash to the floor.

Miss Seeton could only gasp, which made her cough again as plaster dust came swirling from around the stunned shape on the floor. No, not stunned—Dr. Braxted's eyes were open, and moving. She, like Miss Seeton, coughed. She had not, then, been knocked unconscious, but was she otherwise all right?

"Oh, dear," ventured Miss Seeton. "Don't move, Dr. Braxted, until you have ascertained there is no injury."

But there came no answer from Euphemia, now wide-eyed and rigid on the floor.

Miss Seeton had more sense than to ask if Dr. Braxted was all right when it was clear she was not. She asked what she should do to help.

Euphemia continued to stare. Miss Seeton began to worry. Had she hit her head, had a seizure of some sort?

Euphemia's lips opened.

"The devil!" cried the learned and distinguished lady historian. "Oh—the devil!"

Chapter Eight

Miss Seeton was not surprised—she was astounded. She stood speechless, gazing at Euphemia Braxted where she lay amidst ruin and debris, flat on her back on the floor. A gentlewoman was no less subject to moments of stress than anyone else; but on the rare occasions when Miss Seeton felt the need to vent her emotions she found that a modest dash, drat, bother, or blow suited her very well. But of course she had never fallen with such force and banged her head…

"Look!" cried Euphemia, pointing. "Just look at him—upside down!"

Dr. Braxted's tone was so urgent, Miss Seeton's astonishment so great, that after one wary look at the plaster dust and rubble she removed her hat, set it with her bag down by her umbrella, turned around, and raised her hands. Standing with feet apart she began, very slowly, to bend over backwards until she had a safe grip on her ankles and, in the hooped perfection of the Wheel posture or *Chakrasana*, could once more study the painting on the wall. Upside down.

"Good gracious!" she gasped. "It is!"

"Old Scratch himself," said Euphemia, rolling over and scrambling to her feet with a perfunctory dusting-down movement once she was upright. She studied the far from upright shape beside her. "I say! Pretty impressive, Miss Seeton."

Miss Seeton blushed. Yoga was a private matter; one was not supposed to assume a pose with any intention of display. She began, as discreetly as possible, to uncurl.

Both ladies stood together, staring at Henry VIII.

"A mirror," said Euphemia. "I've one in my bag somewhere…"

"As have I."

Both ladies stood staring down at an unmistakeable picture of the Devil. The rich red cloth over Henry's parted knees was now a frowning forehead. The grasping, pudgy hands were the whites of eyes whose brows had been the dark trim of the right-way-up sleeves. The nose was shaped by the dark fur edging of the lavish robe—the tip of the nose was the elaborate brooch—and the mouth, formed of shadows, opened wide to engulf Henry's head, with his crown the beard at the end of the Devil's jaws.

"That," said Miss Seeton, "is a remarkable piece of work. And most unpleasant."

"Answers your question," said Euphemia. "Why Summerset? Because it was a hint—a clue—to those in the know, recusant Catholics, I imagine."

She saw that Miss Seeton did not understand. "You've met my sister." Miss Seeton nodded. "When we had the measles poor Genie had them far worse than me, which is why she needs glasses and I don't. A year or so back she treated herself to some of those new gold frames with eight sides, and when she put them on the first time she almost fell over. The optician tried to tell her she'd grow used to them in time, but my sister has worn specs since we were seven. She knew they weren't right. She took 'em off and turned 'em upside down and—bingo. They'd fitted the lenses the wrong way round."

104

"I trust the mistake was soon corrected…" And Miss Seeton still could not see how it explained the cottage's unusual name.

Euphemia smiled. "It was, though she never went there again. But she said it gave her a different perspective on the world for a moment or two. She let me try to look through them, both ways, and she was right. I really ought to have guessed about Summerset—it's not a misspelling of Somerset, it's an old word for a somersault."

"Oh," breathed Miss Seeton. "Telling one to look at the painting the other way up…"

"And who in the normal course of things ever does that? If I hadn't tripped and fallen, I certainly wouldn't have spotted it. But I did, and," she chuckled, "I did."

Miss Seeton looked into the small mirror she still held, and shivered. "I have always told my pupils that at the start they should try to see exactly what is there—and only what is there, until they have progressed—but this must surely be a unique exception to that rule, because it both is and is not, depending on which way up you look at it. There, that is. And both at the same time, of course. Remarkable," she said again, "but unpleasant."

"Unique, as far as I know," said Euphemia.

"As a fresco, it may be. My knowledge of mediaeval art is limited—but as to unique, forgive me, the concept is far from unknown. My godmother, whose cottage I inherited, also left me its contents, which included the books, many of which belonged to her parents. I dip into them from time to time, and some are most interesting. *Cole's Funny Picture-Book*, for instance, contains several comic faces that can be inverted to form faces equally comic, or intended as such," honesty made her add. "A sense of humour is a very individual matter, and I would rather call them *clever*—a clean-shaven youth with a head of curly hair becomes a bald man with a curly beard, or a bearded man with an elaborate collar is revealed as an old woman in a fantastical hat."

"When we were children," said Euphemia, "I remember we each had one of those twin dolls in a long dress, and when you flipped the dress to the other side there was a different doll in a different dress underneath."

Miss Seeton nodded. She had been given one herself. Or did she mean two? A baby with blue eyes, a baby with brown... "Very clever indeed—the artist, that is. It must, in such perilous times, have been a risk even to sketch out the basic drawing." She glanced at the magnificent chimney breast. "That fireplace must have a few stories to tell."

"Just as I am sure this house *must* have more secrets to unearth." Dr. Braxted flung out her arms, her eyes sparkling. "Priest's holes, secret passages—the smuggling that used to go on in these parts! Oh, Miss Seeton, it doesn't bear thinking about—suppose the builders had gone ahead without the sense to tell the Colvedens! They might have plastered over everything and boarded up goodness knows how many fascinating nooks and crannies!"

Miss Seeton agreed that they might, but privately found it hard to enthuse as Euphemia was doing. The historian saw Summerset Cottage as a fascinating long-term project. The Colvedens, who owned the house, saw it as the future home of Nigel and Louise. She wondered how the family would take this news. Naturally they would be interested, as she was herself, but from their point of view it would be disconcerting to have no idea when the young couple might be able to move in.

She remembered something Lady Colveden, laughing fondly, had shared as a private joke. "His breakfast newspaper," sighed Miss Seeton. "Poor Sir George." But she spoke in vain. Euphemia was still enthusing.

"Luckiest chap in Plummergen, I should call him," she corrected Miss Seeton, with one of her chuckles. "Nobody else owns anything like this!"

Miss Seeton stifled another sigh as she thought of how long it might now take for Sir George to feel comfortable reading *Farmers Weekly* over his breakfast coffee.

Euphemia did concede that a sketch of the complete fresco, even in pencil, would be a slow process, impossible to complete before the light faded. "I'd pop to the shops for new torch batteries, but that's not going to be good enough. I'll go back to the museum—phone the Colvedens if I've time, but there's far more to organise now. Cameras and so forth, as well as students. I hate to leave the place, but I'll be back tomorrow, and far better equipped to deal with all this." The wide-flung arms again. "Isn't it splendid, Miss Seeton?"

It would be churlish to deny her, so Miss Seeton said nothing. She smiled, retrieved her belongings from the floor, shook them free of dust and said goodbye.

On her way home she wondered if Henry the Devil had disturbed her more than she cared to think. Nobody could wish so spectacular a discovery to be lost for ever, but somehow…Tomorrow, whatever the lure of the sunshine, she would not try to sketch the cottage. She would leave Dr. Braxted, and her cameras, and her students, and Henry VIII and—so fanciful—his evil twin, and pay a sadly overdue visit to dear Anne Ranger and her baby at the nursing home her parents owned out on the Brettenden Road. In fine weather it would be a good day for a bicycle ride.

And she might begin work on her mural contribution. Louise had demonstrated how fabric folded over shaped card, or thick paper, and then pressed, could be sewn by hand on other fabric to good effect once the card was removed, without the need for buttonhole stitch and requiring less effort and skill. Even Lady Colveden, still laughing over Nigel's naughty fire-screen, had thought there might be something in this way of layering and stitching similar to the Overlord Embroidery method. After tea, Miss Seeton would sketch her own dear cottage on cartridge paper, and cut out various shapes that—if she could only decide which to use, and find material of the right colours—might make a quilted (or appliquéd) likeness that might, just might, be suitable for submission to the Plummergen Quilt Committee. With pleasing, if perhaps optimistic, visions in mind and Devil Henry completely exorcised, Miss Seeton hurried happily up her front path.

With the aid of the office dictionary, Chief Superintendent Delphick pored over the closely typed pages of the post-mortem report on Gabriel Crassweller. Bob in his corner was quietly amused by muted oracular complaints from the other side of the office in the matter of charts, graphs, tables, and the Queen's English.

"I," announced the Oracle at last, "have reached the conclusion that P.M. reports should come with an interpreter attached. However, they don't, but I have a kindly nature, Sergeant Ranger. Rather than subject you to the torture of this doctor's opinions, I will do my poor best to summarise the findings."

Bob, smothering a grin, sat up and looked alert. "Thank you very much, sir."

"It would seem that Crassweller's car and the definitive tree met at speed after the man fell asleep at the wheel. Barbiturates, no matter what their derivation or how many syllables their names contain, do tend to have a certain soporific effect."

"You mean it might not be suicide after all, sir? It was an accident?"

"It is certainly not unknown for someone to take a pill and then discover a later reason to go out rather than to bed. Careless, but hardly criminal."

"Suicide isn't a crime any more, sir," Bob reminded his superior, who could remember when it had been.

"Or it may be suicide disguised as an accident. As far as I recall, one of the possible side-effects of all forms of barbiturate may be a degree of confusion. It is also not unknown for someone to take a pill, fall asleep, wake up and forget that a pill has been taken…"

"And he takes another," supplied Bob as his superior waited. "And ends up with too much of the stuff swilling about inside him for safety. Shall I get on to his doctor to check the dose he was supposed to be taking, sir?"

"At once, please. And," Delphick added, "should his doctor deny prescribing barbiturates for Mr. Crassweller, it will open up several new possible lines of enquiry. There is a regrettably flourishing black market in such drugs. Crassweller may have had another hidden life besides the homosexual underworld…"

"Or someone else may have slipped him the stuff to bump him off," suggested Bob. "For reasons that Oblon chap and the others will expect us to find out," he added bitterly. "Meaning more paperwork, sir—whichever way you look at it."

"One step at a time, Bob." Delphick balefully surveyed his paper-cluttered office, closed his eyes, and drew a deep, resolute breath. "I beg of you, Detective Sergeant Ranger—one step at a time."

Dr. Braxted stayed late in Brettenden, her address book and telephone in constant use. She spent longer than she wanted tracking down people who could drop everything *at once* to commit their time (unspecified) and effort (guaranteed worth it) to a mysterious Project, no matter how enticing she assured them it was. Having at last exacted promises from two young people who planned to marry once they could afford a flat, she decided she must talk to her sister. Eugenia enjoyed her work at the British Museum, and would still be there.

Euphemia swore her twin to secrecy, and told her what she could. At the end of the thrilled and lengthy recital, Eugenia was silent. "Well, Genie? What do you think?"

"I'm sorry, old thing," said Eugenia at last. "It's a wonderful find, and you could be right about priest's holes and so forth, but I don't think it's unique—not in a general sense. I've a feeling I've read about a fresco along similar lines in Somerset."

"Summerset Cottage," said Euphemia promptly.

"Yes, I know, and very clever of somebody, but this painting I seem to recall is in an old house near Taunton. The county town of Somerset."

"Oh." Euphemia didn't ask if Genie was sure: her twin was generally right in matters of this nature. "Oh, dash it all— and heck!" The learned article she had begun composing in her head as—leaving several motorists badly shaken—she cycled back from Plummergen, was placed regretfully in the Redraft folder. "Oh, what a shame."

"Nonsense. You'd like to find a priest's hole or a smugglers' tunnel, you said. There's more than one of those in the country. Rare, but not unique. Don't be greedy. Think of the fun we'll have tracking down the artist. It could have been anyone! A travelling fresco-painter, devoutly Catholic, loathing Henry, seeing his dissolution of the monasteries and the Reformation in general as satanic destruction of the one true faith—foreign, perhaps—Italian or Spanish…"

"There are some Spaniards on holiday in Plummergen. Sightseeing and taking photos and trying to ask the locals about village history, I heard in the shop. They even drove down Nowhere Lane, and there's nothing much to see there…"

"Oh?" said Eugenia, a smile in her voice.

"Nothing in the open air," amended her sister. "Just trees, houses, a couple of farms at the end. Not even that good a view of the canal."

"Is it worth asking if one of them knows anything about art?"

"I'm not sure their English is good enough. As for art, I told you Miss Seeton was there. She didn't leap up and acknowledge it as the work of the celebrated El Satirico, though she said it wasn't really her period. No reason it should be, of course. And I don't want people to find out too soon." Euphemia sighed. "Even if I'll have to pitch my article in quite a different way now…"

"Cheer up, Phemie. Start hunting out your camera, and a tripod, and lots of colour film. And be sure to let me have decent copies of the prints as soon as they're developed!"

Next morning was one of Martha's days. Miss Seeton explained that she would shortly be taking her bicycle and delivering her little gifts at the nursing home.

Martha grinned. "So long as you don't take the baby a bag of toffees. That's what young Trev Newport did when their first was born, knowing no better."

Miss Seeton smiled. "King Richard III was said by some to have been born with a full set of teeth, though I suspect this may have been a tale put about by the Tudors to discredit him further." Among Cousin Flora's books Miss Seeton had found a copy of *Richard IV, Plantagenet* dating from 1888. She had first been drawn to it by the gold-embossed figures fighting on the brown cloth spine, then by the young man astride his caparisoned horse on the cover. It had been, she found, dipping into the book, a story typical of its era, most likely a Sunday School prize for a boy interested in history. Miss Seeton had been inspired to read around the general topic of the Wars of the Roses, and was persuaded by Josephine Tey's arguments in *The Daughter of Time*. She wondered if that might be why she had so disliked the portrait of Henry VIII, even before Dr. Braxted's momentous discovery. "Although of course that was his father," she murmured.

"He's a father, all right." Martha sniffed. "Four of them under five, and now there's talk there might be another. Some people have got no sense."

"Or no self control," suggested Miss Seeton. "Or at least, very little—though we must remember, Martha dear, that some women dote on babies and when they stop—being babies, that is—they wish to have another. For myself, I regard babies as far more interesting when they stop. When they are small children one may have a conversation with them rather than—than not."

"Doubt if young Anne'll expect you to go coochy-cooing over him." Martha grinned. "She knows you too well, dear."

It was not until Miss Seeton and her bicycle were almost at the gates of the nursing home that she realised she had forgotten the presents.

"Bother," said Miss Seeton. She stopped, dismounted, looked carefully for traffic and crossed the road to start her return journey.

Out from the narrow twisting lane that led to the house of Mrs. Venning swept a large black car. It made straight for the pedalling Miss Seeton. Quickly she closed her hands around the brakes. On tarmac, rubber squealed. Miss Seeton, with a gleaming silver radiator no more than six feet from her nose, rocked sideways and fell off her bike.

Four car doors were flung open. A gabble of Italian? Spanish? drowned out the sound of wheels spinning and an ominous clatter. Oh, dear. A slipped chain. Miss Seeton pondered the contents of her tiny toolkit in its saddlebag, and sighed as she picked herself up. "*Excusez-moi,*" she ventured. It didn't sound as if they were talking French, but it was the best she could do. "Er, aidez-moi, sivoo play?"

"*Madame!*" The two back doors had closed, although the people behind them watched through the windows. "*Señora!* Ten thousand forgive!" The uniformed driver and his front-seat passenger were full of remorse at the sight of the overturned and wounded bicycle, even if the right words failed them. "Zuniga!" snapped the uniformed driver. Zuniga, muttering, climbed from the car.

As the chauffeur dusted Miss Seeton down with a huge white handkerchief from his breast pocket, Zuniga righted her bicycle and looked at the chain. Miss Seeton kept it very well greased. Zuniga addressed the chauffeur in tones of complaint. Something sharp was said. The handkerchief was passed to him, and the chauffeur turned back to Miss Seeton.

"*Señora*, please?" He gestured towards the saddlebag. "Your *herramienta*—tools?"

"Wee," said Miss Seeton, nodding for good measure. Foreigners—one could never be sure how much they understood.

"Side of the road, for blame." The chauffeur eyed Miss Seeton warily. "No harm, yourself? Your *biciclo* alone?"

"Wee." This time her nod was a touch brisk. She recalled some tale about postman Bert, in his van. There could be no excuse, surely, even for tourists? It was not as if they had only just arrived in Plummergen, as she understood it. Of course, she herself did not drive, but one would have supposed the rules of the road must be the first thing one should learn if determined on driving when abroad. Even on holiday.

The chauffeur struggled on with his broken—very broken—apology as Zuniga wrestled with spanners and the back wheel and chain of Miss Seeton's upturned bicycle. Even the apology did not muffle her ears to what that kind (though now sadly besmeared) Mr. Zuniga was saying. And not exactly under his breath. Italian, or was it Spanish, seemed to be a most expressive language. How fortunate that one's own languages were not fluent.

And—good gracious—still more fortunate! An approaching rumble announced the bus, coming up from the village on its way to Brettenden. Suppose it had been going the other way? As she herself had been doing? Miss Seeton saw how close to herself the car had stopped. Fortunate, indeed, and her little mishap a timely reminder to this gentleman as to which side of the road he must use in future.

"Say byan," said Miss Seeton thankfully at last. "Eh… mercy." Zuniga had produced a final clank and returned her bike to its usual position. He wiped the handlebars, and did his best to clean the remaining grease—there was a lot—from his fingers before offering the handkerchief back to its owner.

"*Muchas gracias*, Remendado." Zuniga addressed the chauffeur with what Miss Seeton, thinking back to some of her livelier pupils, recognised as a smirk.

Remendado accepted his property with reluctance, and almost forgot to smile as he and Miss Seeton examined her bike. She pushed down a pedal. It moved. So did the bike.

Miss Seeton smiled at Zuniga and nodded to Remendado. "Mercy," she said again, wheeled the bicycle around the car and, mounting, pedalled back to Sweetbriars.

Remendado returned to the driver's seat and listened to a blast of angry eloquence from the back. Beside him, Zuniga continued to smirk.

In Ashford, fifteen miles distant, Superintendent Brinton picked up his telephone. "Potter?" His voice turned wary. "By some lucky chance, a Potter we've only just recruited that I don't know about—or by some evil mischance, Police Constable Potter from Plummergen?"

At this the young man at the other desk abandoned the report on which he had been engaged. He looked at his superior. His superior groaned.

"Plummergen. It would be." He glared at Detective Constable Foxon, whose eyes were now as bright as his plain-clothes costume. "And you can stop your grinning and start listening, laddie. I might have known things were too peaceful to last."

Foxon quenched his grin and grabbed his extension. Brinton's wary tones deepened.

"Carry on, Potter. What's she done now?"

"It's not so much Miss Seeton doing anything, sir," came Potter's voice along the line, "as things done to her, only they braked in time—and so did she—and she's okay. But it's not the first time, sir. You should've heard the postman—"

"Potter!" Foxon's ears were assaulted in stereo, one blast from the desk and one from the phone. Brinton ignored his pained expression. "Potter, calm down. Who braked? And when? And how does it involve Miss Seeton?"

"It was that Spanish lot who've took Mrs. Venning's house, sir. Driving on the wrong side of the road again, with Miss Seeton on her bike near as a touch having them run into her, only everyone braked in time and she just tumbled off and they fixed her bike for her, no trouble—and off she went back home. I kept behind her nice and quiet in my panda, but she didn't seem to have took any harm."

"Mrs. Venning?"

Brinton waved his puzzled sidekick to silence. "Later. So you were on patrol, and saw it all?"

"What you might call the afterwards, sir, but it all looked pretty straightforward."

Brinton groaned again. "Nothing is ever straightforward when Miss Seeton's in it."

Foxon opened his mouth to protest, but again Brinton waved him down. "Go on."

"Well, sir, far as I could tell these Spanish must of come rushing out of Mrs. Venning's lane and turned towards Brettenden just when Miss Seeton was cycling back from—well, sir, I dunno, but there she was, and there they were. You couldn't have slipped a playing-card between 'em," exaggerated Potter. Mrs. Venning's tenants might not be regular Plummergen, but Miss Seeton was. "She's got good reflexes," he finished, proudly.

"And the Spanish lot?"

"Watched 'em in the mirror, sir, pulling over to the right—the left—the proper side of the road and driving off nice and slow and steady. Sir."

"Hmm. Miss Seeton's all right, then. Good."

"Saw her pedalling north again, sir, when I stopped off home for a cuppa. Her basket had a couple of packages in it. I reckon they'd be presents for young Anne and the baby."

The superintendent visualised the topography of Miss Seeton's village. "Expect you're right. Yes. But apart from their bad driving, there's been no other trouble from the Spanish contingent?"

"Oh no, sir. Very polite, or so we think because the lingo's a problem—they use a phrasebook when they're shopping—but doing their best to fit in, sir. Can't be bad, can it?"

Brinton made him a noncommittal reply, and hung up. He frowned, and pulled open the drawer where he kept his extra-strong mints.

"Mrs. Venning, sir?" prompted Foxon.

"That was before Maidstone kicked you over here and, heaven knows why, said you might do for plain clothes." Brinton looked towards the younger man and winced. "I must have been mad. Plain? Those horrible stripes…"

"My grandmother," said Timothy Foxon, "knitted this tank top for my birthday. I take it as a personal insult that anyone, even you, sir, should disparage Gran Biddle's labour of love."

"If someone knitted a thing like that for my birthday I'd think they hated me. Couldn't you have asked for a nice quiet Fair Isle?"

Foxon grinned. "I'd never dare, sir. You know Gran. You might ask her yourself?"

Brinton grinned back as he inserted a peppermint. He knew Gran Biddle, for whom the word redoubtable might have been invented. He raised one hand in a gesture of surrender. "Peace, laddie. Wear your horrible stripes and leave me out of it. Mrs. Venning: Society widow, wrote children's books. Daughter drugged, she'd been a supplier herself, retired to Plummergen hoping to sort things out. Your lady-friend Miss Seeton and her brolly helped smash at least that part of the supply chain, at the cost of the daughter's life and a complete breakdown on the part of Sonia Venning. She's in a Swiss nursing home now."

"And the house?"

"Let out through a firm of London solicitors. Remember that Russian princess a while back? Some sort of cousin, stayed a few months, paranoid about assassins, after peace and quiet and security. The Meadows has high walls and, I suppose, the right sort of atmosphere." He favoured his young colleague with a long, steady look. And sighed.

"I'd better tell you—but if you're thinking of putting in for sergeant, this will be a good test of how shut you can keep your mouth about things. Understand?"

Foxon was serious now. "Yes, sir, I understand."

"They…aren't Spanish." Brinton paused.

Even now, Foxon was not entirely suppressed. "And here's me thinking they might be reclaiming the long-lost treasure of some sunken Armada ship."

"They might, but it's unlikely. There's plenty of silver in Costaguana." Foxon blinked. "Where there's just been a military coup, yes. And the dictator getting out with a few trusted members of his household, if dictators can ever trust anyone, and after some dodging about on assorted Atlantic coasts arriving in Plummergen." Brinton crunched on peppermint as Foxon stared at him.

"In Plummergen?" said the young man in the striped tank top at last. "That chap who got out of Latin America by the skin of his teeth with machine guns firing at the wheels of his plane? All the gin-joints in the world he might've gone to—even Casablanca—and he goes to Plummergen?"

"Yes," said Brinton. "The Venning place could well be getting known in certain circles as a good temporary refuge for a certain type of person."

Again he paused. Foxon, bright-eyed, was busily thinking.

"You don't suppose there *could* be a hoard of Armada gold somewhere around, sir? They sailed up the Channel, and lots of them sank when the storm came. The *Santissima Nada* was one of them—they say she lies not so very far from the coast, between Romney and Rye—which'd be dashed handy for anyone staying in Plummergen. And there have always been stories. Manville Henty wrote a book about it—her, I mean." He coughed.

"Never read one. Hearty Victorian adventure isn't my style and never was, more-or-less local author or not."

"Or," persisted Foxon, his imagination fizzing, "Julius Caesar! It was one of the reasons the Romans wanted Britain—the lead, the silver. And remember that temple they found in Plummergen the other Christmas, and the hoard that was buried with it—more silver." He sat bolt upright. "That's why they'll have come to Plummergen, sir, all the silver. They knew they'd feel pretty much at home in the place before they even arrived!"

Chapter Nine

Oblon of the Foreign Office was driving the chief super-intendent mad by his prowling up and down, grumbling, between Delphick's desk and that of the rigidly silent Bob Ranger.

"The last we officially heard they were in London, keeping an understandably low profile. Suddenly, they disappear. Rumours of them at Charing Cross, then they turn up in this Plummergen of yours and ask if anyone minds. How can we say we do? They've paid the rent. They try to fit in with the locals. They've hired a car and, yes, nearly killed a couple of people, but they didn't, and generally they've kept to the proper side of the road and done the tourist bit just as if they were on holiday. It's...all wrong!"

Delphick sighed. "Perhaps they really are on holiday. After a military coup and a hair's-breadth escape from a show trial and a firing squad, followed by frantic rushing from one airport hotel to another in the hunt for political asylum, even the toughest dictator might fancy a rest."

"Possibly." Oblon did not sound convinced.

"All that packing and unpacking. Having to sweep the walls for bugs, check under the beds for explosive devices—always looking over their shoulders for assassins, even in

London. An out-of-the-way house with a high wall round it in a quiet village in Kent might suit them very well."

"Getting away from London, I can understand." Oblon prowled to the window and looked out from the umpteenth floor of New Scotland Yard at the vast expanse of the metropolis. "But why Plummergen? We've kept a discreet eye on them since we learned where they were, and we cannot make out what they're doing. And not knowing the reason makes us uneasy. You two are the acknowledged experts. Why Plummergen, I ask you?"

Delphick glanced at Bob, who remained silent. "There are historic precedents," he said quietly, "and fairly modern history, what's more."

Oblon the expert in foreign affairs looked peeved. Nobody likes to have their ignorance exposed, even with only one (tactfully still silent) witness. "Precedents?"

"Charles Louis Napoleon Bonaparte, later the emperor Napoleon III, settled in England for the first time in 1838." As the Crassweller investigation failed to go anywhere in particular, Delphick had refreshed his overburdened mind with periodic dips into the office encyclopaedia. "After years of European to-and-fro pursuit of the French throne, in 1871 he ended up in Kent." Oblon winced. "Chislehurst," the Oracle added. "But undeniably Kent—where he died in 1873."

"Before my time." Weakly, Oblon grinned. "Oh, well." He pulled out the visitor's chair, and sat down. "Go on. I'm intrigued."

"More recently Haile Selassie of Abyssinia, later Emperor of Ethiopia, fled his country after the Italian invasion and came to England in 1936."

"The same year we packed our Nazi-loving Duke of Windsor off to France."

"One in, one out," murmured Bob.

Delphick frowned. "I hope you're not suggesting Haile Selassie had fascist sympathies. Abyssinia, after all, was invaded by the forces of Mussolini, who was very quick to join the Hitler bandwagon when the opportunity presented itself."

Oblon waved a dismissive hand. "I meant Edward. One shouldn't speak ill of the dead, but there was rather more support for the Nazis among our aristocracy than anyone these days cares to remember. What happened to Haile Selassie?"

"He ended up in Somerset. Bath, eventually, but he went via a rather downbeat resort on the Bristol Channel called Burnham-on-Sea."

"Good God."

"No doubt saltwater paddling gave him a taste for the waters, for which Bath is so well known. More recently still, Her Imperial Highness the Princess Katerina Andreyevna Stakhova. She, I would remind you, not only went to Plummergen, but stayed in the very same house that El Dancairo is renting now."

"Precedents," agreed Oblon. "The princess is a distant cousin of the owner, but—oh, very well. If you don't know why he's there, you don't." He favoured the chief superintendent with a piercing gaze. "Do you know anything yet about Gabriel Crassweller—?"

Delphick exchanged looks with his sergeant. "We know nothing beyond what you already know that we know. Unless there is, somewhere, further information we have not yet seen."

Oblon seemed puzzled. His gaze swept the small room crowded with files and folders, the trays that could be classified as neither In nor Out now that all were full to overflowing. "I'd say you've got everything there is. What makes you think you haven't?"

Both Delphick and Bob noted the practised circumlocution. Neither said anything. Both regarded Oblon thoughtfully.

He seemed unconcerned, but he pushed back his chair and stood up. "Thank you for your time. You have clarified my thoughts to a certain extent, but the Plummergen aspect remains...problematic. Please continue your efforts in the Crassweller case. Such matters cannot afford to go unresolved. Questions are being asked at the highest level, and time is becoming of the essence. The draft reports submitted over recent days have eliminated several possibilities, but there must still be aspects that could usefully be pursued."

Before he could say what those might be, he had whisked himself out of the room.

"Ho, hum," said Delphick to Bob.

"He's good at his job, sir. Didn't tell us a bally thing, but picked your brains very nicely."

"Yes, I wonder why. He knew about the Russian princess. He must have known about Haile Selassie—barely forty years ago, and the FO has a long memory. He could probably have quoted chapter and verse on the military campaigns of the 1830s, and told us what Charles Louis had for breakfast in prison."

"Prison?" Bob was curious, but Delphick dismissed the query. "Irrelevant, Bob." The sergeant made a note to check the encyclopaedia in his next breathing space.

"Plummergen, however, may well be relevant," Delphick went on, after a pause. He was frowning. "It may be."

"To an outsider," said Bob, "I can see that it might look a bit...odd, sir."

"No doubt." Delphick's frown deepened. "Plummergen. Now, I wonder…"

Miss Emily Seeton was taking tea with Miss Cecelia Wicks, and admiring the older woman's delicate work for her contribution to the Plummergen Mural.

"Hexagons," hissed Miss Wicks, whose friends suffered torments when conversing with her. Sibilance was infectious. The ears of both Miss Seeton and Miss Treeves naturally suffered more than most: but everyone liked the old lady, and none would dream of upsetting her by suggesting she might spend more money than they suspected she could afford on new dentures. "Basted over separate pieces of paper and subsequently stitched by hand, as you can see."

She indicated a small basket, its blue lining faded after a lifetime's use, at her side. It was full of dainty coloured shapes no more than an inch across. "Old correspondence," said Miss Wicks. "A set of compasses from my schooldays to make six intersecting circles on one of last year's Christmas cards and, once cut out, traced for all subsequent copies."

"As we did in handiwork…" Miss Seeton hesitated. Both *lessons* and *classes* held equal danger, but she gave up trying to suppress her hisses as everyone always did. "At school," she temporised. "It is useful for children to learn that geometry has a practical value in real life, as well as teaching them to handle sharp instruments with care."

Miss Wicks beamed. "Scissors, too, can be sharp, yet despite a little stiffness first thing in the morning—" she wiggled her fingers "—I found it easy to prepare these shapes."

"And you sew them right sides together?" Miss Seeton's eyesight was good, but she could barely make out the stitches. "Miss Wicks, how long do you think it will take?"

"My dear," said her elderly friend, "one never knows the hour, so one must waste as little time as possible. Once I have finished piecing my small mosaic frame I can sew it to the central stitchery—a likeness in Spanish-work of my cottage, taken from one of Mrs. Welsted's postcards." Once more she indicated the basket with its tiny six-sided shapes tacked over scraps of old letters. "I baste these when my eyes need a rest, later in the day. They say it was brought to this country by Catherine of Aragon—the Spanish-work, that is." Miss Seeton blinked. "Sometimes it is called blackwork. I've been sewing the basics of my history panel in my spare time. I had so many choices. For some days I was unable to decide between Queen Anne's request for a glass of water, and Sir Philip Chute raising the standard for Henry VIII. Out of interest, which would have been your preference, Miss Seeton?"

Miss Seeton blinked again at this second casual reference to the monarch who had in so dramatic a manner entered her life. First, his wife—one of his wives—then Henry himself. "Queen Anne," she said promptly. "The clothes," and really it was no more than true. "Such colour—such luxury."

"Such fun," agreed Miss Wicks. "Those enormous sideways hoops, and the panniers—the silken stomachers, the lace fans, the jewelled shoes..." She touched her guest gently on the arm. "My little hexagons are mere cotton, Miss Seeton, and for the surround of my blackwork picture will do very well. But, although Mrs. Welsted stocks a surprising variety in so small a shop, for a queen I now realise that it must be something special..."

Miss Seeton guessed the little hexagons had once belonged in garments for which Miss Wicks had no further need. Elbows wear out eventually, but other parts remain usable to a greater or lesser degree. "I fear that my own stock of fabric is far from extensive, and could hardly be thought luxurious…"

"Oh, my dear!" Miss Wicks almost giggled. "No, I must not ask you—for more than a small favour, and of course I shall insist on reimbursing you at once. It is simply that I should not wish to offend Mrs. Welsted, who always does her best to oblige, by requesting what I am sure she does not have in stock. And busy as I am with my two submissions for the Plummergen project I cannot be sure of the next occasion I shall have time to visit Brettenden."

Miss Seeton's own submission (should she submit it) would be far more modest and far less time-consuming. She smiled. "You must tell me what you would like me to buy," she said. "I know there is an art shop, it's where I obtain my supplies, so I would expect there also to be a shop that sells fabric. I can easily ask."

Miss Wicks looked back to the days before her pension had seemed to shrink so much. "There used to be a dressmaker and modiste, Jeannine Claire, and most stylish costumes she created, in rich and sumptuous fabrics. She also stocked glass embroidery beads in different colours."

"For the jewels, of course."

"Indeed yes, though I would not wish her to suppose that I want them in any spirit of—of commercial competition. Some scraps of silk or satin, a small assortment of beads—sufficient for one modest picture, certainly not for a rival establishment." She glanced around her tiny sitting room. "They speak of cottage industry, Miss Seeton, but I should say that this cottage, while its owner certainly does her best to be industrious, hardly counts. Would you not agree?"

And Miss Seeton, smiling at her friend's little joke, agreed that she would.

Euphemia Braxted was not a selfish woman. She loved her work, and found discovery of any sort enthralling, but never grudged a share of the fun to those who could be trusted to enjoy it as much as she did. Having coaxed Felix Graham (studying for a PhD) and Miss Madeline Staveley (aspiring MSc) into abandoning their studies to help with the investigation of Summerset Cottage, she made sure the young folk would have the chance to make discoveries of their own.

Euphemia carried a broom with the rest of her paraphernalia, having made early telephone arrangements with Crabbe's Garage the day after the sudden appearance of Devil Henry. Enthusiastic Dr. Braxted might be, but not stupid. Nobody with any sense carried a broom, a yardstick, two cameras, assorted lights and a tripod on a bicycle, never mind tape measures, notebooks, and sandwiches. All three historians, heavily laden, were collected from Brettenden Museum by Jack Crabbe's taxi at half-past nine and were in Summerset Cottage by ten.

After the requisite exclamations of wonder as they peered in the mirror and took it in turns to lie on the newly swept floor, Felix and Madeline asked what happened next.

"I've taken a fancy to this chap." Euphemia indicated the fresco. "The artist, not Henry, I mean. A talented chap, and brave. While I take photos of his masterpiece you can hunt through the rest of the house tapping the panels, banging on floorboards, measuring every room, drawing plans on the lookout for any indication of secret passages or priest's holes."

"And for any more loose plaster," added Madeline.

"Golly! Neither of us thought of that." Euphemia had explained her sister's interest, and repeated Eugenia's view that there was likely to be a priest's hole even without a smugglers' tunnel. "A second picture? Oh, wouldn't that put us one up on the Taunton place!"

"You never know, in a house this old," said Felix.

The clatter of the young couple's feet was a background constant as Euphemia set to work. She propped the wooden steps against the wall, balancing her yardstick on top for accuracy of scale. As she took photo after gloating photo, Felix and Madeline moved from room to room calling out measurements, stamping, tapping. They found nothing, but were as eager when they finished in the scullery as they'd been when they started in the parlour.

Further clattering in other rooms, then up the stairs. Overhead, their footsteps echoed even more in the empty house. The Colvedens had ensured that the auctioneers appointed to dispose of the contents had done a thorough job of clearing.

Suddenly, a shout. Euphemia's ears pricked. Some fevered tapping, back and forth along one wall. Euphemia, who had wanted a closer look at Devil Henry's nose, climbed off the steps and set her measuring stick against the wall. She waited, her heart bumping.

Down the stairs came Felix and Madeline. They rushed through the hall and erupted into the parlour. "Found it!" they chorused.

Two notebooks were brandished as one. "We've checked and double-checked," said Felix, pink about the ears.

"The largest bedroom is two feet shorter than the room underneath." Madeline was breathing hard. "There's a recessed alcove that hides the difference, but upstairs, once you look, you can tell. However, the wall doesn't sound very hollow—there's a dead patch at one end—and we can't find how you get in."

"But it's there!" finished Felix.

"Come on, then," said Euphemia. She did not check the measurements. If these two said the rooms didn't match for size, they didn't.

Together they hurried up the stairs and went into the largest bedroom, where Euphemia began her own tapping. "Hmm," she said. "When this was built the wood was all new, and the plaster hadn't decayed. If we're right about what's behind this wall, nobody in those days would have spotted anything unusual without a decent tape measure."

The other two nodded. It made sense. Had the secret room, if that was indeed what it was, been as easy to find then as now, no Jesuit priest taking refuge there would have been safe for more than five minutes. If as long.

Euphemia let out a sigh. "My sister said that every design is different, for a priest's hole, so that anyone finding one couldn't use the same tricks to find another. She said that sometimes you gain access from another room—or even another floor." She tapped again at the dead patch. "I suspect that what we have here is a staircase, starting in the roof."

Madeline clapped her hands; enthusiasm was catching. "A priest's hole and a secret passage—a vertical passage, but who cares?—in one!"

"Bull's eye," crowed Felix. "Now all we have to do is find the way in."

They moved out to the landing, and looked up.

"If the builders come to take their stepladder back," said Euphemia, "they'll be right out of luck. It's our only way of reaching that trapdoor."

"Then we'd better hurry," said Madeline, "in case they appear."

Three wide smiles beamed around the landing. Felix ran down the stairs, and returned with the paint-splattered steps over his shoulder. He positioned them under the trap.

"Me first," said Euphemia. "You'll each get your turn, but if it proves to be a tricky job I'm the one who should take the risk—not that there really is one. The attic was cleared as well as the rest of the house, Sir George said, so it shouldn't require too much force to open the trapdoor. We should be safe enough."

Madeline and Felix grinned. They shared Euphemia's excitement. Common sense suggested that she should ask around the village for the loan of a longer ladder, but now common sense took a back seat. All they had to do was hold the steps firmly and not look beyond their mentor's ankles as she scrambled up into the attic.

"Maddy," said Felix, "you stand by me. Okay, Dr. Braxted…"

Euphemia had guessed correctly: the trapdoor was heavy, but it did not stick. With a push and a sideways shove, it opened. She reached up to drag herself over the edge.

"Mind you step only on the rafters," warned Madeline. Her father had once put a foot through her bedroom ceiling while inspecting the hot-water tank.

"Teach your grandmother," cried Euphemia. "In a previous incarnation I could have been a platelayer for the railways…"

Her voice faded as, switching on the torch squeezed into her cardigan pocket—her pockets were always double-lined for just such eventualities—she began to pick her way across the attic floor. Felix and Madeline exchanged looks.

"You're taller," said Madeline. "You keep an eye on her."

As she held the ladder he climbed up, and poked his head through the square, shadowy hole through which Euphemia had vanished.

"They certainly cleared this place right out," called Euphemia. She coughed. "Apart from the dust."

At first he could see erratic shadows from her torch on the rafters, which were bare and gave straight on to the tiles.

Occasional points of daylight flickered through but the roof, for all its years of neglect, appeared reasonably sound.

"I'm going to start tapping the ceiling—the floor," shouted Euphemia from the distance. "But I'll be careful!"

"I'm not bothered about her damaging the plaster so much as herself," said Madeline. She explained her reasons. "When my father put his foot through the ceiling, his trouser leg was ripped to shreds and he was terribly cut and bruised. My mother sent him for a tetanus jab and said he could pay for a new pair himself because now they were only fit for the bin, and she wasn't going to waste her time sewing when it was all his own fault. But she did get some peas out of the freezer for his sprained ankle."

"A heart of gold," observed Felix.

The two young researchers waited. The tapping stopped. "No luck as yet," announced Euphemia. "But my sister told me a wrinkle or two…"

"She seems to be examining the rafters," said Felix, as muffled grunts came periodically from the darkness. "Good grief—she's doing gymnastics."

Another grunt, a creak, a shriek. "Bingo!" cried Euphemia. "Good old Genie! One of the cross-beams…" She spluttered into silence after a long burst of coughing.

"Are you all right, Dr. Braxted?" Madeline was concerned.

"Catching my breath," called Euphemia, wheezing slightly. "A cloud of dust blew out when the thing opened—suction, I suppose."

"It's open! You found it!" babbled Felix and Madeline together.

Euphemia coughed again. "Some sort of counterbalance, I think. You have to put all your weight on it—and now I can see steps. I'm going to explore!"

"At least we know where they go," said Felix to Madeline. "If the worst comes to the worst we can always find a pickaxe and chop her out through the bedroom wall."

"Don't joke."

He climbed down the steps and hurried with Madeline back to the bedroom. They heard Euphemia's footsteps on the hidden stair. There was a bump. "Safely down," she shouted. "Are you there?"

"Yes!"

"Good. A feeble light through some sort of shaft," reported Euphemia. "Ventilation, probably—look for it later from outside. A chair…a table…and—my God!"

Both young people jumped. They demanded to know what she had found.

"That—that devil!" burst from Dr. Euphemia Braxted. "I'm coming back *right now!*"

Chapter Ten

Euphemia reappeared, looking grim. "You can go and see for yourselves, but be prepared for a nasty shock. Don't drop the torch." She saw Madeline's face. "Nothing so nasty as you're thinking, my child! Maybe I should have said *unpleasant,* only that lacks sufficient…force. Evil, perhaps."

Felix went first. He came back. "I'd say wicked—or devilish, and entirely in keeping with our friend on the parlour wall."

Madeline looked from one to the other. "Just tell me," she said. "I'll make up my mind afterwards if it's the sort of thing I want to see."

"Nobody decent could *want* to see anything of the sort," said Euphemia. "But there it is. Sir George will have to be told, of course—he's a magistrate. He'll know what to do about—about a two-way radio with German instructions on the dials."

Madeline stared. Euphemia remained grim. "*Sender* could just about be English, but there's no arguing with *Empfänger.* It means 'receiver' in German—and there's an umlaut over the 'a' if anyone needed further proof of…treachery."

"It must have been there since the war," said Felix. "Maybe even before. Who lived here then? It can't have been installed without their knowledge."

"Once you know it's there, you can even see the aerial draped under the ridge of the roof," said Euphemia. "If the people clearing this place spotted it they would have thought it was something to do with the electricity supply."

"Devilish," Madeline said faintly. "Do you suppose…I mean, I wonder if that sort of thing is—is catching? An evil atmosphere—maybe even ghosts…"

"My dear child," said Euphemia, "the people who painted the fresco, the people who lived here, were devout Catholics. Their ghosts *may* haunt this house, not that I imagine they do but, if they did, they would be courageous and, by their own lights, honourable ghosts entirely out of sympathy with treacherous English Nazis four hundred years later. The first owners of Summerset Cottage would have wanted the overthrow of a Protestant crown for religious, not for personal or—or mercenary reasons."

Madeline shivered. Euphemia sighed.

"There were more upper-class Nazi sympathisers before, even during, the war than we like to think," continued the unconscious echo of Duncan Oblon. "Some were merely fascinated by that devil Hitler—look at Unity Mitford—but others thought the lower orders really should be ground under the heel of the discerning rulers, by whom they meant themselves. You're both too young, but I remember people like that. Whoever lived in this house during the war will have been of the same kidney."

Felix cleared his throat. "I know Sir George must be told, but perhaps he's not the most obvious person even if the house does belong to him. Shouldn't we tell the police?"

It was decided at last that Felix and Madeline would go to the police house in search of PC Potter, while Euphemia would make for Rytham Hall.

"But first, we hide the evidence," she decreed. "And the stepladder. We'll shut the trapdoor and put the steps somewhere they won't immediately be found. There may be surviving family members, even friends, who wouldn't care for the word to get around that the people who lived here were a gaggle of Hitler-lovers…"

In Ashford, Superintendent Brinton devoured a bun. Foxon was not long back from the canteen, and the superintendent was a distracted man. Paperwork bred nothing but paperwork. No sooner did one in-tray shrink than another wodge appeared. It wasn't as if he could offload it on young Foxon, even if the lad had the rank, which he hadn't. Brinton had the rank, and was paid for it. It wouldn't be fair to pull that rank and dump everything on his subordinate. If there were nervous breakdowns around, Superintendent Brinton claimed the monopoly. Besides, Foxon had a way with him, for all his fancy clothes and persistent chirpiness. These buns had the thickest icing in the canteen, he'd bet a bob or two—

The telephone rang. "Mmph," he grunted through a stodgy mouthful, then a gulp. Choking, he gestured that Foxon should listen on the extension. Foxon set down his mug. "Potter?" cried Brinton. "Not again!"

"Well, sir, I thought you did really ought to know, even if you might say 'tis thirty years too late…"

Brinton banged down the handset and clutched his hair. "Nazi spies in Plummergen. That's all I need. If it wasn't bad enough with El Dancairo and his chums playing at dodgem cars, now we've got to watch out for elderly ex-Nazis breaking into empty houses to retrieve incriminating chunks of 1930s technology. This just about takes the perishing cake."

"Bun, sir," amended Foxon. "Have some more—you'll feel better."

Brinton glared, grabbed his mug, gulped heartily. He bit again into his bun.

"You could always cancel your standing orders, sir," said Foxon while his superior's mouth was still full. Brinton glared at him again.

"And I don't see how you could possibly blame Miss Seeton for any of this," persisted the young man in the striped tank top. Brinton swallowed the last of his bun.

"No, I couldn't. And yes, I can. You know very well why those standing orders were set up. If I'm not kept informed of anything—everything—that happens within five miles of that perishing village when that woman's in it, blue bloody mayhem will ensue."

"But, sir, you say it always does anyway."

"I know it does, and no need to rub it in. If Potter keeps me as up-to-date with things as he can, at least we have a slight—far too slight—advantage when the mulligatawny finally reaches the boil."

"But Miss Seeton wasn't even living in Plummergen during the war! And she's the last person who'd ever dream of— of consorting with enemy agents."

"I never said anything about *consorting*. Dammit, I never *thought* she was that sort—is, I mean. But she can't help it, she and that brolly of hers just stir things up. Pure unadulterated mulligatawny. I'll bet if asked about the war she'll say something about popping down from time to time to visit her cousin, and there'll turn out to be some sort of link no-body's heard of before…"

Foxon raised a further objection. "I thought they didn't let you pop anywhere during the war, sir. *Is your journey really necessary?* and all that."

"Shuttup, Foxon."

Foxon looked pained.

"I hate you, Foxon. You think I'm being unfair to the old girl, don't you?"

"I thought you liked her, sir. That umbrella you gave her for Christmas…"

"I know, laddie, I know. It's just that things do tend to happen when she's around, whether she means them to or not—"

"*Not*, sir," declared the loyal Foxon.

"—but I don't want to end up having to—trying to—stop a pitched battle between the Plummergen locals and a gang of jackbooted neo-Nazis who believe that Hitler's alive and well, being egged on by a load of Latin American fascists who say he's living next door to their mothers." Brinton once more clutched at his hair.

"Plummergen," he groaned. "I wonder if—"

The telephone rang. He picked it up. His eyes rolled. "Sir George Colveden. I might have known. Yes, put him through. Foxon, if you so much as smirk I'll—Yes, Sir George, what can we do for you?"

Foxon did not wait to be told. He seized his extension. He watched his superior's face. Brinton had gone from red, to white, and back to red. Foxon wondered when his boss had last had his blood pressure tested. Better not ask.

"Thank you, Sir George. Yes, disturbing. But you can leave it with us now, sir."

Their handsets cradled, the two policemen looked at each other. Foxon broke the silence. "You were starting to wonder, sir, when that phone call interrupted you—hardly a coincidence, when you think about it, and maybe a bit of a nudge?" Brinton favoured him with an old-fashioned look. "You wondered, sir—and so do I—about having a word or two with the Oracle. After all, he is our acknowledged Plummergen expert…"

In an office on the umpteenth floor of New Scotland Yard, the telephone rang. Delphick picked it up. "Yes?…Hello, Chris…Yes, a while…Plummergen? Spies?" He looked at Bob Ranger, who was all ears. Anne and Ranger Minor were in Plummergen. Delphick put a finger to his lips and indicated that Bob should listen unobtrusively on his extension.

The handsets back in their cradles, the two Scotland Yarders looked at each other.

"A strange coincidence, Bob, even if at present I don't see how Nazi sympathisers in the last war, right-wing to a man—and woman—can relate to the treachery we currently suspect in the matter of the People's Republic of Stentoria. But it does give me to think."

"Me too, sir. Is that why you didn't want Mr. Brinton to know I was listening?"

"The death of Gabriel Crassweller is under wraps for as long as we can manage to keep it so, yes. The intelligence leak has to be found, and possibly exploited, in some manner neither you nor I will ever properly understand—at least, I hope we never do—beyond knowing that the whole convoluted affair demands the utmost secrecy, and that people in authority keep breathing down our necks. I heartily wish we were rid of it all."

"Me too, sir. Tons of bumf and eyes on stalks and beggary zero to show for it."

"Yet we should always remember that just as 'no' is as much of an answer to prayer as 'yes'—prayer asks a question, and both negative and positive as answers have equal weight—then so must a negative be as valid a response to investigation as a positive." Delphick fell silent, contemplating his telephone.

"How is Anne?"

Bob looked at him. "Fine, she says, and her parents haven't told me otherwise. I phone every night. She says she can always catch up on sleep during the day if it's a bit late when I call."

"Your son continues to flourish?" The chief superintendent returned Bob's look. "One likes to show an interest in the lives of one's subordinates."

Bob Ranger's face became one enormous grin. "Shall I ask them to book you a room at the George and Dragon, sir?"

If Delphick's expression was austere, his voice held a smile. "As you recall, the question of god-fatherhood was raised not long after all the—entirely understandable—excitement had, happily, died down. But before committing myself to accepting the compliment, I might be well advised to study at closer quarters than hitherto the responsibility which I would be assuming for a fair number of years."

"The George it is, then. When, sir? And for how long?" Delphick favoured him with a look as old-fashioned as any of Brinton's. "She isn't going anywhere, as far as I know."

"So I would expect, in her still-delicate condition."

"She went to see Anne the other day." Sometimes all you could do with the Oracle's sense of humour was ignore it. "Lovely weather for a bike ride, apparently."

The Oracle surrendered. "Even if she did have a near-miss with a car."

"Shall I hunt out some photos from the files for her to sketch?" Bob's eyes were alight with amusement.

Superintendent Brinton would have said it was small wonder Bob Ranger and young Tim Foxon got on so well.

Delphick told Bob to leave the motorway at Maidstone and take the cross-country route through Headcorn and Brettenden rather than continuing via Ashford, in case their arrival should be reported to Superintendent Brinton. "It's hardly a border incursion," said the Oracle, "but I'd prefer as few people as possible to know about us for as long as possible."

"Which won't be long, sir, once we reach Plummergen. The tom-toms will have been beating ever since we booked you into the George."

"Is a man not permitted to visit his godson?" demanded the chief superintendent.

"That won't fool anyone, the minute they spot you going to see Miss Seeton."

"Is a man not permitted to visit a colleague?" demanded the chief superintendent. "A colleague, moreover, who could be said to have been absent without leave for rather longer than the authorities would like, and who should therefore be taken to account for this lapse of professional etiquette."

Bob grinned. "That won't fool 'em either, sir. You know it won't."

"Then I rely on you, as a proud and doting father, to explain our appearance in these parts to the best of your ability. Fathers tell their children fairy stories every night. The experience will help you start as you mean to go on."

Bob was serious. "Anne will guess there's something up, sir."

"Anne is a nurse, her father is a doctor, and her mother is likewise accustomed to keeping her professional counsel. Try your best to let nothing slip regarding Crassweller, but don't agonise too much over it if you do. Oh, and stop the car."

"But we're almost there, sir."

"Yes, and you are even closer to your destination than I am. Swap seats, Bob, and I'll drop you off at the nursing home and proceed to the George by myself." Delphick smiled. "Or do you doubt my driving ability?"

"Perish the thought, sir—and thanks." The exchange was duly effected, and Delphick smoothly set the car in motion.

Having left his passenger he drove the anonymous car warily past the narrow entrance that led to Mrs. Venning's house. No careless Costaguanans emerged to collide with him, and he reached the George unscathed. He grinned as he saw the large chalked A-board messages, one on each side of the entrance to the hotel's modest car park.

When is a Steak Dinner never too Deer?
Venison our Menu!

With a price-list for different size or cut, two veg. of choice, and chips or mash.

Before taking his overnight bag from the boot he walked past the A-boards to check that Charley Mountfitchet had copied these dreadful puns the other way round for the benefit of those approaching from the other direction. He had, of course.

Hadn't there been something said about a historic painting the other way round? Bob said Anne had mentioned it—that Miss Seeton was there when it was found, that the village had talked of raising the devil and the closeness of Halloween, which was the usual nonsense because it was weeks until the end of October.

"Mr. Delphick!" The landlord of the George and Dragon bustled out, seeing his chance to help the police with their enquiries. In another life Charley Mountfitchet would have liked to be a private eye, with trench-coat, fedora and, if based in California, dark glasses too. He drew the line at chain-smoking, however, and knew enough about drink to give that aspect of the hardboiled life a miss as well. "Grand to have you back, Mr. Delphick! Young Bob says you're here to see your godson?" He spoke loudly, for the benefit of listening ears.

Delphick thanked him and agreed that he was, adding quietly that it was a kind thought, but probably a wasted effort. Charley grinned. "Fancy a drink, Mr. Delphick?"

"A little early in the day for me, thanks."

They were at reception. Charley, having opened the flap, was busy on the other side at the register. "I suppose a cup o' tea would be more in your line right now, sir?"

"It might," agreed Delphick, filling in the final details. "But I'll unpack first."

"Take your bag up for you?"

"Pump all you like, you'll get nothing from me." Delphick winked at the landlord and picked up his bag. Charley, resigned to disappointment, handed him his key.

After unpacking, Delphick picked up the photographs removed by Bob from the Crassweller file—they were in a brown envelope stiffened with card. It seemed sufficiently anonymous. Delphick brought it with him as he came back down the stairs.

In anticipation of the chief superintendent's visit—Bob had telephoned his adopted aunt the previous evening—a special fruit cake had been requested from dear Martha, who really preferred to let the flavours mature before cutting, but on this occasion was willing to make an exception for an old friend.

"So you must have at least one slice, or her feelings will be hurt." Miss Seeton lifted the teapot lid to stir.

"I'd hate to do that. I might even manage two, although Bob is really the man for cake."

"And gingerbread," smiled Miss Seeton, pouring. "Dear Bob…"

They chatted generally for a while, and then he explained the reason for his visit. Miss Seeton, remembering the retainer fee, did her best to understand.

"In matters of—of national security, which I fear does feel—forgive me, Chief Superintendent—a somewhat sensational term to one who leads such a very quiet life as you know I do…" Had she been rude? The police were, after all, there to uphold the law and thus keep everyone in the country safe. Which must therefore be a matter of national security. Yet it seemed more like a film, or a television play, than anything that could reasonably be applied to herself, who had nothing to do with the sensational. Her only involvement with the police, after all, was being paid by Scotland Yard for drawing whatever they might ask her, whenever they asked. "Naturally I will do my best, but I'm not sure how good a likeness can be drawn of someone I have never seen except in a photograph."

"I won't say too much." Delphick sipped his tea and ate a cucumber sandwich. "All I want is one of your IdentiKit sketches." The term Miss Seeton herself applied to those lightning flashes of insight came easily, after so long. "Your first impression of the man—and if I tell you about him it could distort that impression, so I won't. Instead, I'll ask if you enjoyed yourself in the north."

Miss Seeton, reassured, resumed her general chatting. Delphick showed particular interest in the yellow-crowned night heron, about which he, like so many, had read in the newspapers. The television coverage had been willing, but hardly effective.

"Because birds," pointed out Miss Seeton, "fly."

"I suppose you made a sketch or two," suggested her visitor. Miss Seeton went to the bureau and retrieved one of the blocks she had filled partly on holiday, and completely on her return. She flipped through pages. "May I take a look?" Delphick held out a hand.

"Rather dumpier than I would have expected," he observed at last. "Herons in this country have a more streamlined feel about them."

"That would be the heavier body, and the thicker neck. Had it been a black-crowned night heron, rather than yellow, it would have had shorter legs, which would have made it seem even more dumpy. But the black and white stripes on the head are eye-catching, are they not? Such a striking contrast against the grey."

Delphick agreed that they were, and went on leafing through the sketchbook. "Hello—so you attended a performance of *Macbeth*."

"Oh, no," said Miss Seeton. "Rather too violent for so young a child as little Marguerite, even if the story is part of her Scottish heritage."

"Oh?" Delphick took a closer look at her sketch of the three weird sisters on the stairs.

Miss Seeton saw what had caught his attention. She turned pink. "Oh dear, so foolish…the house—Nigel's, and dear Louise. Martha has told me of the family who once lived there, and Lady Colveden was so amusing about dear Sir George, and why he always encouraged her to call on the sisters rather than go himself. I suppose it must have confused me—the Fates, you see, with the builders taking so much longer than expected, as, sadly, does so often happen, and now not before Christmas as they had hoped. Fated, as one might say—and of course, three sisters."

"But not Chekhov?" The Oracle smiled as he continued to leaf through the sketchbook. "I see no cherry-trees or sea-gulls, Miss Seeton—but this, now, is an intriguing piece."

A dark-haired man in uniform, complete with jackboots, was emerging from a large car. Three blurred figures hovered in the background. A bicycle lay on its side in the road.

"So careless," said Miss Seeton, "but really so fortunate, after what happened to poor Bert, that the matter was not more serious. One of the gentlemen very kindly replaced my chain and I was able to ride home, and of course it will have served as yet another reminder that they are in England, rather than Spain."

Delphick shot her a quick look. "You thought they were Spanish?"

"They were driving on the wrong side of the road, and they didn't sound French. My languages are not good, and they may have been Italian, and everyone drives that way on the continent, don't they?"

"They do…You saw all of them?"

Miss Seeton frowned. "Now you come to mention it, I didn't. Only the driver, and the man beside him, who mended my chain. The others in the back opened their doors, but once they saw I was unhurt they closed them. One can understand they would not wish to get in the way. The passenger complained, I believe, about the grease, and was rather…emphatic when cleaning his hands afterwards, but he did a splendid job and people don't care for others looking over their shoulders when they are engaged on a complicated task, do they?"

"No, as a rule they don't." Delphick said no more about the sketch, but his thoughts were busy. He brushed cake crumbs from his fingers and finished his tea. "Business after pleasure," he told his hostess with a smile. "Now, ungracious though it sounds, I must make you sing for my supper."

Miss Seeton smiled back as he reached for the brown envelope. "What do you make of this chap, Miss Seeton? Take a good look while I clear the tea things for you."

There was time for him to rinse everything thoroughly and set it on the draining board before he heard her stirring. He hurried back from the kitchen. "Well?"

"I—I'm not sure," said Miss Seeton. "A most interesting face—the bones, in particular—but there is somehow a strong impression of—of concealment…" Did she mean the homosexuality, until so recently a crime, or the life he had been leading as a spy? She was staring unhappily at the result of her labours. "Only I fear my sketch has become confused somehow with Summerset Cottage, and I don't really see how it can be of any help."

Gabriel Crassweller had been a tall, elegant man with aristocratic features and an air of distinction many genuine aristocrats would envy. His nose was chiselled, his lips refined, his eyes dark, and shadowed. How, then, had Miss Seeton contrived to show him as plump—if not fat—with slits for eyes, a mean mouth, and a double chin? And yet it was unmistakeably Gabriel Crassweller at the same time as…

"Bluff King Hal?" said Chief Superintendent Delphick.

Chapter Eleven

Miss Seeton hesitated, then explained that the original portrait was a remarkable piece of work. Dr. Braxted of Brettenden Museum planned a thorough investigation of the whole house, which would delay the builders still further…

"Easter, rather than Christmas?" Delphick shook his head. "Poor young Colvedens. Still, I can't see Sir George chucking any spanners in the historical works—he'll know his duty to posterity. It sounds fascinating. Would Dr. Braxted give me a guided tour, if I asked you to introduce us?"

He saw her hands move swiftly and then settle, with a visible effort, to rest. Firmly, she twisted her fingers together. Delphick recognised the signs.

"Did you sketch it—him?" he asked gently.

She glanced at the bureau, and murmured that she had tried, although it had not turned out as she expected.

Delphick's interest quickened. Such unexpected drawing—Miss Seeton's special drawing—was the reason for her generous police retainer. Her intuitive skill might embarrass her, but this almost psychic ability to see beyond apparent reality to the deeper truth was often of the greatest assistance in a confused investigation. He opened the drawer where her sketching gear was kept, and pulled out a block at random. "This one? May I look?"

Mutely, she nodded.

"Yes, I see." Here was the devil, raging omnipotent in a vicious electrical storm above, presumably, the house in which the German wireless had been found. Yet again, she had seen the truth before anyone else could have done so…

"No." Miss Seeton flushed. "Not that one—the generator blew up, you see."

He carried on searching through painstaking depictions of scenery, birds, animals…"Ah." Here were her scribbled notes—colours, tints, shades in pencilled black and grey, lines indicating the appropriate planes and sections of Henry's fat white face. He looked more closely. No, he saw nothing that could have upset her the way it clearly had.

"You—you'll have to look at it upside down," she brought out at last.

Upside down? Costaguana was situated well south of the equator. Had she somehow confused two dictators, Hitler and El Dancairo? Might she be thinking of the rumours that periodically erupted of Hitler's escape from his bunker to the Latin American jungle where, even now, he was planning a comeback?

"Dear me. Upside down. Must I stand on my head? Not many people have such skill as yours, Miss Seeton."

Of course, he knew about her yoga. Now she was no longer being asked to accompany him to Summerset Cottage, she began to relax. "Dr. Braxted can lend you a mirror. In my case I could bend over backwards, but it was easier for her with the one from her bag, even though of course it is not just upside down but the other way round, too. And while students might not mind, I imagine that you, Chief Superintendent, would. Even if they have cleaned the floor, which with plaster isn't really possible without a vacuum cleaner—and, naturally, the electricity is off. Your jacket appears to be of high-quality cloth, and even were you to remove it your shirt and trousers would still be in some danger."

"Thank you for the warning, and I'll also offer thanks on behalf of my wife. No reason to annoy her when an easier method could work just as well."

"Oh, it will, and one cannot help but marvel at the skill of the original artist. Dr. Braxted's sister from the British Museum is trying to find out who he might have been. I don't know if they knew about yoga in Tudor times, though of course they had tumblers—acrobats—and perhaps squared paper, too, for the basic design. And they would have had to burn it every time they worked on the picture, in case they were betrayed."

It would all eventually make sense. He seized on the one point that made sense now. "Dr. Braxted—yours, that is, not the one at the British Museum—will she be there if I stroll round in a few minutes? I take it we can't phone to ask."

Miss Seeton smiled. "From what Lady Colveden has said, and what little I myself have seen, I think it unlikely there ever was a telephone in Summerset Cottage. But it is only a few minutes' walk away, and Dr. Braxted is a true enthusiast. I imagine you would be almost certain to find her at work there as long as the light remains good."

Delphick thanked her and took his leave, with the envelope of photographs and Miss Seeton's sketch of King Henry Crassweller. He wondered about the Three Sisters and the Devil In The Storm, but couldn't yet see how they fitted in. What he could see was that she was still not entirely herself. Bob, he knew, intended to call on his adopted aunt later. He could ask for the other sketches when she'd calmed down properly.

As he entered the George and Dragon he met Doris, the hotel's live-in waitress, general factotum and indispensible assistant to Charley Mountfitchet. She also worked on reception if required, and was another friend of long standing. She beamed at him.

"Welcome back, Mr. Delphick. Hope you enjoy your stay. How you and young Bob stick London week after week, I can't think."

"Nor can we," he said, disappearing up the stairs. "That's why we come here."

Having hidden Miss Seeton's sketch, with the photographs, under the mattress, he went back down to reception.

"Doris, I'm told that somewhere nearby there's a lady historian on the loose?"

"Dr. Braxted, yes. Her and a couple of youngsters are down Nowhere Lane in the house where young Nigel's going to live one day. Very keen, she is. Going to put Plummergen on the map, only it's a big secret for now until she's written it all up in some book or other."

Delphick, being the Oracle, could translate "book" as "magazine" or, in this context, "academic journal". He nodded encouragement, and Doris explained how he would find Nowhere Lane and he couldn't miss Summerset Cottage. But…

"They say she's keeping the doors locked and letting nobody in bar the police—so you'll be all right, Mr. Delphick, only you'll have to explain who you are in case she sets that young man of hers to chase you off the property!" She was still chuckling as Delphick thanked her for the directions, and hurried away.

Euphemia heard steps on the path, peered through a window, and saw a tall stranger in a tweed jacket. A rival historian! He had somehow learned of her discovery, and was after a spot of academic poaching. She flung the window open.

"This is private property," she shouted. "Go away at once, please!"

"Madam, I am a police officer." He held up the warrant card he knew she couldn't read from so far away. "I understand the law of trespass, but Sir George Colveden can vouch for me, if asked."

The heads of Madeline and Felix appeared at upper windows. "There are three of us here, as you see." Euphemia hesitated. "I'll take a look at that card of yours…"

She was fulsome in her apologies, and he assured her that he understood her caution. He had heard from Miss Seeton, and from Superintendent Brinton of Ashford, that she had made some remarkable finds of considerable importance in historic terms "both ancient and modern…"

Euphemia contemplated him for a moment, then nodded. "Come through and I'll show you Henry the Devil, but I imagine it's another devil that interests you more."

"Very probably." Delphick followed her into the parlour, and was honestly astounded by what he saw when Euphemia produced her mirror. He kept looking from Henry to the Devil, and back again. He shook his head.

"I can only borrow Miss Seeton's word," he said at last. "Remarkable."

Dr. Braxted sighed. "Not unique, so my sister tells me, but still an amazing find, though it's what we found in the priest's hole that shook me up rather more." She lowered her voice. "I wouldn't say so in front of those youngsters, but I had nightmares last night. The people directly involved—the three old girls who lived here—are dead, but that's not to say a few of their cronies aren't hiding somewhere in the wings waiting to see what else might still give them away. And there are the servants. From what PC Potter told me, and Sir George, they pushed off almost as soon as the death of the last old girl had been reported—though it was all above board, officially." She paused. "As far as anyone knows."

Delphick made a mental note to ask Brinton what exactly was known about the previous inhabitants of Summerset Cottage, masters and servants alike.

"Sir George sent us a longer ladder." Euphemia led the way up the stairs. "He said it would be safer than balancing on steps, and the very least he could do, though he wasn't keen to go scrambling about in the roof at his age. Of course, when young Mr. Colveden brought the ladder *he* was up there like a shot. He said not only was he his father's official representative, but he was also the chap who'd be living in the house once all the work was finished, so he thought it was the very least *he* could do."

"They're a close family," Delphick said. "They share a sense of humour."

He noted how the heavy wooden ladder had been wedged against one wall. The rungs were awkward to reach, but safer to climb than if the bottom rested, free to slip, on bare boards. Nigel might be a cheerful young man, but he was no more irresponsible than his father. He would take due precautions for the safety of anyone working on family property.

"Where a Colveden can go, and a Potter before him, so can a Delphick." The Oracle wondered how Superintendent Brinton, not noted for his lack of bulk, would have responded to the challenge. He'd send young Foxon, of course. "Could I borrow a torch?"

On his return, he was thoughtful. "The house belongs to Rytham Hall, but I assume the contents were the property of the late Saxons and now of their heirs, if there are any. An intriguing legal conundrum. Does this include a wireless set clearly marked as the property of a Third Reich that no longer exists?"

"And a good job, too! The sooner that devil's mouthpiece is gone from here, the happier I shall be."

"The proper authorities will be contacting you before long, I'm sure. Both Sir George and PC Potter have reported your discovery to Superintendent Brinton at Ashford, and he will be in touch with the right people. It may well turn out it's all so far back in history that another historian, specialising in the Hitler years, will be the one who sorts everything out for you."

Euphemia's eyes narrowed. "You can always," he added quickly, "keep the door of the parlour shut—locked—while it's being sorted. I won't breathe a word about Henry, and I'll warn my colleagues not to say anything either."

She brightened. "Careless talk costs academic lives," she said, adapting the poster slogan of the Second World War. "I intend to write this up for publication, Chief Superintendent, and that's how it goes, for people like me. Publish—or perish. This is the most exciting find I've made in years! And all thanks to Miss Seeton."

He might have guessed his old friend was somehow involved. He struggled not to laugh out loud when Euphemia explained how it had been tripping over the umbrella that led to her first upside-down view of the fresco.

"Remarkable," was all he could say at the end of the tale. Dr. Braxted had flung out her arms, clasped her hands, and thrown herself wholeheartedly into the re-enactment. She'd be devastated if anyone took the fun and the fame away from her now. "I'll do my very best to stop people talking," he promised again.

She beamed at him, then stiffened. Delphick heard them, too: brisk, heavy footsteps, coming along the path. Euphemia uttered a warning cry, and flew down the stairs to guard the door. Delphick followed in her wake, hearing other steps clattering above, and windows being opened.

"This is private property," Euphemia shouted. "Please go away!"

"Is Chief Superintendent Delphick still with you?"

"It's all right, Dr. Braxted." Delphick hurried across the hall. "My sergeant has come to find me. I imagine he dropped in on Miss Seeton and she sent him along."

Euphemia opened the door, took one look, and burst out laughing. "I can't see him in my priest's hole," she spluttered, as Bob Ranger—six foot seven and seventeen stone—hovered outside.

Bob looked from Dr. Braxted to Delphick. "Miss Seeton said you were probably here."

"She was right." The laughter bubbled in Euphemia's voice. "Come in. I'll share one of my professional secrets with you, but I doubt if I could share the other! They don't make shoe-horns big enough."

Bob was as impressed by Devil Henry as everyone else, swore to the utmost secrecy, and agreed that climbing ladders and creeping across rafters to corkscrew down a Tudor staircase was probably not justified unless a major crime had been committed—

"Treason is a crime," snapped Euphemia.

"—with a realistic chance of bringing the criminal to justice," he finished, watching the martial glint in her eye.

"Hmm. Yes." She subsided. "Unless the servants know anything, or we find lists of names—which I doubt we will—I suppose you're right."

"Have you found any papers at all?" asked Delphick. "The Germans are an efficient race. If we grumble about our paperwork, they positively revel in theirs."

"Mice," said Euphemia. "Plenty of old droppings up there, and nests galore. Any code-books or similar that haven't already been chewed to shreds will have crumbled away, or were never there at all, or were there and then taken away and destroyed when it looked at last as if we really were going to win."

Delphick nodded. "You could use such incriminating documents to light fires. Risky to put them out as salvage, but bundles of paper spills wouldn't be noticed."

"The Saxons cooked on an enormous kitchen range," said Euphemia. "The servants must have spent hours black-leading it, poor things. Or I should really say the servants did the cooking, not the Saxons. But I do remember that if you already possessed a reliable means of cooking during the war, then without a dashed good reason for the change you weren't allowed to install anything more up-to-date for the duration."

Bob grinned. "From what I've heard of the Saxons, they were barmy enough to put in for a smart new electric cooker or an improved gas supply at the height of the Blitz, and stick to the kitchen range years after the rules were relaxed out of sheer bloody-mindedness at their demands being refused in the first place."

Euphemia turned to the fresco. "Imagine if such unpatriotic vandals had known about this!" She flung out her arms. "I wouldn't put it past them to have whitewashed the whole thing over—or taken the wall down for firewood!"

"But they didn't, and it's going to make your name," said Delphick. "And when you've completed your researches I believe the Colvedens are going to let *you* take the wall down, for your museum."

Euphemia beamed, nodded, and pressed on the two detectives an invitation to view the kitchen range and the scullery beyond, because of the floor tiles. It would have been heartless to decline, yet to both men the tiles looked merely old and worn, though Euphemia tried to explain how the pattern of wear clearly showed various generations of kitchen layout, and how many times the sink would have needed re-plumbing.

"Whew!" said Bob as they finally made their escape. "I heard she was keen, but…"

"I'd call that an understatement. And how are things at the Knights'?"

"So-so, thank you, sir. Anne's been telling me about the cottage, and the Saxons—you know how this place thrives on gossip—and how they were seen at midnight on D-Day burying something in the garden here, or in the spinney round the back where it borders the graveyard. They say it was probably their German uniforms, ready for when Hitler came, but I'd have thought with a great kitchen range like that they could easily have burned them—if they even existed—and no questions asked."

"Except for the buttons. A domestic range would have been insufficiently hot to melt them beyond recognition."

"I'd have cut 'em off first and chucked them in the canal."

"You, Sergeant Ranger, have a criminally trained mind—and you aren't in shock, as they doubtless were." Delphick looked at his subordinate. "Yet you do appear somewhat anxious. Is all well with Anne and the baby?"

"Ye-es, sir, but it might be better, if you don't mind, to postpone your visit until tomorrow. They had a bit of a crisis last night at the nursing home and nobody got much sleep—except his lordship, of course." The proud father grinned. "He's an adaptable little cuss and was full of beans when I saw him, but poor Anne's exhausted. A new patient was brought in last night, a real emergency—caught dancing nude along the ridge of his roof telling everyone to call him Icarus."

"Real name, Plummet?" the Oracle couldn't resist asking. Bob looked blank. "Sorry," said Delphick. "I take it that he didn't fall off."

156

"Oh—plummet, sir. I get it. Jolly good." Bob coughed. "They had quite a time with him until Dr. Knight could get hold of the chap's proper doctor and find out what he was meant to be taking that he'd stopped." Anne's father had been one of London's top neurologists until retiring early for reasons of his own health. His private nursing home had once been Plummergen's cottage hospital. He selected, rather than was allocated, his patients when possible, but he would never ignore a genuine emergency.

"I'm sorry," said Delphick, "but I fear the pleasure of meeting my prospective godson must be postponed beyond tomorrow. Give my apologies to Anne, but I've been thinking. You have called on Miss Seeton. How did she seem?"

"Pleased to see me, sir. She told me you'd gone off to look at Nigel's house—and I admit she didn't seem too happy about the place, but having seen that creepy painting I can understand why…"

"Come into the George," invited his superior. "You'll be able to phone the Knights and explain we'll be heading back to town this evening."

Bob was surprised, but had more sense than to ask why when, as they came through the door, they saw Maureen ambling across the hall. A duster drooped from one hand, and she looked bored. She heard their footsteps, stopped, and slowly turned round.

"Oh," she said. She saw Bob and nodded at him, one local to another.

"Good afternoon, Maureen," Delphick said. "Or perhaps we are moving towards good evening? Hello, in either case, and at the same time I'm afraid it must be goodbye. We're returning to London, so I won't need my room after all. Could you find Charley or Doris so that I can settle my account?"

"Oh," said Maureen. Her lightning wits were a village joke. "Hello." She frowned. "Mr. Mountfitchet's down in the cellar. Dunno about Doris."

Delphick knew when not to insist. "We'll just slip up to my room to collect my things. Perhaps by the time I'm back one or other of them will have appeared. If you see them before I do, could you please tell them I would like to check out at once?"

"But…you've not long checked in. Doris told me."

"And soon I'll be checking out. I'll go up now." He went, beckoning Bob to follow.

In his room he rummaged under the mattress for the envelope of photographs with Miss Seeton's sketch. "She drew this for me, having studied these. What do you make of it?"

Bob contemplated his adopted aunt's IdentiKit drawing. "Well, it's Crassweller all right, but there's a lot of Henry there too…"

Delphick had moved to stand in front of his sergeant. "And upside down it's the devil, as well. Exactly the same as the Summerset fresco. Miss Seeton was most insistent that this—" he tapped the sketch "—should be looked at upside down. At first I thought she meant the fresco, but now I've had time to think…"

"Yes, sir?"

"I wonder," said Delphick slowly, "whether she might not be trying to tell us we've been looking at the whole Crassweller business upside down from the start. Which is why we're going back to London tonight."

"Upside down?" Bob was repeatedly turning the sketch in his hands. "You mean it's somehow the wrong way round, sir?"

From the other direction. Mirrors. *Venison the menu…*

"Not suicide," said Delphick. "Somebody else administered that polysyllabic barbiturate to Gabriel Crassweller. Not suicide—but murder."

Chapter Twelve

Miss Seeton regretted the brevity of Bob's visit, but at least she had seen her adopted nephew, and received further news of Anne and the baby, so that when he telephoned to say he and Mr. Delphick must return to London sooner than expected, she entirely understood. It was, after all, their job. She hoped her little IdentiKit sketch had been of some help. Mr. Delphick (Bob assured her) was delighted. Miss Seeton, relieved, packed her sketching gear away and settled to the pursuit and practice of appliqué, as demonstrated by Louise to herself and Lady Colveden, and also by Miss Wicks, with her neatly basted geometric shapes.

Miss Wicks! Miss Seeton almost dropped her scissors. She had promised she would buy her some fabric—she had forgotten! It was no excuse that she had been distracted by sketching the secret List of Local Legends and History. The schoolchildren had long since put the finishing touches to the painted map foundation strip. Assembly and stitching-on were well under way as panels—done in cross-stitch, needlepoint, or quilted—were handed in. Miss Wicks had been one of the first to submit her contribution, the wrought iron balustrade of her cottage being represented by a length of exquisite crochet lace, the whole picture framed in dainty hexagons. Miss Wicks would never rebuke a friend for breaking a promise, but…

"Tomorrow," promised Miss Seeton firmly. Today she was busy cutting her own shapes out of cartridge paper. When one looked at anything closely, and broke it down into its true form, as she always told her pupils, the possibilities were endless. Like designing one's own personal jigsaw puzzle, only with lines rather than wiggly edges. Miss Seeton knew that in theory you could make curves from multiple short straight lines, and knew that in real life she never would. Or certainly not with fabric. Straight lines on their own would do very well. A window, a door. An individual rectangle? Or several smaller oblongs in slightly different hues of the same colour, to indicate reflections of the outside world on glass, or paint? A pitched roof—a lozenge and a parallelogram in different shades, and there it was, almost in three dimensions…

Next morning Miss Seeton, her shopping list in her basket and her basket over one arm, selected an umbrella. Yes, the dark blue. Dear Mr, Brinton, so thoughtful to have had her initials embossed on the handle. Though maybe her hat now seemed a trifle shabby. She might pop into the milliner's while visiting Jeannine Claire, to see the latest Monica Mary creations…

Her mind on hats, Miss Seeton headed for the bus. Passing Miss Wicks's cottage, her conscience prompted her to wave at the front window where the old lady, she knew, sat at work in the natural light that was so much more comfortable for the eyes than the artificial yellow of electric bulbs—daylight apparently held a bluish tinge. Which, apparently, explained the comfort. Artists, of course, preferred a north light, without the sun, although in Australia and New Zealand they would presumably prefer a south light. Upside down again. It was all very puzzling, when the sun itself could only be described as yellow. She recalled Mrs. Thorley, the physics mistress at Mrs. Benn's school, saying this was all to do with scattering wavelengths. On whichever side of the world you happened to be. Perhaps one day someone would invent a lightbulb that showed colours as they really were, even at night.

She thought she saw an answering wave, and her conscience pricked again. Her own submission to the Plummergen Mural would be modest, a plain likeness of her cottage offered as her contribution to the community spirit of which the dear vicar had preached with such enthusiasm last Sunday.

It had taken Molly Treeves a long time to explain to the Reverend Arthur why Plummergen's women had turned Dorcas overnight, and what a splendid chance it might be to bring everyone in the place together. A realist, Molly knew that any togetherness would not last, but even a brief truce was worth encouraging.

Miss Seeton waved again, and hurried on. Miss Wicks could knit, tat, and crochet, too. She enjoyed her work so much. It would be churlish not to bring back the widest possible selection of fabrics, whether from Madame Jeannine or some other shop. She could tell her elderly friend that it was mostly scraps, costing half of what they really had: her conscience might then leave her in peace.

There were several others in the queue for the bus. With a nod and a smile for all, Miss Seeton took her place behind them.

Miss Nuttel and Mrs. Blaine, with the advantage of living opposite the bus stop, were as usual second in line. They tended to watch until someone arrived and then bustled out to join her (or them) to find out where she (or they) proposed to go, and why.

"No point hanging around outside in a draught," Miss Nuttel always said; and Mrs. Blaine always agreed.

Mrs. Newport and Mrs. Scillicough had parked an assortment of offspring with their long-suffering mother and arrived together from the council houses. "Brettenden," they replied as one to Mrs. Blaine's polite enquiry after their destination.

"Yes, a change of scene can be welcome from time to time," Mrs. Blaine probed further, "can't it? Especially the shops."

"Sometimes," said Mrs. Newport.

"Spice of life, variety," said Mrs. Scillicough.

"Most things we need are right here in the village," pointed out Miss Nuttel.

"Not all of them," said Mrs. Newport. "You're off shopping too, aren't you?"

This was close to a challenge. How best to answer while giving nothing away?

"A change of scene," repeated Mrs. Blaine. Mrs. Newport gazed at the basket carried by Mrs. Blaine. Mrs. Scillicough remarked the linen bag poking from Miss Nuttel's coat pocket.

They were joined by Mrs. Skinner and Mrs. Henderson. These ladies lived in houses close enough for each to keep, with little effort, a wary eye on anything suspicious her rival might do, by day or by night. Neither need fear that an outright march could ever be stolen by (or on) either side, which inevitably struck both as unfair, and gave them a feeling of justification when in unspoken agreement they chose to ignore the vicar's words about community spirit. "Haven't missed the bus, then," said Mrs. Skinner. "Good."

"Plenty of time," snapped Mrs. Henderson. For once she had been a little slow to notice the opening of Mrs. Skinner's front door. The shoes Mrs. Henderson wore now were the pair she normally kept for around the village. There was plenty of wear left in them, but after a while they tended to pinch her toes. Mrs. Henderson was not looking forward to her day out in Brettenden.

Miss Seeton was reminded of squabbling schoolgirls. And with a hint of reproach said: "Jack Crabbe is always reliable, of course. We have no more than two or three minutes to wait, which on a beautiful morning like this can surely be no great hardship."

"Fancy a change of scene yourself, Miss Seeton?" enquired Mrs. Newport.

"Just a little shopping." Neighbourly interest; how fortunate one had been in Cousin Flora's loving bequest. Her dear cottage, her many friends…"The art supplies shop, mainly, because I have used all my cartridge paper in my poor attempts at design…"

Everyone looked at everyone else. The last few weeks had been difficult for the seamstresses of Plummergen. Secrecy became endemic. In a place with gossip as its lifeblood, this had sent blood-pressure soaring. While people would admit to a stake in the History and Legends Quilt, they refused to give details. But if Miss Seeton, rather a late starter in the Sewing Stakes, was careless enough to let something slip, then…

Mrs. Blaine, domestic half of the Lilikot partnership, simply had to know. "It sounds as if you have something too elaborate planned, Miss Seeton." She tittered. "Being a teacher, of course, you have such an advantage—so many new ideas we in our quiet little village would never dream of."

Miss Seeton looked startled. "Oh, no. My needlework has always been practical rather than decorative—like Goldilocks, or do I mean Curlylocks? I may well *sit on a cushion and sew a fine seam*, though of course at this time of year there are few strawberries to be had—" Mrs Blaine, whose marriage had been childless, failed to catch the nursery-rhyme reference—"and sadly my stitches are nowhere near as fine as my Cousin Flora's. But I would never attempt anything one could call elaborate. Just a simple depiction of my house in appliqué, thanks to dear Louise, and in plain cotton because I understand that anything more luxurious can fray if handled inexpertly, or stretch, as well as slipping."

The cartridge paper design—cheating! Professional tricks none of them knew! An incomer trying to outshine the locals!—was about to be disputed when the bus came along. Everyone climbed in. Miss Seeton moved to the back, leaving room for those less agile—so beneficial, her yoga—who might get on at later stops and be glad not to have to squeeze their way down the aisle. Jack Crabbe, of course, was a perfect gentleman and would never leave the stop until everyone was safely seated, but if she could help in any small way she was more than happy to do so.

Miss Nuttel, glancing over her shoulder, nudged Mrs. Blaine in her well-padded ribs. "Up to something," she muttered. "Smiling to herself, and not speaking to anyone."

"Plotting, you think?" Mrs. Blaine wished she wore make-up so that she could take out a mirror and powder her nose while she snooped to the back of the bus.

"Could be." Miss Nuttel, gardener, pondered. "Strawberries in September? Odd."

"That must be the drink talking." Mrs. Blaine's black eyes glinted. "Vodka doesn't smell, remember. If it had been whisky or brandy she'd have reeked."

"Explains why she's sitting by herself," agreed Miss Nuttel. "Thinks nobody will notice."

"She could still be plotting something. Or she might have an accident. There's so much more traffic in Brettenden. You know, Eric, I think we should keep an eye on her—for her own sake—while she's out and about by herself in a strange place."

"Civic duty." Miss Nuttel nodded. "Only what the vicar said, isn't it?"

Where Miss Seeton was concerned, the Nuts were accustomed to lurking. Had they not, on her first day in Plummergen, gone to pay a call and found her curtains shut in the middle of the afternoon? Checking round the outside of the house they could see no one in any of the ground-floor rooms. She was upstairs! Their suspicions were naturally aroused. Such behaviour, in a newcomer who ought to anticipate visits of welcome, was abnormal. Abnormality could be a pointer to…perversion. Or worse. Had they not always suspected her of involvement in witchcraft, demonology, the Black Arts in general? Guided by the Ouija board, had they not on another occasion checked round the house for indisputable proof of her malignant tendencies, and had she not thrust an arm from her bedroom window—a first floor window—and conjured up some unknown, unseen, unnamed Force to strike Miss Nuttel senseless to the ground?

Not all the protestations of Martha Bloomer then or later could persuade them that the sacrificed baby they had both seen that dreadful night—its throat cut, its blood falling into a basin on Miss Seeton's draining-board—had been bramble jelly dripping through a muslin bag. It was irrelevant that Erica Nuttel had never cared for the sight of blood. It was no over-heated imagination that had caused her sudden collapse. Miss Seeton, they knew, was a skilled practitioner of the very darkest of dark practices.

Yet few ever seemed to believe Miss Nuttel and Mrs Blaine, so strong were Miss Seeton's evil powers, so cleverly did she seem to throw her sorcerous dust in village eyes. This time, perhaps…

In Brettenden, accordingly, the Nuts lurked.

Miss Seeton had meant to go to the art supplies shop, but again her conscience pricked her. She had made a promise—and Jeannine Claire: Modiste was in the same part of the high street as Monica Mary: Milliner. She would call first on Miss Brown, to ask where she acquired her ribbons and trims for the lavish creations that adorned so many local heads. It would most likely be a London wholesaler, though it might be a shop within walking distance, where she could go afterwards if neither Miss Brown nor Madame Jeannine had interesting scraps to spare.

The Nuts watched Miss Seeton glance at the art supplies shop, hesitate, shake her head, and walk on. Signalling? They looked, but saw nobody paying particular attention to their quarry. "Just shows how cunning she can be," said Miss Nuttel.

Miss Seeton, unaware of pursuit, came to the hat shop and went in. Through plate glass the Nuts watched her in animated conversation with Miss Brown, who after some minutes vanished to the back of her shop. She returned with a pale blue paper bag that Miss Seeton received with a nod and a smile, before putting it in her neat wicker basket.

"Could be anything," said Miss Nuttel.

"Drugs, Eric?" quavered Mrs. Blaine.

"Disguised, whatever it is."

Surveillance continued. After further animated conversation Miss Seeton began to try on hats. A number of hats. More than once. In the end Monica Mary helped her reach a decision, and the Nuts rejoiced. It is possible to spend only a certain length of time in front of a shop window, no matter how stylish the display therein, before people start to notice.

Banknotes were produced. Miss Seeton handed them over. Miss Brown returned some of them. Further animated discussion. Miss Seeton smiled, shook her head, nodded, and a pale blue cardboard box tied with silvery string made a neat parcel for her to bear proudly from the shop before carrying on down the high street.

"Drugs," agreed Miss Nuttel, sadly. She could never buy another hat from Monica Mary Brown—and that meant in future going all the way to Ashford.

As they hurried after their still oblivious quarry the Nuts were accosted by Mrs. Newport and Mrs. Scillicough. The sisters, of a younger generation, had seen nothing in the hat shop window of any possible interest, and wondered why Nutcrackers and the Hot Cross Bun were so clearly lurking. Then Miss Seeton appeared with her hatbox, and trotted away. They wondered no more.

"Up to her tricks again, I suppose?" Mrs. Scillicough nodded towards the retreating figure, and was ready to join the chase if it seemed likely to prove worthwhile.

"With Miss Seeton, you never can tell," said Mrs. Newport.

Miss Nuttel, busy watching Miss Seeton, did not answer. Mrs. Blaine hesitated.

"We...don't know," she admitted at last.

Miss Nuttel was still watching. "There!" she announced. "Look—going into Jeannine Claire's place right now." Her indignation was great. First, the hat shop, now the dressmaker! At this rate they'd never feel safe shopping anywhere in Brettenden again.

"She did buy a new hat, Eric," said Mrs. Blaine. "Maybe she just wants a—a matching costume." She herself hadn't bought a new hat for ages. Or a new frock, either. Eric said they must be as self-sufficient as possible, and save money—and the planet—where they could. Mrs. Blaine knew she always had her sewing machine to make a blouse, or a dress, but the effect was never as good, and she certainly couldn't make a hat with all the ribbons and trims that Monica Mary used.

In tacit agreement everyone remained at a safe distance from Jeannine Claire: Modiste. Nobody wanted anyone else

167

to gain the fact-finding advantage, and four people in front of a high-class shop window would definitely attract attention.

Miss Seeton came out, and bustled away.

"Not long enough for a fitting..." Miss Nuttel prepared to follow.

Miss Seeton stopped, turned, and hurried back down the high street. Plump Mrs. Blaine was left behind as the others melted into shop doorways. Miss Seeton inclined her head but said nothing, hurrying on to renew her stock of cartridge paper before she forgot again. Mrs. Blaine had time to peer into the wicker basket.

She made her report. "Another paper bag!" she announced, as doorways disgorged the loiterers. "Bigger—and pale pink!"

"Drugs, then," said Miss Nuttel grimly.

While Mrs. Newport generally harboured suspicions of Miss Seeton, Mrs. Scillicough was never sure. This, however, was not one of her doubting moments. "Drugs? Gammon!" she scoffed. "Stealing a march on the rest of us, that's what she's doing."

"How?" demanded her sister. The Nuts stared.

"Caught her at it, didn't we? In and out of that posh Jannen shop with her paper bags—and when she said it was going to be just plain cotton, too." It was hard to tell which had annoyed Mrs. Scillicough more: Miss Seeton's blatant attempt to outdo the rest of the village in the matter of quality fabric, or the fact that she hadn't thought of any such scheme herself.

"Well!" said Mrs. Newport, thinking fast. "Using fancy material, and ribbons! Two can play at that game."

"Three," said her sister, promptly joining her in the dash along the high street towards Jeannine Claire: Modiste and the possibility of satin, lace and velvet offcuts.

Miss Nuttel looked at Mrs. Blaine. Mrs. Blaine sighed. "Dutch courage, I expect," she offered, but her heart wasn't really in it, and Miss Nuttel could think of nothing in reply.

Without her hatbox Miss Seeton might have managed, but with her basket, handbag and umbrella too she knew that rolled sheets of cartridge paper would be awkward to carry, no matter how many rubber bands the shop used to secure them. She had decided to buy instead one small packet of assorted colours—only to find the shop had sold out, with the next delivery not due until next week. Drat. This meant choosing between buying several small packs of individual colours, or one middle-sized assorted pack, neither of which would fit so well in her basket.

"Have a carrier bag," suggested the girl behind the counter. "Nice strong handles, and free advertising for us." She and Miss Seeton were old acquaintances.

"Perhaps I should have left the hat for another day," said Miss Seeton, "but Miss Brown was so persuasive, and I know she never makes the same design twice, except in different colours, that is."

"A bit like you," said the salesgirl, unfolding a smart grey carrier bag. Miss Seeton had already explained about hexagons, and appliqué, and the varied shapes that could make up her cottage, and how she could not quite decide which; and the girl had said that she too enjoyed sewing, and was happy to advise on the best method for stitching through cartridge paper, and the best place for Miss Seeton to buy...

"Needles," murmured Miss Seeton as she passed the Nuts, who had ducked into another providential doorway when she emerged from the art supplies shop. Needles, of course, she already possessed, but the salesgirl had warned that just as she should never use her sewing scissors for cutting paper or card—Miss Seeton blushed—so she should keep her sewing needles for fabric, thread, and nothing else. She must buy either a packet of darning, or a packet of heavy-duty needles from the haberdashery section of Messrs Lance & Lance, that celebrated department store (tel. Brettenden 73) and, once back at home, label it carefully and keep it in a different part of her sewing box to avoid confusion.

"Needles," echoed Miss Nuttel.

"We were right after all," said Mrs. Blaine. "It's too bad of her."

Miss Seeton was so preoccupied with the damage her thoughtless cutting of paper might have done to her needlework scissors—though it had been only once, when she somehow mislaid her little crafting knife and she was in a hurry, or maybe twice, she couldn't be sure—that she walked slap into a man who, busily chatting, was coming with his wife from the opposite direction.

"Oof," said the man.

"Oh dear," said Miss Seeton, and in her confusion dropped nearly everything except her pale blue hatbox. "Oh dear, I'm so very sorry. I should be far more careful about allowing my thoughts to wander in such a busy street."

Three heads bumped as Miss Seeton, the man, and his wife bent to retrieve her bag, basket, umbrella, and smart grey carrier, as well as the shopping that had spilled from her basket across the pavement. "Oh dear," said Miss Seeton again, as they straightened together.

"No harm done." The man held out her handbag as his wife scooped up the contents of the basket and repacked it as best she could. "And your brolly, too. Handsome piece."

Miss Seeton smiled as she accepted her belongings from his wife, but continued with her apologies as he went on admiring the umbrella with its hand-stitched leather cover for the handle, and the neat gold initials embossed thereon.

"Very nice. Looks like real gold, too."

"It is," said Miss Seeton, adding quickly: "Only my initials, of course—I believe the police are not highly paid, and it was given to me by an acquaintance in the police force—and silk, too, as is the one Superintendent Delphick gave me some years ago—but it was Superintendent Brinton who gave me this. So very kind of him." She was delighted, on Mr Brinton's behalf, that his present had so caught the attention of her new acquaintance, although was he, indeed, so new? His face, his wife's, seemed familiar. "But I would," Miss Seeton hurried to explain, "have been just as happy with nylon because it is the thought that counts, not the financial expenditure, and a superintendent cannot be paid as much as a chief superintendent, naturally."

"Friends in high places, eh?" The almost-familiar man looked a little surprised, and his wife was frankly staring. Miss Seeton blushed. Would it be presumptuous to call Superintendent Brinton a friend? They had known each other for several years, but somehow it wasn't quite the same as dear Mr. Delphick—yet both were colleagues, in a professional sense, even if her little art consultant fee was paid by Scotland Yard rather than by the county constabulary.

"I have been acquainted with Superintendent Brinton for several years," she said. "The umbrella was a special present one Christmas. He was kind enough to say that I had been of some assistance when the bank was robbed and the treasure was found—though not so much the chest in the vault as the Roman treasure at Rytham Hall—and not gold, but silver—jugs, and bowls, and dishes—and no hallmarks, naturally, and no coins, which puzzled me as I had always understood they were needed to pay the ferryman. Funerary goods, I believe, and you can see them in Brettenden Museum, together with the mosaic." Miss Seeton, whose modesty discouraged her from chatting to anyone, especially strangers, about her own affairs, warmed to her theme as she told these strangers—or were they indeed strangers?—of the elaborate and unusual design of the floor of the Temple of Glacia at Rytham Hall, and of the rarity and beauty of the hoard of Siberius Gelidus Brumalix that had been found there.

"Need a deal of polishing, from the sound of it," observed the wife ruefully.

"Now then, Agnes," chided her husband. "We've done with all that at last."

"But—forgive me, but it is *Roman* silver," protested Miss Seeton. "Polish, I assure you, would be most unsuitable. Only the purest soapsuds, and then a rub with chamois leather or soft flannel once it has been thoroughly rinsed. The fine detail would be lost over time if one were to use ammonia—or powdered pumice—or Bluebell."

Agnes pulled a face. "Horrible smell," she said. "Still, I knew a kiddie once that drank half a can of the stuff, though it says poison on the tin—too young to read, see."

"How dreadful," said Miss Seeton faintly. She would have thought the smell, never mind the taste, would have discouraged any child from such a foolish act, whether or not it could read. "I hope the child survived."

"Yes, but Sam never used anything but paste ever after," said Agnes, "just in case."

"Or washing soda and aluminium foil, for small pieces," said Sam. "But that's all in the past, and not needed for this brolly anyway."

"No, indeed." Miss Seeton, receiving her umbrella, slipped it on her arm and patted the royal blue handle. "Gold, of course, does not tarnish."

With final apologies, a friendly smile, and a nod, Miss Seeton parted from Sam and Agnes and continued needle-wards to Lance & Lance. She did not notice Miss Nuttel and Mrs. Blaine hovering in the near distance.

But they had noticed her. And her distracted mishap. And the people with whom she had collided.

"Oh, Eric," said Mrs. Blaine. "Nobody ever sees them now they've moved away—so why is she talking to the Brattles?"

Chapter Thirteen

The way to the Foreign and Commonwealth Office was now familiar to Detective Chief Superintendent Delphick and Detective Sergeant Ranger. Their reasons for this third visit, however, differed from the two previous occasions on which they had interviewed a small multitude of his colleagues in the department to which Gabriel Crassweller had belonged.

"Before, we were after motives for suicide," said the Oracle, as they left Scotland Yard on foot in search of a taxi. They'd learned the first time that, brandish their warrant cards as they might, parking spaces were at a premium in Whitehall. It took longer to find one than the effort was worth. "Now, we aren't. We'll try a return to basics. Why would you, knowing him, murder Gabriel Crassweller?"

"Because he was a traitor, sir. And I'm a patriotic bloke."

"Why not report him to the authorities and let them deal with him?"

Bob considered. "I've got no outright proof? Any more than we've managed to find, sir—so far, that is. Besides, whoever I told might be in on it too, and then I'd be the one for the chop, most like."

"No easy way of telling sheep from goats? Yes, that's a possibility."

Bob was inspired. "Or the authorities know about him already, and want to try that turnaround trick Oblon mentioned, keeping him as a...a sleeper," the jargon came with an effort, "and playing the misinformation game on the Stentorians to pass on to the Soviets, sir."

"Also possible. And in our country's best interests, in the long term. If that's the case, then, why kill him rather than leave him to mislead the Reds with or without realising it?"

Some further thought. "I'm a patriotic bloke who's illogical?"

"Or, perhaps, convinced you know better than the authorities. You think it too risky to keep him alive—perhaps for fear he might encourage others to follow his path...Yes, that is likewise a possibility. You are conceited enough to think you always know best."

Bob grinned. "Sounds more like a politician than a diplomat, sir."

"So young, and so cynical." The Oracle fell silent as they walked together, neither now looking for a taxi. Their conversation was not of the sort to be overheard by a third party. "Someone who sees him- or herself as judge, jury, and executioner all in one—who can't believe they can possibly be wrong in whatever they choose to do."

"They all struck me as pretty bright, sir. The high-ups, I mean, those at Crassweller's level—you'd need to be, wouldn't you? For a job like that?"

"Bright enough to conceal your machinations, certainly. What's really needed here is an expert on the corkscrew workings of the human mind, not a couple of humble Scotland Yarders. Sadly, your father-in-law is trained in neurology rather than psychoanalysis."

"How about hypnosis, sir?" suggested Bob. "Or a lie detector?"

"Both can be fiddled, as I understand it—and by trying either, we give our suspicions away. We'll just have to rely on copper's instinct, the way we've done for years, and carry on as if we still believed it to be a suicide."

"You know, sir, I'm not sure I'm cut out for an actor. Assuming Miss Seeton's right, that is."

"How tactful. You mean, assuming that *I* am right. You know Miss Seeton's sketches invariably show us the truth. However, because this truth is filtered through her eyes, it is the interpretation of what she thinks she's seen that has to be correct. I could be entirely wrong in my interpretation."

"You aren't usually, sir. It's got to be worth a try. And nothing else plausible has come up, has it?"

"Only in a totally negative sense—which, as I've said before, is as valid an answer as any positive." Delphick thought back over long, intense days of background reading, theorising, interviews and note-taking. "We found no motive for suicide. We found no evidence that he was being blackmailed—the man had money in the bank. There was no illness to cause him anxiety. His workload was no more than it had been for years. True, the drug found at the post mortem was not prescribed by his doctor, but in these days, sadly, drugs are all too readily obtained by those who seek an illicit thrill. It could indeed have been self-administered—but, as Miss Seeton with her latest upside-down portrait has now led us to suspect, it was in all probability administered by a third party."

"All forty-seven syllables of it," said Bob.

"Yes, but if I can't pronounce it I won't waste time trying. Crassweller took or more likely was given whatever-it-is, crashed his car, and died. We will leave the details to those who understand them, and accept that the stuff is not impossible to obtain and is virtually undetectable by whoever ingests it until the general effects make themselves known."

"Until he goes woozy," said Bob. "The way druggies like to feel. Trippy."

"Except that he didn't drug, did he? Or smoke. The man could be almost an ascetic, if he hadn't so clearly enjoyed an after-dinner drink or two."

"So someone could have slipped the polysyllable stuff into his port and waved him off in his car and just waited for the bang when it didn't mix with the booze."

"Someone certainly could. Most probably it was someone he knew—and apart from work he appears to have known very few people." He sighed. "Despite several days of rigorous questioning we have obtained no especially helpful information from any of his colleagues—and now it looks as if we must interview the whole lot again, asking the same questions as before, but with a different slant and without giving ourselves away."

In thoughtful silence, they walked on.

They climbed the steps beside the statue of Robert Clive, and entered the elaborate grey building of the Foreign and Commonwealth Office, with its chandeliers and painted ceilings. "Ladies first, I think," said Delphick, mentally reviewing the various people they were about to interview for the second or third time.

Miss Edith Brownlow, whose demure floral blouse had a neat kitten-bow tie rather than a pussycat, had been personal private secretary to Gabriel Crassweller from the moment he reached the appropriate step on the promotional ladder. As he had continued to rise, so had she, refusing every lure thrown to her by others promising higher grades and more money if she would come and work for them. Before even greeting her interrogators, Miss Brownlow pointedly double-checked the door of the office they had borrowed. After the preliminaries were over she said firmly that neither her loyalty nor her discretion could be questioned, whether her country or her boss might be under discussion.

"Gabriel—Mr. Crassweller," she corrected herself, her handkerchief to her eyes, "knew he could rely on me. When he had to go abroad he always took me with him—he would never have dreamed of anyone else. I can summarise reports and type speeches faster than anyone I know, which isn't immodest, Mr. Delphick, I merely state a fact. Mr. Crassweller's thought processes were…lively. Few people would be able to follow his unusual leaps of logic and make them coherent—but I can. Could."

Again she raised the handkerchief and dabbed gently at her eyes.

Once she had gone, they looked at each other. "This time round," said Delphick slowly, "I'd say she's foxing. That handkerchief didn't seem necessary. Did you notice that once or twice when she sniffed, she didn't blink?"

"I wondered about that, sir."

"Yet I can't think what she can be covering up more than she's covered previously—if she is. Or has been."

"First impression she gave us was that she was totally devoted to him, sir, but sort of resigned to the fact he was a…a hopeless case. When they started out together homosexuality was still against the law, remember."

"And Miss Brownlow would have been suitable camouflage? Yes. I wonder why he let the opportunity slip."

"He might've preferred her doormat impression in the office to her toothbrush in his bathroom."

Delphick pounced. "Impression? Yes. She's been acting the part of a devoted subordinate—and acting well—but my bet would be she's every bit as bright as the rest of them, and clever enough not to let anyone find out. There may be talk in the real world about Women's Liberation, but in the corridors of power any sort of change takes a long time. Subterfuge must be the name of the game."

It was Bob's turn to pounce. "As subterfugeous as taking over Crassweller's leaks now he's gone? Maybe that's what she wanted all along, sir, knowing the work as well as ever he did and how to benefit the most efficient way."

The Oracle agreed that such an idea was not to be dismissed, adding that if anyone could bring Women's Lib to Whitehall he thought Miss Brownlow probably could.

Next to be interviewed was Harry Gilmore, several years younger than Gabriel Crassweller, but only one grade lower in the FO hierarchy. "I'm redbrick, not Oxbridge," he said cheerfully. "Hence the tie—socialist red rather than old school." He was apparently untroubled by the nuances of class and education said to exist in government. "Now poor Gabriel's gone, there's a chance for me to move up—or Walter Marrable," he added, with the first hint of bitterness. "Walter's second generation, you see."

"His father worked here?" Delphick's research had already given him the answer, but he wanted to see what Harry really thought.

"His father's the ambassador to Costaguana—or was, until they recalled him when the trouble flared up. No doubt he'll be back there before too long."

"The Reds," offered Bob once Harry Gilmore had left the room, "believe in rising by your own merit and social equality and so on, sir, not handing it to you on a plate because of who your father is."

"He was open about his socialist sympathies, which don't seem to have done him much harm in the promotion game.

Or is he really Stentoria's tame English Red from Redbrick? Although perhaps a little blatant for our purposes…"

"Double bluff," said Bob. "He's bright enough for that. Triple, even."

Walter Marrable, by comparison, seemed born to be an ambassador. He was tall, sleek, well-dressed in pinstripes and very well groomed. Delphick's quick appraisal of the cost of his shoes made him think with considerable envy of his own mortgage.

"Either Ambrose Denarcott, or myself," said Mr. Marrable, when asked who was likely to inherit the services of Miss Brownlow *because you can't let a woman like that go to waste, can you?* Walter Marrable agreed that you couldn't. "Made a touch at her myself, a year or so back," he admitted, "when poor Gabriel looked so shaky—not politically," he hastened to add, "never that. Very patriotic chap, our friend Crassweller. But he had a run of bad luck—pneumonia, twice, and the second time almost did for him. Edith covered for him during his absence, of course, and made more than an adequate job of it."

He settled back in his chair, and smiled. "Of course, she's too old to get much further on her own, but with me to help she could have done it, and maybe now, she can."

"Time will tell," said Delphick. "Do you know if Mr. Denarcott make a similar approach?"

"Gabriel was really very ill," protested Walter Marrable. "One has to look out for oneself in a place like this—in a career like mine. Ours. I've no doubt Mr. Denarcott did, and will have received the same answer as the one she gave me."

"As I understand it, Mr. Marrable, Miss Brownlow has been professionally associated with Mr. Crassweller for some years. Is this the normal way such matters are arranged?"

Walter Marrable said such was generally the case, but should events conspire against the female—junior—half of what he might almost be prepared to call a partnership, then it was every man, or even woman, for him (or her) self.

"Your own secretary has not been with you for long," deduced the Oracle.

"Slipped up and had a baby, and the same sort of thing happened to Ambrose—except that his girl had the sense to get married first. Inconvenient for both of us, of course."

"Of course," echoed the Oracle. "Thank you, sir."

He looked at Bob as the door closed. "Your views, Sergeant Ranger?"

"Started off smooth, then gave himself away, sir. I don't think he liked Crassweller that much—but surely a chap like him wouldn't bump off another chap, no matter how much he envied him, just to get his hands on his secretary?"

"Would he not? Remember that old saying about love and war, Bob, and everything being fair. In-fighting, competition and skulduggery would seem to abound in this place just as on the wider political stage, except that the outside skulduggery is rather more dramatic in its presentation. For an ambitious man, the perfect secretary is essential. Mere adequacy wouldn't be enough."

"Miss Brownlow says she's good, sir, but maybe she's exaggerating."

"When she knows we can ask elsewhere? I doubt it. She probably takes down the six o'clock news verbatim from the radio every night, to keep in practice." He smiled at Bob's evident chagrin. "So now who envies whom, Sergeant Ranger?"

"Let's talk to Ambrose Denarcott," suggested Bob, sheepishly grinning. "He might know if she does."

"Why, yes, Chief Superintendent." Ambrose seemed surprised that Delphick had even bothered to ask. "I believe it is part of standard secretarial training for the FO."

"Along with flower arranging," murmured the Oracle.

"Naturally. Ambassadorial servants are as likely as anyone else to fall ill." Mr. Denarcott was amused, but courteous. At his grave inclination of the head Bob Ranger was put in mind of a plump, bobbing wood pigeon—not that you got many of those in London, more the rats-with-wings type, but in the open countryside wood pigeons could be a pest. Now the soft greyish pink of Denarcott's double-breasted waistcoat was a definite reminder, along with the starched white collar…

"A good secretary," enlarged Ambrose, "must be able to take most reasonable eventualities in her stride. Mine, for instance, faltered on only one occasion of which I have personal knowledge."

The pigeon bobbed and bowed again, inviting the inevitable question and sharing the joke that he knew what he was doing, and so did Delphick.

"The one occasion being…?"

"It was a few years ago. We—I—had to travel abroad. There was a revolution. The populace was unusually restive, with the result that the entire British Consulate had to be evacuated to the embassy of…a certain foreign power that does not use the same alphabet as we do. And the telephone switchboard was of the manual type…"

"Dear me," was Delphick's only observation.

"I suspect even Miss Brownlow might have found herself at a loss," Ambrose said, with a wry smile.

Delphick smiled back, sharing the joke. "And will Miss Brownlow be coming now to work for you, sir?" It was almost an afterthought.

Ambrose Denarcott continued to smile, perhaps a little more broadly. "That remains to be seen, Chief Superintendent."

"Another smooth one," said Bob after he was gone. "I reckon it's him, sir—doesn't look ruthless enough to be a killer, so it's another double bluff."

"Another?" Delphick was amused. "So far, you have given me plausible reasons to suspect Miss Brownlow of removing Gabriel Crassweller from her path for thwarted ambition—Mr. Gilmore, the socialist sympathiser playing a classic bluff—Mr. Marrable, smooth and envious of a man with a superlative secretary—and now Mr. Denarcott, for similar reasons."

Bob grinned. "I didn't like his waistcoat, sir, not so much the colour as the mother-of-pearl buttons. A bit too much of a good thing. And didn't he remind you of a wood pigeon? All that nodding and bobbing." He stretched cramped fingers. "They do a grand pigeon pie at the George and Dragon, did you know? If you're not too worried about lead shot, that is."

"I shudder to think what dread wordplay Charley Mountfitchet might concoct for pigeon pie," said his superior. "Now Nigel Colveden is back in the neighbourhood, I suspect the worst. And, talking of the worst, who shall we see next?"

They saw, they questioned, they noted; they returned to Scotland Yard, and they analysed. It took them two long, hardworking days of concentrated cross-checking.

"And we might just as well not have bothered," concluded Bob at the end of a further unproductive morning. He yawned, pushed aside what he devoutly hoped would be the final heap of paperwork, rocked his feet heel-to-toe under the desk, and shook his head to ease the tension in his shoulders.

"I know you say a negative's as good as a positive, sir, but this is a bit much. Whatever it is, we've missed it."

Delphick was silent. Bob pushed back his chair. "Blood sugar boost, sir?"

Delphick finally focused a blank gaze on his sergeant's face. "By all means walk off some of your fidgets by taking the scenic route to the canteen. I need to think…"

When Bob finally reappeared he found the telephone off its hook, and his superior with Miss Seeton's Devil Henry VIII sketch on the blotter in front of him. Delphick was turning it from one orientation to the other, and back again.

"She must be right," he said, without lifting his head. "Which means we must be wrong. Tea? Thank you. The buns seem somewhat the worse for wear, so do keep them for yourself—after which, please rustle up a car while I phone the George and book a room. I really think it's time for me to pay a proper visit to my prospective godson."

This time they went straight to the nursing home. Mrs. Knight welcomed them in the hall, and smiled reassuringly at her son-in-law. "Both fine. One is fast asleep and the other looking forward to seeing you—both of you." Another smile. "You haven't seen the little monster yet, Mr. Delphick."

"Regrettably, I've missed my previous chances through pressure of work. I won't stay too long now, but I should indeed like a peep at the newcomer. I need something to cheer me up, and I believe he will. Bob hasn't stopped grinning since he arrived."

"Hope he's not neglecting his work," came a cheerful boom as Dr. Knight appeared. "He's paid to be a policeman, not a proud father—even if he has an excellent reason for pride," added the reason's proud grandfather. "A splendid, healthy specimen after the initial worries, but now I'd say he's an example to us all."

"We'll have him playing for the police eleven before he knows it," agreed Delphick.

"Could make him even healthier." The doctor accompanied the visitors into the private part of the house. "Had a chap here the other day, worried he might be crumbling to pieces through lack of this, that and the other his body wasn't absorbing properly, or so he said. Been reading too many articles in the popular press, if you ask me. Diet deficiency's rare in a developed country. Variety, plus a little of what you fancy from time to time, should be good enough for most people."

"As you no doubt told him." Delphick could sense an imminent punch line.

"Not exactly. But I asked what he'd done about it before deciding to consult me, and he began spouting a list of God-knows-what mineral supplements—zinc, iron, magnesium." He snorted. "These health food people must make a fortune out of his sort. I asked if he'd had his blood tested for deficiencies and he hadn't, the idiot, so I said I'd be more than happy to do it for him, and sell him a bag of garden soil at the same time. There's boron in soil, I said, not to mention selenium. More for your money. So, if our young Tarzan spends half his leisure time rolling in the mud the way his father does, he'll get all the minerals he needs without paying a penny."

Anne was by the window, admiring alternately the garden's autumn flowers and the contents of a wicker basket that rested on a coffee table beside her. The basket was lined with blue gingham, and could be heard snuffling rhythmically to itself.

"I do hope he won't grow up to be a pig," said Anne, her proud smile inviting them all to come and join her gloating. "He not only sounds rather porcine at the moment, he looks a bit that way, too. Mr. Delphick, would you be happy god-fathering a pig?"

"Pigs," he reminded her, "are more equal than others—which does suggest a degree of intelligence, this being infinitely preferable to stupidity." He reached into the basket, and gently touched a chubby hand. "Perhaps I will take the risk after all. And thank you for the compliment. A hint of red in his hair, I think. The Tamworth is both a handsome breed of pig, and athletic. This should bode well for any footballing aspirations…"

Dr. Knight returned to his patients, and his wife told Anne to sit where she was and, with Bob, talk to their guest while tea and cake were prepared. "Always assuming Mr. Delphick wants any," she added, vanishing into the kitchen. "I gather Miss Seeton has asked Martha for another fruit cake."

"Ah, Miss Seeton." Delphick winked at Anne. "How is your adopted aunt? No ill effects from our recent flying visit?"

"Not that I've heard," said Anne, "though we've been hearing quite a lot about her. I haven't gone into the village much—Mrs. Venning's Spaniards have had a couple of close shaves and I'd rather not risk it—but the village seems happy enough to come here." Again she looked with pride into the snuffling basket. "Even Miss Nuttel and Mrs. Blaine, which was a surprise."

"Mrs. Blaine gave him an odd sort of fetish thing she'd made," said Bob. "She said it was a toy elephant, but it has the oddest proportions."

"Only since we had to wash it," said Anne, fair-minded. "The wool stretched and the stuffing distorted a little—"

"A lot," Bob corrected her.

"—and, yes, it does rather remind me of something sinister. But I'm sure it was a kind thought, and we won't tell her."

"Does it shriek when you pull its ears?" Delphick enquired. Anne blinked, then giggled. Bob looked puzzled. Delphick smiled.

"The mandrake," he told his subordinate, "is thought to scream when it is uprooted. Your talk of sinister fetishes somehow reminded me. In the good old days a dog would have string tied to its collar to effect the uprooting, because the mandrake's curse on those who dug it up was fatal."

Anne made a face. "Poor dogs. Thank goodness that sort of superstition's dying out—except, of course, that it isn't. You know how they are in Plummergen. They're saying Miss Seeton's been conjuring evil spirits and raising the devil down by the churchyard."

"What rubbish," spluttered Bob. "This is the nineteen-seventies, not the fifteen-seventies."

"One sees the logic," said Delphick. "For the story's genesis, that is. Local imagination will have run wild from the moment the builders told everyone what they saw when that chunk of plaster fell off the wall—and wilder still when Dr. Braxted was so very secretive after being called in to investigate further."

"And then when she asked Miss Seeton inside to sketch it for her," said Bob sourly.

Anne sighed. "They're blaming Dr. Braxted, too, and those nice young things she's got helping her, only they can't decide if they've been starting a coven—remember all that witchcraft nonsense a few years back?—or raising the devil, because of the painting."

Bob grimaced. "We've both seen it, and I can't blame Nigel and Louise for not wanting to keep it there when you know what happens if you look at it upside down."

"Apparently," said Anne, sensing Delphick's unspoken interest, "some of the council house kids dared each other to get into the cottage and lie on the floor and look."

"As children do," said Delphick.

"Same old story," said Bob, still simmering at the insult to Miss Seeton. "One minute it's egging each other on to knock-down-ginger, then they try a spot of shoplifting. Then breaking into houses or bashing old ladies on pension day to fund the drug habit, and they end up peddling drugs themselves if they aren't already in quod…"

Delphick laughed. "Bob's been working very hard, Anne. It's not like him to be so gloomy."

"No, it's not." Anne's eyes twinkled. "But if he's had as little sleep as I sometimes get I can find an excuse for him." She sobered. "They're saying lights have been seen in the general area of the cottage in the middle of the night, and of course they blame poor Aunt Em. Some of them even say it's the ghost of Hitler she's trying to raise—"

"What?" yelped Bob, then clapped a hand over his mouth as the basket gave a violent wriggle. Anne hushed and soothed for a few moments.

"Because of the Saxons, and the Nazi sympathies," she went on quietly. "Some people say she's been looking for the uniforms they think were buried in the Kettle Wedge after D-Day to, well, to reinforce her chances of making the spells work."

Bob rolled his eyes, and was speechless.

Delphick nodded. "To give verisimilitude to an otherwise bald and extremely unconvincing narrative? I can understand that."

Bob muttered something vicious under his breath.

"It could well be true that something was buried there, though not necessarily uniforms," Delphick went on. "Is anyone suggesting it might have been anything else?"

"A chest of Nazi gold," said Anne. "For bribery purposes if the invasion had worked out. But uniforms are much more likely, because how else would you get rid of them?"

"Chuck the metal bits in the canal and burn the rest," said Bob, who still thought his idea had possibilities. Anne shook her head.

"You'd be at the mercy of the Brattles if you tried that. Lady Colveden told me there's an enormous range in the kitchen, which is probably the only place big enough to burn so much fabric without spending ages chopping it into pieces small enough for an open fire. If the servants caught you playing about with dampers, and using the poker, and clearing ashes from the grate when you've never done such a thing before, they'd be even more sure to smell a rat."

"Leaving you open to blackmail." Delphick smiled his most oracular smile. "I believe a similar theory was proposed once before, Bob—but I should say Anne is right. As for you, you'd better learn fast to say that she's right even if in your heart of hearts you don't believe a word of it. Believe me, and take the advice of an older man who's been happily married for years!"

Chapter Fourteen

Delphick drove away from the nursing home by himself, letting the Ranger family have as much time together as possible; they'd really had very little so far. He would telephone from Sweetbriars in good time for them to say their goodbyes before his return with—he hoped—another drawing from Miss Seeton.

She was as ever delighted to see him, and spoke happily of fruit cake and Martha's kindness, and gingerbread in case Bob came along later.

Delphick shook his head. "I've told him to stay with Anne until we leave. You'll have to make do with me."

"Very wise." Miss Seeton was pleased. "Families ought to be together—except during working hours, of course. And very kind, Chief Superintendent."

"Practical, certainly. Bob has been working amazingly hard, day after day—and the days have been long—for very little result. He's nowhere near as cheerful as he might be, and he deserves a spot of relaxation." He smiled. "And, of course, the resulting benefit to me in efficiency terms will be more than adequate a reward."

"Oh, but I thought—oh, dear, was my IdentiKit drawing of no use after all? I'm so very sorry. Of course, it explains why you have had to come back again. And such a waste of time…" She glanced towards the bureau. "Lady Colveden said, you see, that the committee needed my sketches for the quilt, and she will be collecting them later, but I'm sure a day would have made little difference, and had I only known my sketch was wrong—yours, I mean, the one you took away—I would naturally have made a further attempt before you left, or if you had telephoned later to ask, I could have put it in the post to save you the journey, when you are so busy."

"Please don't concern yourself, Miss Seeton. The sketch was a great help, believe me. Between us we managed to eliminate…certain considerations, and were able to start on an entirely new line of enquiry. Which is why I'd like your entirely new opinion of the case, now that you know how helpful you've been." He smiled kindly at her. "As ever."

Her anxious look turned to a blush of pleasure. "I do try my best, Chief Superintendent, and will certainly try again."

"I'd be glad if you would—but there's no desperate hurry to show you these new photographs. Think of Bob and Anne. We have time, surely, for a cup of tea and a slice of cake? Afterwards, I can satisfy my curiosity and see what you've been doing for Lady Colveden. What is it? For the tapestry? Or should I say mural?"

"Or quilt." She managed a smile. "They all seem acceptable, in Plummergen terms. People are using so many different stitches and styles, you see, that it is more for convenience, rather than technical accuracy. Which has upset some of the purists among us, or at least confused them. Mural, for instance, means anything that may cover a wall, which of course it will, and in the case of a painting, one can also say fresco. Rather like the…like that found in Nigel's house—and as, unlike so many others, I am no needlewoman, the correctness of the terminology doesn't bother me as perhaps they would feel it should."

"It certainly doesn't bother me," he assured her.

She was still thinking. "*Embroidery* would cover most aspects. The Overlord Embroidery uses appliqué, as I myself am trying to do. But I beg your pardon, Mr. Delphick. Lady Colveden gave me the list of everyone's ideas for the quilt—the History and Legends wall-hanging, not the map, which is of course straightforward in design—and asked me to sketch them to help in the design and final layout, and where necessary to plan the size of the sashing, and the correct number of cornerstones."

Looking as baffled as she herself had felt on first hearing these words, he laughed. "I won't ask for a translation, Miss Seeton, but it seems you're all making good progress."

"Let me assure you, Mr. Delphick, that it is no use trying to pump me for information. I am sworn to the utmost secrecy." Her eyes danced. "As, indeed, is everyone, apart from dear Miss Wicks, who is more than happy to say she is one of those showing Queen Anne arriving in her royal barge to take a glass of water—such beautiful fabric, and such delicate stitches—but everyone was asked at the very start what she—or, indeed, he—might wish to submit, and although, I gather, they all seemed happy enough then, especially the children, to discuss in general terms the finished article there is now a—a decided spirit of competition in the air, especially with the deadline of the Henty anniversary so close."

"I must admit I've never heard of the chap." The Oracle helped himself to a sandwich. "G. A. Henty, yes. Sir George and the Admiral share a collection of his books, I believe."

They chatted for a while about the Colvedens and other friends; about the wedding; how the display of photographs and presents had led to the current enthusiasm for needlework; how Miss Seeton was grateful to dear Louise for showing her how to appliqué, and to Miss Armitage for explaining the mysteries of the sewing machine. Delphick noticed that, even when she was relaxed and laughing gently at herself for her lack of stitch-craft, Miss Seeton seemed uneasy if Summerset Cottage drifted into the conversation. It was understandable; that Devil Henry fresco wasn't pleasant when you knew it for what it really was, clever thought the artist had been—but it wasn't like her to be so squeamish. Superstitious. If that's what she was being.

Or did it mean she knew there was more to be discovered? And was worried about what that discovery might be?

The tea things cleared away, Miss Seeton took her sketchpad and pencils from the bureau, then stood irresolute. "Lady Colveden has asked me to keep my sketches for the quilt secret from everyone but the committee. Policemen, naturally, can be trusted more than most—but I did give my word."

"Then I'll look at some of your books, if I may." His eye was caught by half a rainbow arching across the worn black cover of a book near the bureau. "*Cole's Funny Picture-Book*? I've never heard of that, either."

"It belonged to my Cousin Flora. I recall looking through its pages when I was young, and not caring much for the pictures. Clever, but somewhat bizarre for a child. I had meant to show it to Dr. Braxted—you see, upside-down drawings are less unusual than she thought—and yet somehow I haven't managed to find the time."

Or haven't wanted to, thought Delphick. "You've been too busy with the quilt sketches, of course. But might I give you this new set of photos and ask for your latest impression, while I study the bizarre and clever work of Mr. Cole?"

From the corner of his eye he watched her take the photographs from their envelope and set them on the table in front of her. She moved those she had seen before to one side, the new ones closer. She might have been shuffling a pack of cards as she arranged and rearranged them. She stared; she concentrated. He began an ostentatious flipping through the picture book so that she wouldn't be distracted by his interest. Then, to his surprise, he became intrigued by Mr. Cole's—yes, bizarre—view of life, and as he read on, and contemplated the pictures, he became absorbed.

He spluttered. Miss Seeton, flushed, looked across at him.

He was contrite. "I'm sorry to have broken your train of thought, Miss Seeton, but it was the whipping machine for naughty boys. It made me think of carpet-beaters. Efficient, to say the least, but I do see what you mean about bizarre."

She nodded. "Children, of course, have a decided taste for the macabre, which is why they enjoy ghost stories so much, and scaring each other with turnip lanterns in the dark at Halloween, and pretending that peeled tomatoes might be dead men's eyeballs, or that twigs are their finger-bones and toes. But they always know it isn't *real*, and I always felt the whipping machine was one step *beyond* what one might call normally frightening, because of factories—production lines, you see—it might just have worked."

"This style of drawing was popular at the time, I imagine." Delphick studied the pictures. "Think of Edward Lear—odd proportions, huge heads, and spidery writing for the speech bubbles. I've never greatly cared for it either."

He saw that he had not, in fact, interrupted her; she had already set down her pencil and had been watching him as closely as he at the start had watched her. "As you say, Miss Seeton, not real. Distorted. Perhaps the artist needed glasses, and the lenses of the time weren't sufficiently precise. Astigmatism, perhaps, or anisometropia." He closed the book. "As for artists, what have you to show me now?"

She moved instinctively to cover what she had drawn, He recognised the signs. She was unhappy with her sketch and felt guilty about letting him down. He held out a hand.

"I should like to see it, please."

"I think I must be a little tired," she said. "With so many quilt sketches, I suppose. Otherwise I'm sure I would have... that is, I'm sorry, but I looked and looked and simply couldn't think of anything else..."

Delphick looked at the drawing. It was still recognisably Gabriel Crassweller, and yet it was at the same time another drawing of Henry VIII as the Devil.

Delphick frowned. Miss Seeton went on apologising. He ignored her.

The doorbell rang. "Lady Colveden," gasped Miss Seeton. "I didn't realise the time. Please excuse me..."

Delphick went on staring at the sketch. It was swift, and—for all Miss Seeton's evident doubts—sure. This was what he wanted: one of her instinctive, inspired drawings that went right to the heart of the matter. Most of her work was painstaking, accurate—as a photograph is accurate. She might draw something from real life, but there was no true sense of life, no animation, in too many of her pictures. Anyone with even a modest talent could produce them. But this...

She was telling him the case was still upside down. That he was still missing some vital point. That he still saw Gabriel Crassweller in completely the wrong way.

He needed to think. He heard voices approach the sitting room. He folded the drawing, swept up the photos, and bundled everything inside the envelope.

He rose to his feet as Lady Colveden came in. There followed greetings, and pleasantries, and Miss Seeton, relieved to see that he hadn't minded too much about the sketch or he wouldn't have taken it, ventured to tease him about his interest in the quilt, and told Lady Colveden that their secrets had been protected by herself at great personal risk.

"From the little I've heard it sounds fascinating," he said. "I'll be sure to come and see it when it's on display. I had no idea so small a village had so much of interest to show. Bob and Anne tell me there has been an almost unprecedented degree of enthusiasm, and the church roof is guaranteed to benefit from everyone's efforts."

"Even mine," said Miss Seeton, "though it is not finished yet, I fear."

"Don't leave it too late," warned Lady Colveden, "the way a few people seem to be trying to do—though they'd better not for the quilt, which of course is why we needed your sketches. For the overall layout," she explained to Delphick, who tried to appear politely interested when all he wanted was solitude, and time for thought.

Lady Colveden sensed his preoccupation. Miss Seeton, responding to the gentle hint as to the purpose of her ladyship's visit, hurried to the bureau and withdrew a stout cardboard folder.

"And of course," she said, handing it over, "as well as my sketches, I must give you back the list."

"The most secret of secrets." Lady Colveden smiled. "The master plan," she couldn't help telling Delphick, "as to who intends to sew what, and how many of each topic. Miss Seeton's sketches will be invaluable in the final planning."

"Unless anybody changes her mind," he suggested absently. He knew the value of Miss Seeton's sketches, and he wanted to consider this latest one in private—and as yet he couldn't…

"They'd better not," said her ladyship. "Now we have the sketches we're about to start work." She patted the pocket of her jacket. It jingled. "I'm meeting the rest of the committee at the village hall shortly, and we're going to lock ourselves in. If anyone tries to talk to us, well, they can't."

He saw his chance. "Did you walk here, Lady Colveden? Yes, I thought you wouldn't want to waste such a lovely afternoon. Allow me to offer you a lift. I have the car nearby and I'm collecting Bob from the Knights', so we'll be going right past the door. Miss Seeton, I must thank you for the tea, and for your help—" he waved the envelope "—and wonder if I might trespass on your kindness and ask you to telephone Bob while I escort Lady Colveden to the village hall…"

The car turned into the nursing home and Delphick saw Bob, bright-eyed and with an evident case of the fidgets, waiting by the most convenient flowerbed.

"Miss Seeton telephoned," his sergeant greeted him, snatching open the passenger door and cramming his bulk inside.

"As I asked her to," said Delphick. Saying goodbye to his family must have disturbed his young sidekick more than expected.

"No, sir—I mean, yes, you did, and she did—but just as I was leaving she telephoned again."

Delphick put the car in neutral, and waited.

"She said she'd had another try at what you wanted," said Bob. "She said it hadn't worked out the first time—"

"But it did."

"—because she must have been distracted by thinking of the quilt sketches, only once she'd handed them over to Lady Colveden she thought she'd try again. So she did, sir."

"And she thinks we would be interested in the result." It was not a question.

"That's how it sounded to me. She was a bit muddled about it—wavering a bit, the way she sometimes does—but she said it just sort of happened, sir, and she thought she'd better let us know because those are the kind of sketches we pay her for, and she knew we were going back to town and she was worried about wasting time if she put it in the post."

"She could be right." Delphick put the car in gear, swung round and out of the drive, keeping an eye open for vehicles on the wrong side of the road, and once more headed in a southerly direction.

Miss Seeton wondered about offering tea and gingerbread, but hesitated.

"Anne's been stuffing me with biscuits and cake, thanks," said Bob, as Delphick looked at the sketch she had completed just a few minutes previously. "May I see, sir?"

Under a dark and stormy sky two complete strangers, one male, one female, carried between them a chest, or a very large strong-box, decorated with flowers as they emerged from a building that seemed to have strayed from Threadneedle Street.

"The Bank of England." Bob recognised it at once.

Delphick caught Miss Seeton's quick intake of breath, and saw her shake her head. "A local bank, Miss Seeton?" He saw her nod. "Who are these people?"

"I'm not sure, though I may have seen them occasionally on the bus, but I met them the other day in Brettenden, when I dropped my umbrella. We exchanged a few words, as one does, because it was my fault for not paying proper attention, and they very kindly picked up my things for me. So careless. Mr. Brinton gave it to me—the umbrella, that is—and the man I'd bumped into teased me a little about having friends in high places when I explained why I was so thankful it had not been damaged through allowing my thoughts to wander."

Delphick considered the faces of the two strangers. Recognisable, should he meet them, but unlikely to stand out in a crowd. What had Miss Seeton noticed about them that was so remarkable she had felt the urge to draw them? "What did you talk about? While they were collecting up your bits and pieces."

"I'm not sure there was any conversation, as such. It was, as I explained, merely an exchange of pleasantries." Delphick said nothing.

She made an effort to remember. "I know they admired my umbrella, with its leather handle and gold initials, and we talked about the Roman treasure—the silver—and the mosaic found at Rytham Hall, yes, and I told them it was all in the museum…"

Delphick pointed at the chest the two carried. "Why the flowers? Brettenden, like Plummergen, is in Kent. Are they perhaps Canterbury bells?"

She brightened. "Oh, yes, of course—or rather, no, but it was the mention of silver, you see. A little anecdote about a child who drank half a tin of Bluebell polish and, thank goodness, survived. I remember that he, or possibly his wife, said they were glad not to have to do such work any longer."

Delphick and Bob studied the faces again. "A retired butler, perhaps. Servants of a sort, anyhow."

"Ye-es, that does seem a possibility…but it is only a vague impression of a chance encounter some days ago, and I haven't really given it any further thought…"

Try as she might, she could recall nothing more, and began to look a little anxious. He had no wish to put pressure on her, and was busily thinking.

He was still thoughtful as once more he took leave of his hostess, promising that he would be talking to Accounts and she could expect the usual cheque in due course.

"But for what," he said to Bob as they drove up The Street, "I'm not entirely sure. First, she looked at the new photos of Crassweller and produced a near duplicate of Henry-as-the-Devil—strongly suggesting that we are still looking at it all the wrong way round."

"Double indemnity, sir?" suggested Bob.

"I think so, yes." Delphick shook his head. "As for the bluebells of Brettenden and the silver treasure and the museum…"

He turned to Bob. "Ashford," he said. "The police station. I think we need to show that sketch to Superintendent Brinton."

Chapter Fifteen

Brinton regarded the entrance of the Oracle and his sidekick with misgiving. "What's she done now?" he demanded. "And don't tell me she hasn't. I won't believe you."

"Good afternoon, Superintendent Brinton." Delphick politely ignored Foxon, struggling to suppress a splutter at his corner desk, and motioned Bob to take a visitor's chair while he himself dragged the other from under a teetering pile of files and folders he then crammed on top of a cupboard already full to capacity. "How reassuring that your paperwork is in a similar state to ours." Foxon began to go slowly red in the face. "We do not suffer alone, Sergeant. Charming weather for the time of year, don't you think?"

Brinton closed his eyes. "The minute the front desk phoned through, my heart sank. The only reason you ever come into these parts is Miss Seeton." He opened his eyes in a flash of irritation as the younger members of the party shifted indignantly on their chairs. "And not a word from either of you two champions. Tell me the worst and get it over, blast you, Oracle."

The two elder men were old friends, and all four were colleagues of long standing. "She's drawn a sketch on which I'd value your opinion—opinions," the chief superintendent corrected himself, inviting Foxon to join the party. "May I show you?"

Brinton grunted permission, and Delphick made his selection from the contents of the brown envelope. "Observe the stormy sky," he said of the treasure-chest drawing. "She has already produced one sketch with a similarly inclement feel to it—that of the Plummergen house with Nazi connections. I can't help but wonder why this later picture—of a possibly retired possible pair of servants—makes me think of the other drawing, unfortunately, left behind in London. But can you see the similarities, Sergeant Ranger?"

Bob warily agreed that he could, insofar as one stormy sky could be said either to resemble or to differ from another when the same pencil was used to depict them both.

"Miss Seeton told me this particular sketch was inspired by a brief encounter she had with a couple of strangers in Brettenden, except that she seemed to feel some doubt that they were indeed strangers. Have you any idea what the servants who ministered to the late Miss Griselda Saxon looked like?"

"Name of Brattle," said Brinton. "Nothing officially known. Sorry."

Foxon likewise expressed ignorance of anything beyond the name.

Brinton pondered. "Potter said as soon as their late employer was decently under ground they pushed off, as far as anyone in Plummergen knows. They never made much of an impression about the place, he says. They mostly shopped once a week in Brettenden. Never spoke to anyone on the bus. Didn't mix with the village crowd any more than she did. Came from London originally. Agnes and Sam, I think."

"But no criminal record," said Delphick. "At least, under that name."

"No."

Delphick was puzzled. "As soon as she was buried. Didn't they even stay around to see if they would benefit from her will? It's usual to leave a small bequest to any servant not under notice at the time of the employer's decease."

"Far as I know she didn't leave a bean to anyone," said Brinton. "She didn't have even one small tin of beans to bequeath. According to Potter, everyone who thought about the woman at all, which most of the time nobody did, knew that she lived there more or less at Sir George Colveden's discretion—peppercorn rent and so on. He'd promised the father, as I recall the story. Just after the war."

He tapped the sketch with the blunt end of a pencil. He wasn't as clever at decoding Miss Seeton's efforts as Delphick, but here he had local knowledge to assist him. "If that's supposed to be the Brattles, could that mean they were feathering their nest at her expense? And didn't want to hang around to answer awkward questions?"

"Possibly. They're carrying the box out of, rather than into, the bank. That could hint at some form of appropriation—removal—of funds formerly thought secure."

"I'd have thought a bank was pretty secure," said Brinton.

"And honest," said Delphick. "The tax people will want to know, and the bank will be legally bound to tell them—the basics, anyway."

"Keep it under the mattress or up the chimney and nobody need ever know a thing." Brinton grinned. "Especially if you disappear before they pounce on you."

"Bury it in the garden, sir," said Foxon. "Buried treasure."

The other three looked at him. "Well," he protested, "that's what I'd do, and I bet that's why so many rumours about metal detectors have been bubbling up recently. Someone's looking for it."

"Metal detectors?" Delphick regarded the young man with interest. "In Plummergen?"

Foxon and Brinton exchanged glances. It was the superintendent who finally spoke.

"Potter says people have been seeing lights moving around in the middle of the night, down by the churchyard near some bit of land that used to belong to this blasted cottage there's been so much fuss about."

Delphick nodded. "We've heard something of that, thanks to Mrs. Ranger's numerous visitors, or rather, her son's admirers." Bob looked startled, then smug. "There has been talk of ghosts, among other phenomena."

Brinton snorted. "Ghosts! Poachers, more likely, or courting couples—the nights aren't cold yet, though a churchyard's not a place I'd choose myself."

"But, sir," said Bob, "if the Brattles have got this money in Brettenden—and we don't even know that it exists, or if it does, whether it's missing—but if they have, why should anyone be looking for it in Plummergen?"

"Last known address," said Brinton.

"If they aren't local, that's where they'd have to start looking," Delphick agreed. "Yes. I wonder if we should think about looking there ourselves?"

This surprised everyone. He hesitated before enlarging on his theory.

"It's not the idea of buried treasure," he said slowly. "I would imagine that any money hidden in those parts has long since been moved elsewhere, by the Brattles—or by someone else. And it's that someone—or a plurality of same—in whom I am interested. There could be other metal items there." He glanced at Bob. "Buttons, or shoulder-flashes, or belt buckles there wasn't time to cut off and chuck in the canal."

Bob acknowledge this with a faint grin, but Brinton was quick to protest.

"Isn't that perishing wireless proof enough of treachery?" he demanded.

"It is indeed, but the war isn't so very long ago, remember. If we knew how many—if any—uniforms were buried there in the middle of the night of D-Day, we might also know how many traitors there were then—and still could be. With Germany divided as it now is, there may well be some whose sympathies have moved to the, ah, still-defiant East rather than staying with the thoroughly conquered, and now accommodating, West."

Brinton raised the same objection the Oracle himself had raised in London. "Hitler was right-wing, the Reds are left—nobody's going to switch sides like that, are they?"

"Nobody who's not a fanatic, and thus already halfway round the political bend. I'd say it's unlikely, but not impossible." And something else to consider during the drive back to London, enough having now been said to explain his interest without going into details. "As for these metal-detector rumours…"

Brinton looked at Foxon. "You heard 'em first, laddie. Let's all hear 'em now."

"It was nothing definite, to start with," said Foxon. "Mr. Brinton will remember how there was some trouble with our Choppers a while back, and Hastings had trouble with a motorbike gang too, so I swapped duties with a lad from Hastings for a spot of—of undercover infiltration, sir."

"Arbuthnott," supplied Brinton at once. "Nicknamed Sleaze—with good reason. Foxon here deludes himself into thinking he's a snappy dresser, but this Hastings bod's as scruffy as they come. Fitted into the Chopper crowd of leather-jacketed thugs and tearaways as to the manner born."

Even now Foxon found the time to look pained. "I really can't imagine why Mr. Brinton doesn't care for my taste in clothes, Mr. Delphick. The Hastings lot, Hastings being generally classier than Ashford, are more sympathetic. DC Arbuthnott and I adapted pretty well to our respective gangs, and after it was over we sort of kept in touch in case a repeat performance was ever wanted."

"And was it?" Delphick was waiting for the metal-detector connection. "Is it?"

"Just rumours, sir. Sleaze comes over to Ashford from time to time, partly to keep his hand in but mostly because Hastings've been having drug trouble and they're trying to find the distribution route after it's left the coast—" Brinton grunted confirmation "—and the word is that someone from Plummergen went to buy a metal detector in Brettenden and couldn't find one there and was sent to Ashford instead."

"Which is how the Choppers heard about it." Brinton rolled his eyes. "Lazy baskets, our local yobs. Someone else spends the money buying the gadget and doing all the hard work trudging up and down muddy fields and digging holes, then in they waltz with bicycle chains and coshes, and scoop the lot for themselves."

"Hence your remark about buried treasure." Delphick nodded to Foxon. "The connection with Plummergen and the Brattles may be tenuous, yet it's surely no less a possibility than the little conundrum posed by Miss Seeton's earlier hints regarding long-lost Nazi sympathisers—whether there are any present-day survivors of the group that seems to have included the family for whom the Brattles worked."

He saw Brinton's expression as he picked up the sketch. "She's been right before," he reminded everyone. "The sketch suggests there's money involved. And if she says there's money involved, even if she doesn't exactly tell us how, then in some way money is likely to be involved. These Brattles, if that indeed is who they are, know something. How long ago did their employer die?"

"Not long enough for them to be in the telephone directory or the electoral roll," Brinton said, anticipating the next question. "If they keep to themselves the way they've apparently always done, it could be months before anyone officially takes notice of them."

"And we still can't be sure they are in fact worthy of official notice. Miss Seeton hints that they are, or I think she does, but it's all a matter of interpretation, which, gentlemen, is purely subjective."

"You could try asking her," said Brinton glumly. Delphick, about to return to London, might just delegate the asking to him. In which case he'd get Foxon to do it. The lad liked the old girl, and she liked him, and they didn't make each other feel uncomfortable the way he tended to feel with MissEss, like her or not. Oh, he liked her. Didn't understand her, that was the trouble. He preferred his life, and his cases, to be straightforward. A whisper, a hint from a snout that a job was planned—you laid an ambush, you grabbed the chummies, you produced the evidence, you saw them jugged. The logical progression. A hint, but with facts to back it up. Not purely subjective interpretations of artistic guesswork produced in a village miles from the action by a respectable spinster who seldom left the place...

After a lengthy pause as Brinton gloomed, and the two younger men didn't know what to say, Delphick suddenly sat up. "We could try our own spot of metal detecting," he suggested. His own purely subjective speculation had given a sudden, illuminating lurch. "Or, while we're in London, you could. Do let us know what you find. If a shop here in Ashford sells metal detectors, no doubt you could borrow or hire one. As the area of particular interest is close to the churchyard you might care to let the vicar know, but if you promise not to dig up any bodies I don't see that he can object. Sergeant Ranger, we must be off."

He pushed back his chair, replaced the sketch in its envelope, checked his watch, and looked pleased. "Goodbye, gentlemen—for the present," he added, and hurried his sergeant through the door before Bob could do more than utter a quick farewell.

He was still catching his breath as Delphick unlocked the car and buckled himself into the driver's seat. "Hurry up. We've no time to waste."

"I gathered that, sir." Bob was still breathless, but this did not stop his brain working. "You've had an idea," he said. "About Miss Seeton's sketch?"

"Sketches, plural," the Oracle corrected him cheerfully. "Those two she's drawn that are upside-down in spirit, and more or less identical. She apologised because she thought her imagination had let her down when she was tired. It hadn't. She drew the first to tell us we were looking at the case the wrong way round—Crassweller didn't commit suicide as we'd been led to believe, he was murdered. She's now drawn the second to tell us that we are still looking the wrong way round—that, just as we've begun to think, he was indeed no traitor but instead a loyal and honourable servant of Her Majesty."

"Yes, sir," said Bob warily.

"A patriot, then—and yet the man was murdered. We thought the motive could have been professional jealousy, one way or another; thwarted ambition, class envy, even coveting the man's secretary—"

"We were only theorising, sir."

Delphick ignored him. "At one time we even thought the murderer might be a patriot who disapproved of the risky game being played by the authorities. Taking the law into his own hands when Crassweller remained alive to be turned, or used as some sort of double-bluff conduit feeding false information to the other side..."

"We changed our minds, sir," said Bob as Delphick paused.

"Gabriel Crassweller was murdered," announced the chief superintendent, "by someone in a good position to know the man was no traitor, because it was the traitor who murdered him—before Crassweller could reveal his activities and identity to the authorities. And *that* is what Miss Seeton's drawings are trying to tell us, Sergeant Ranger."

Clarissa Putts, widowed mother of the post office's Emmy, worked three days a week in Brettenden's biscuit factory rather than on the land, in a shop, or as a domestic in Plummergen, even on the two days when the bus didn't run and Clarrie had to survive without all the gossip and giggles among her workmates and (in summer) the air conditioning.

Like everyone else involved in the mural and quilt projects she seized every moment for stitchery, and had forged ahead with her portrayal of her dark-haired daughter's coronation as a blonde-wigged Miss Plummergen at the summer fete. The wig had been Clarrie's idea, and she was proud of it. Emmy didn't have much gumption. She wasn't as dozy as her friend Maureen—who could be?—but she often needed a prod. Clarrie had more than once tried to persuade her to get a job at the factory, wearing a crisp blue overall and a neat muslin cap, but Emmy preferred the extra half-hour in bed and the short walk to work, as well as the money for five days' employment rather than three.

Clarrie had plied her needle late into the previous night, and needed more wool for her cross-stitch. She was waiting outside Welsted's on the dot of nine.

"Morning, Mrs. Welsted." The draper's wife unlocked the door to the ping of an overhead bell. "I'd like another hank of this shade, if you haven't sold out."

Mrs. Welsted checked the serial number on the wrapper, hurried to the drawer and hunted through its contents. "You're in luck, Mrs. Putts, the very last one. We've more on order, though. It'll be here next week, if you need it."

"Don't think so, ta," said Mrs. Putts, opening her purse. "Though you might keep one back for me, just in case. But today with luck did ought to see the finish of it."

Her luck was out. As she handed over the money a second, more energetic ping had announced the arrival of Mrs. Blaine, with Miss Nuttel in tow. It was obvious that Mrs. Blaine was there on a similar errand to Mrs. Putts. It was likewise obvious, from the darting look in the Hot Cross Bun's black eyes, that the tail end of Clarrie's remark had been overheard, and correctly interpreted.

"So you've almost finished your panel, Mrs. Putts?" said Mrs. Blaine. "Of course, it takes time to produce really *careful* work, don't you think? Good morning, Margery," she said, as the daughter of the house bustled in from the back room. "I need something a little darker than this, please, and another hank of this green."

It amused the Welsted ladies that, after an initial burst of enthusiasm for the tapestry project, when people were happy to discuss their plans and ask for advice, secrecy was now paramount. Nobody would tell anyone else what they were doing, or how far along they'd got. The vicar had hoped for a spirit of co-operation, but it seemed to Margery and Mrs. Welsted that it was more a competition than anything else.

Clarrie Putts changed the subject. "Anything more about them lights in the middle of the night?" she enquired. Mrs. Blaine bridled at the snub; Miss Nuttel frowned.

"Nothing's been said," said Mrs. Welsted, "and anyway I'm sure it wasn't ghosts or devil-worshippers, whoever it was." Mrs. Welsted played the organ in church, and knew the vicar wouldn't like to think of any of his flock listening to such nonsense, whether or not there was anything in it. Mrs. Welsted always tried to keep an open mind. "Poachers, most likely, or kiddies larking about when they should by rights have been in bed. But of course ever since that picture turned up in Summerset Cottage, there's been talk."

Mrs. Putts was pleased with the success of her diversion. Whatever her daughter might lack, Clarrie Putts had plenty of gumption. "Grave robbers, more like," she said, with a mischievous eye on the Nuts. She nodded as their eager curiosity turned to shock. "Oh, yes. The word's been going round Brettenden that someone from here went there trying to buy a metal detector…"

The sensation was all she could have wished. "A metal detector?" Mrs Blaine cried. "But—who? And why?"

"Tombstones," said Miss Nuttel, when Mrs. Putts could think of no plausible answer. "Not always there to mark the spot. Hinges and handles, Bunny."

"Six feet under?" scoffed Margery Welsted. "Need to be an expensive machine, surely. How many people could afford one?"

"And what could they be looking for?" Mrs. Blaine wanted to know.

"Just saying what I heard at work," said Mrs. Putts.

"Smugglers," suggested Miss Nuttel. "That Henty chap. You told me, Bunny, about a book where they buried kegs of brandy—" She broke off as Margery stifled a giggle. Miss Nuttel flushed. "Of course. Wooden barrels in those days, not metal."

Mrs. Putts, intrigued by the hare she had started, felt she must add a little support to the chase before going home to finish the sewing project only begun because of the wedding of…Nigel Colveden.

"The Colvedens," she offered, "being the richest folk in these parts could afford one all right. Maybe they were practising in the churchyard before…before they went looking for another Roman treasure along at the Hall."

Mrs. Blaine's eyes gleamed. "Perhaps they've already found it. That would explain why they wouldn't put the presents on display there, wouldn't it? They probably have a whole row of silver cups and plates and jugs they didn't want anyone to see."

"Gold, even," said Miss Nuttel.

"That'll be why nobody's seen the lights again," said Mrs. Putts, and vanished before the flaw in their collective logic should be spotted. She hadn't the time to argue days of the week and phases of the moon: she wanted her sewing finished.

Plummergen has never allowed a flaw in its logic to spoil a good story. Mrs. Blaine's wool having been paid for, the Nuts hurried up The Street to the post office. Within minutes everyone knew that the Colvedens—the Colvedens!—had been breaking England's strict laws on Treasure Trove and, rather than reporting a hoard of gold on their land, had kept it all for themselves.

"Melt it down, probably," said someone with visions of ingots before her envious eyes. "Then they can sell it and no questions asked because of having no hallmark to say where it came from."

"Pawn it," said someone else, more realistic. "You wouldn't get as much, but anything'd be better than nothing."

"A crucible in the kitchen range…"

"Dan Eggleden's forge, only they'd have to go fifty-fifty…"

"With Sir George a magistrate, you'd expect him to know better."

"It'll be all her ladyship's doing, mark my words, with him too busy on the farm to know what she's up to."

"That man from Scotland Yard took her away in his car the other day, didn't he?"

This was too much for Mrs. Stillman. "All he did was give her a lift to the village hall to meet Miss Treeves and Miss Armitage."

"And they locked themselves away smartish," someone pointed out in triumph.

"Because of the Tapestry Project," retorted Mrs. Stillman. "Keeping it all secret as they were asked to do by—Now, Emmeline Putts, just you stop your goggling! Your mother's as close as anyone else about what she's sewing, isn't she? Are you going to stand there and try to tell me Clarissa Putts is in league with the vicar's sister and Miss Armitage?"

Emmy blinked, and said she supposed she wasn't, only it did all seem a bit queer.

Nobody disagreed, but nobody could say they knew why it was queer, it just was. And it showed that you couldn't trust anyone, could you? The Colvedens, for all they'd lived years in the village, were incomers. Thick as thieves with Miss Seeton, what was more, that other incomer whose presence had never been properly explained, cousin or no cousin, and the police always dragging her off here, there and everywhere, which never happened before she turned up, did it?

And the Scotland Yard man, they could be sure, wouldn't have missed the chance to interrogate Lady Colveden when he gave her that lift in his car...

Speculation ran merrily riot. A protesting Mrs. Stillman could only roll her eyes, and sigh for the folly of her customers, and glare at Emmy Putts whenever she appeared on the verge of offering an opinion.

But it was not until the next morning that, having seethed and speculated to its heart's content and happy exhaustion, Plummergen was given the ultimate proof that it required.

Chapter Sixteen

Delphick was unusually silent during the journey back to London. Bob had seldom known him in such a mood. They hardly spoke at all until they were back at Scotland Yard. Bob began making for the lift.

"I'm tired of paperwork," said the chief superintendent. "I prefer face-to-face."

"Yes, sir." As did any honest detective—able to watch a suspect's expression, hearing the voice, reading the body language…Files were for filing clerks, not coppers.

"Come on." Delphick turned and led the way out again. They strode in silence, until he hailed a taxi. "The Foreign and Commonwealth Office, please."

Hmm. He could tell from the Oracle's voice, it was no good asking questions. But Bob wondered…

"We wish to speak with Mr. Oblon," Delphick told the clerk at the FCO's front desk. "Tell him Chief Superintendent Delphick and Detective Sergeant Ranger are waiting in the hall—and will wait until they see him," he added as the clerk, checking down a list he tried to keep discreet, seemed about to deny the very name of Duncan Oblon.

He caught the Oracle's wintry eye. "If you'd like to take a seat over there, sir."

"A seat where we will wait," Delphick reminded him.

Bob sat beside him and watched the desk clerk busy at the telephone. "Pity neither of us can lip-read, sir."

To his relief, Delphick smiled. "The ability to read upside down would be another useful skill. Quite as useful as your shorthand. You can practise during the long, sleepless nights of teething. And learn sign language, too," he added as the clerk replaced the handset on its cradle and gesticulated to a burly man hovering in the near distance. Some quick muttering at the desk, then the burly man straightened and came over to them.

"I'll take you up in half an hour," he said. "Mr. Oblon is in a meeting just now."

"We'll wait," Delphick said for the third time.

Bob chuckled. "Like *The Hunting of the Snark*, sir."

"What I tell you three times is true? Quite so. You have hidden depths, Sergeant. I had no idea you knew Lewis Carroll beyond Alice and her friends."

"Had to read it to my sister's kids one Christmas—anything to keep them from under her feet, she said, and out of the kitchen. Before I met Anne, of course. But that bit sort of stuck. You could just as easily argue the Bellman," a reference to the poem's protagonist, "was dreaming up any old excuse to make the whole thing plausible to his shipmates, couldn't you?"

"In the manner of the lady protesting too much," said the Oracle. He'd become almost cheerful during these last few minutes, after staying quiet for so long. He'd obviously finished his brooding and was set for action now he'd made up his mind about…whatever he'd finally decided. He hadn't brought a warrant, so it was most likely they were here for more interviews, or to gather additional facts or figures or—heaven help him—files from Oblon before doing them.

When they were at last ushered into the small office inhabited by Duncan Oblon the man seemed puzzled, and slightly irritated.

"I am a busy man, Chief Superintendent." He indicated a crowded turret of paperwork in-trays on his desk. "And I have cut short my meeting on the assumption that you have—or believe you have—good and sufficient reason to arrive unannounced in this way. I would be grateful if you could tell me, and quickly, what that reason might be."

"It would be worth asking Mr. Fenn to join us," said Delphick. "Also your colleague, Mr. Greene. From...the ministry."

"Greene? Ah—yes."

Delphick's smile was thin. "Welles, or even Lime, if you prefer. The third man at our first meeting, however he wishes to be known."

Oblon shot him a look. "You have news?"

"I have a theory, and I have a question, but I would prefer to discuss both of them with all of you, if possible."

"I'm afraid it isn't. Fenn, as far as I know, is out of the country."

"Somewhere in the neighbourhood of Stentoria?" Oblon said nothing. "And Greene?" Oblon shook his head. "Then it seems I must put my theory to, and ask my question of, you alone."

"Please do." Oblon looked pointedly at his watch.

"Sergeant Ranger will take notes. Mr. Oblon, I will ask my question, wait for your answer, and give you my thought-processes, should you require them, afterwards."

"You've had every possible co-operation so far," bristled the Foreign Office representative. "Great heavens, half our filing cabinets must be empty! You can have no reason to suppose our co-operation is likely to be refused now, when it would appear that you may at last have a lead. What is it? Why did Gabriel Crassweller kill himself?"

"He didn't," said Delphick. "He was murdered." Oblon blinked, then grew very still. "And the question I would have liked to put to you and your colleagues together is—which of you decided he could die?"

Bob Ranger's jaw, like his pencil, dropped. Oblon stared. Delphick waited.

Delphick sighed. "My theory seems to have been proved."

"Nonsense," brought out Oblon at last. "Utter…nonsense! I've never heard such…such a scandalous—slanderous…"

Delphick shook his head. The silence was broken only by the scratch of Bob's pencil, and the sound of a turning page. "You protest too much," said the Oracle at last. "Too much for an innocent man. I don't suggest for one moment that you were directly involved in drugging Crassweller and arranging for the car crash, but either you or Fenn or Mr. Greene must have been instrumental in setting the crime in motion."

Oblon winced. "Crime? You can't call me a criminal."

"The man who orders the trigger pulled, or who by conscious omission allows that trigger to be pulled, is as guilty of the crime as the man who pulls it."

Bob was now note-taking on automatic pilot. He knew he'd wonder later if he'd heard correctly, and pinch himself to make sure. Better make sure now. He moved one large foot to press heavily on the toes of the other. Ugh. He wasn't dreaming. The Oracle really had waltzed into the Foreign Office and accused a high-up of colluding in murder with the Special Branch Ass. Comm. and a ministry—which ministry?—bloke, and the man wasn't denying it. Talk about seeing the case upside down and the wrong way round, it was back to front and bees-over-titifolah into the bargain.

Oblon resumed his staring. Delphick stared back. Bob held his breath.

Oblon's gaze shifted. There was a pregnant pause. "We had our suspicions," he said at last, "but we had nothing to do with the murder—yes, he was murdered, I believe we have to grant you that, but I'd like to know how you reasoned it all out. And what you intend to do about it."

He looked at Bob, with his notebook. "Might I request that the good sergeant abandon his squiggles for the moment? All along I was in two minds about the wisdom of his initial involvement in this case—he's a young man at the start of his career—but you would insist, Chief Superintendent."

"Young—and trustworthy." Delphick nodded to Bob to carry on. "And no more susceptible to threats, veiled or blatant, than I am."

Oblon was horrified. "Threats? I didn't mean us, man, I meant *them*!"

"Ah, then it was—excuse me—a friendly warning. Against whom?"

Oblon looked puzzled. "I thought you said you knew. That you'd worked it out."

"I worked out at long last that I was deliberately chosen for this job because it required someone of or above a certain rank, able to bring sufficient clout to the investigation to worry a few suspects into possibly unwise moves. Moves on which you or your colleagues will, no doubt, have been keeping the very closest watch."

Those who work for the Foreign Office do not blush, but Oblon wriggled on his chair and chose not to meet the chief superintendent's eye.

Delphick bowed. "I thought so." He glanced at Bob. "At first, when we so clearly were getting nowhere, I wondered if I'd been handed what seemed an impossible task through

217

the machinations of someone who wanted me, for reasons completely unknown, nobbled—perhaps to clip my investigatory wings for over-confidence, a case of professional jealousy, but more likely to deflect me from some other investigation that could be handed over to someone...more suitable. Suitable for whatever obscure task the cloak-and-dagger people might have had in mind."

"Such things can happen," conceded Oblon. "In this instance I am not prepared to say whether or not it did."

"It hardly matters. It was Sergeant Ranger who first pointed out that the files we were given to study were incomplete." Oblon frowned at Bob. "We saw, or rather were permitted to see, nothing produced by a computer—even though it is to be hoped that the security of this realm would warrant the most modern, efficient information storage and retrieval system in the world."

"The Treasury," said Oblon, "keeps a close eye on expenditure."

Delphick ignored this. "It eventually became clear, or perhaps I should say was brought to our attention—" Oblon jumped "—that we were looking at the case the wrong way round, just as somebody intended. As was required. We were meant to do no more than blunder about stirring things up to force somebody's hand into even more unwise moves that would result in some definite proof upon which you and your colleagues could finally act."

Oblon was still concerned with the first part of the Oracle's argument. "Brought to your attention? By whom?"

Delphick ignored both questions, and fixed Oblon with an accusing eye. "It could have gone terribly wrong. Suppose we had blundered into something...dangerous?"

The Foreign Office mask replaced Oblon the man. "Highly unlikely."

"I notice you do not say impossible."

"Let me assure you that we were indeed keeping a very close watch. Fenn and the man you call Greene saw to that side of things. You were in no serious danger for very long." Oblon looked only at Delphick. "Either of you," he added. "Or your families."

Bob dropped his notebook. The Oracle's voice grew several degrees colder. "You said you had not wanted the involvement of Detective Sergeant Ranger. Or, by inference, that of his family."

Bob sat bolt upright, and drew a deep breath. An icy flash from Delphick's eyes kept him quiet. It was an uphill struggle. He suddenly saw that his job—the job he enjoyed—had put everything he most cared for in the world at serious risk of harm. Anne, the baby…

The Oracle was still speaking. Coldly. "We should, I suppose, thank you three gentlemen for your…consideration. Perhaps, in due course of time, we will." Bob was not so sure. His pencil stabbed across the page in a furious scrawl.

Oblon did not look at him. He addressed the chief superintendent. "Who exactly brought the—yes, deception if you like—and the dubious nature of the death to your attention? If there's been another leak, when we've taken so much trouble to channel and to contain this one…"

"All I am prepared to say at this stage is that we were put in the picture—pictures," he amended, for the sake of accuracy. Just because he'd been caught up in a mirror world of duplicity didn't mean he had to hedge and haver and double-speak as if he'd caught the same blasted disease the rest of them had.

"Pictures?" Oblon stiffened. "P-pictures? What do you mean?"

"To be blunt—" began Delphick, and broke off as he saw Oblon's eyes widen, then narrow. Bob, wondering how you pot-hooked an emotion, squiggled *he looks worried—no idea why*, turned a page, and added in vicious shorthand *and I hope it hurts him!*

"To be frank," the Oracle began again, and suddenly saw Oblon seem to relax. "In short, neither I nor my sergeant take at all kindly to being made cat's-paws in whatever convoluted game you and your Intelligence cohorts are playing."

"The great game, as Kipling would call it." Oblon no longer looked worried. "You and the good sergeant have, for beginners, performed admirably." For the first time he risked meeting Bob's eye, recoiling at the controlled fury in the good sergeant's face and movements. He tried to rally. "The Department—departments, that is," he mimicked the Oracle's accuracy, "will be most grateful."

Delphick set his jaw. It was like trying to catch smoke in a butterfly net. Just as at their first meeting, when he'd had to press for what it was they'd wanted done, now apparently they'd done it—with no more idea now what "it" might be than they'd had back then. "Why should anyone be grateful? What the hell is it that we have done?"

Bob Ranger couldn't remember when he'd last seen the Oracle lose his rag this way. Which made two of them. Seemingly they'd been duped into spending days, if not weeks, looking into a murder the authorities had already decided to cover up, with possible risks not only to themselves—they were paid to take risks, after all—but to their families. Except…

"That's how you knew they were in Plummergen!" Bob burst out.

Oblon had been framing one of his diplomatic speeches, but was deflected as he worked out what the sergeant meant. Then a forced, thin smile curved his lips. "But of course." He seemed surprised anyone should need to ask. "A watching brief—discreet, naturally—was kept pretty much the whole time. As I explained. Although it was something of a surprise when they appeared in that village of yours, we never harboured any serious doubts about the Costaguanans—apart from their driving ability, that is."

The feeble joke did not work. Delphick was speechless. His sidekick, controlling himself with an effort, rushed to his support. "You mean we were never in any real danger—Mr. Delphick and…and the rest of us?"

"For a short time, perhaps, had—ah—certain persons learned our intentions before the matter had been properly settled. After all, we could hardly set up a watching brief until we knew definitely who it was we were meant to be watching. Once you—the chief superintendent, that is—agreed to undertake the task, it was—"

"*What* task?" Delphick was almost shouting. "Once and for all, man, and in words of one syllable if you can, just tell me what we have been doing!"

There was a long pause as Oblon contemplated the two irate detectives, evidently making up his mind. He reached for the telephone and dialled a number neither could see.

"Oblon here. Delphick and Ranger are with me…Yes, very little doubt…Not too happy…I rather think so…Refer to the Grey Committee?…The OSA—yes, of course…"

He replaced the handset. "You ask what you have been doing. You have been buying valuable time for what we may call the relevant authorities, by deflecting suspicion—and proving our case beyond any doubt, as we could tell from the response of…a certain person as your investigation progressed." He coughed. "I explained on a previous occasion that when we find a security leak, we…try to take advantage of it."

His tone became grave. "If, however, we are forced to accept that we cannot perform a successful boomerang—my apologies for the jargon—if we realise we can't hope to turn the leak to our advantage with misinformation, then we must find other ways of dealing with it."

"The way someone dealt with Gabriel Crassweller?" Bob brought out. Delphick continued to hold himself in check.

"That was unfortunate. While we had suspicions of...a certain member of staff, we didn't have enough certain knowledge on which to act. The intention, naturally, had been to wait until we were sure, but it seems we were not the only ones to have suspicions. As far as we can ascertain, Crassweller found out what had been and was still going on, and took the matter into his own hands by challenging his colleague to refute his accusation before putting the matter before the appropriate authorities."

Bob snorted. Delphick spoke, bitterly. "The action of a true gentleman. One simply can't believe one of our chaps would be such a treacherous cad, what?" It was a vicious imitation of the uppermost of the upper-crust voices that prowled the corridors of power. "Got to give the man a chance to stand up for himself, what? Jolly bad form to sneak behind his back. No doubt he showed his suspect colleague the original of that photocopied Stentorian Bank counterfoil, and was gent enough to accept whatever explanation he was given." He shook his head. "The credulous idiot."

Oblon sighed. "I take your point. If only he hadn't done the decent thing, Crassweller would probably still be alive, but his death did confirm that we were right to suspect...the guilt of that certain person, for various reasons into which I would prefer not to go unless you insist." He leaned forward. "Please believe me. There really are some matters of which it would be better for you and your sergeant—I'm relieved to see he has stopped taking notes—to remain ignorant."

"Such as the name of the certain person." Delphick shook his head as Bob, with a guilty start, breathed heavily and prepared to resume his squiggling. "Does this mean that at some point in the future there will be another car wrapped around a tree? Or don't you people like to repeat yourselves? Oh, I beg your pardon, it wasn't your doing, but theirs, whoever They might—Ah. The Grey Committee. A suitably anonymous colour for, one has to hope, some different group of Them. The word 'dikast' comes to mind."

"Ah," said Oblon. He saw that Bob, still simmering, was puzzled. "A civilian judge in ancient Athens," he explained.

"One of six thousand," added Delphick. "Or, in this case rather fewer?"

"It would be better not to press for details. You can trust me—" Bob snorted again "—when I tell you that the matter will be dealt with. Your successful investigation will draw to its close with a conclusion of murder by person or persons unknown. The report will be accepted. The death penalty is no longer imposed for murder, but there are…certain exceptions."

He nodded to the Oracle. "Your knowledge of the law, Chief Superintendent, should enable you to name those exceptions."

"Setting fire to one of Her Majesty's dockyards," said Delphick slowly. "High treason. Piracy. And…espionage."

Oblon inclined his head. "Quite so."

There was a long, thoughtful silence.

"A judge and jury…" began Delphick at last, but then he broke off. "After Burgess and Maclean, and then Philby, you wouldn't want the publicity, of course."

"We would not." Oblon looked uncomfortable.

"The Cambridge spies," said Delphick, still thoughtful. "There have been rumours of a fourth, even a fifth, man. We could always re-check the files to see which of our shortlist of suspects didn't go to Oxford…"

"But you won't. What good would the knowledge be to you beyond the satisfaction of professional curiosity? I promise you, the matter will be dealt with. The judge may not wear robes, but the jury—those who decide the final verdict—will be the person's true peers. Equals. People doing similar work, in the same world, understanding, even experiencing, the same pressures and temptations—*and not succumbing to them*, Mr. Delphick. Loyal, trustworthy subjects of the Crown."

There was a further silence.

The silence continued.

Oblon broke it in the end by pulling open the drawer of his desk. He withdrew a slim folder, and set it on the blotter. He opened it, his gaze moving from Delphick to Bob, and back. What he saw in their eyes seemed, eventually, to reassure him.

"In real life," he said quietly, "you cannot hope to win them all. Real life has its flaws. Only the Almighty can achieve perfection. We mere mortals must do the best we can with what we can. I ask you to believe that you have done your country a great service—"

He produced two closely printed forms on foolscap paper.

"—and I must ask you both, please, to sign the Official Secrets Act."

Delphick signed first, without speaking. He rose, in silence, to leave.

Bob scrawled his reluctant signature and handed the form back across Oblon's desk. The sleeve of his jacket clipped the corner of Oblon's in-tray turret. Everything crashed to the floor. Papers carpeted more than half the office.

"Sorry, sir. Clumsy of me," said Detective Sergeant Ranger, and followed the Oracle from the room without another word.

Chapter Seventeen

An unmarked police car made its roundabout way from Ashford to Plummergen, arriving in the middle of the morning. Heading north it crossed the Royal Military Canal, turned down Nowhere Lane, and stopped near a discreetly parked panda. Two young men got out to greet a third man, rather older, in uniform.

"Potter's talked to the vicar," Brinton had told Detective Constable Foxon, "and he'll be there to keep an eye on things while you dig. Potter," he added as Foxon grinned. "Not the vicar, no matter how much the old boy likes to play in his vegetable patch. The fewer people on this wild goose chase, the better."

"And unless we find the golden egg we don't dig, sir. Is that right?"

"Depends how often the thing goes beep, laddie. You should know, you went to the shop, you had the lecture. If it beeps, you said, something's there. Could be an old tin can, could be a broken spade, could be somebody's loose change or—and pay attention, Foxon—the buckle from their trousers. Or the buttons from their tunic. If the thing makes the right sort of noise, you and young Whatsit start digging. Potter can shake the sieve."

News of police activity near the churchyard did not go unnoticed in Plummergen. PC Potter, warned by Brinton to keep it as quiet as possible—there were also warnings about chasing wild geese—had been torn between walking down The Street and risking questions, or driving there and making it official. He wondered about plain clothes rather than uniform, but that too would cause undue comment. In Plummergen there were always curtains on the twitch, and people going in and out of shops close to the Nowhere Lane turning.

Margery Welsted, popping down to Mrs. Wyght's for half a dozen currant buns (elevenses) and a sliced brown for toasting (supper tonight, sardines, and breakfast tomorrow), saw PC Potter driving down the lane and—she waited, to be sure—not coming back. She could see he'd gone beyond Summerset Cottage. Could be heading to one of the farms. Reminders about warble fly and sheep-dip, perhaps.

Perhaps not. Margery continued to wait. Watching a blacksmith at work made excellent cover, and Dan Eggleden was a pleasure to watch. He could shape and fit a horseshoe faster than anyone for miles, and his wrought-iron balustrade for Miss Wicks's cottage was a matter of village pride.

Above the roar of the bellows, the rage of the fire and the clang of the hammer on red-hot metal nobody could have heard the approach of the unmarked police car, but Nowhere Lane was almost directly opposite the forge, and the movement as the car slowed caught Margery's eye. Waving to Dan, she turned to see Detective Constable Foxon from Ashford, with another young man at his side, follow in the wake of Police Constable Potter. And, likewise, not coming back.

Margery hurried to the bakery. There was nobody there but Mrs. Wyght. Plummergen prefers a larger audience when it has news to impart. With buns and bread in the string bag she'd crocheted herself, she returned to the draper's and told her mother something seemed to be happening down the lane.

"More people looking at Summerset Cottage," suggested Mrs. Welsted. "Reporters, maybe. They say Dr. Braxted is going to be famous."

"No, it was the police. Two cars—Ned Potter in his panda, and that young Foxon from Ashford with another lad, both trying to look as if they were just out for a drive, as if anyone'd go down Nowhere Lane when it goes nowhere except to the end."

Mrs. Welsted's interest grew. "Problems at one of the farms? Though nothing's been said this morning that we've heard. Course, they might only just have found out and dialled nine-nine-nine."

"They weren't flashing their blue lights, or using the siren."

"Trying to keep it secret." Mrs. Welsted pursed her lips. "That would fit with Dr. Braxted, all right. Won't let anyone into the house except those youngsters from Brettenden, and the police—and she shouts if you even go up the path."

True. Margery began to wonder if she hadn't made too much of her casual sighting. The cars might have parked farther from Summerset Cottage to be out of the way of passing traffic, not that there ever was much…And as neither of the Welsteds could find any plausible excuse for either to stroll past to see what was happening, and exactly where, they agreed they must wait upon events. They knew it wouldn't be long before someone came in and told them more.

It wasn't. And it was a lot more. Mrs. Skinner came in for another skein of red wool (her quilt panel depicted the French raiders burning the church in 1380) and said that as she walked past the forge Dan Eggleden had just stopped work, and in the distance she'd heard noises from Nowhere

Lane and thought it best to slip along to make sure it wasn't anyone up to mischief.

"Men's voices—thumps—a sort of rattling. Made me think of them Spaniards along of Mrs. Venning's—castanets, and dancing—and I couldn't think why anyone, even foreigners, should want to start dancing about like that so close to the churchyard."

"Hardly respectful," agreed Mrs. Welsted, church organist, her lips again pursed, this time in disapproval. "Let the dead rest in peace, I say."

"Well!" said Mrs. Skinner, relishing her hold on her audience. "And that's what I thought, too, only, with them being foreign—and Roman, what's more—they'd think different from us, I thought. They have *festivals*, don't they? Seen them on the telly."

"Mardi Gras," said Margery, who enjoyed her food.

Mrs. Skinner didn't care to have her narrative interrupted. "So what I thought *was*," she went on, "they might be trying to raise the spirits of the dead, in broad daylight, their ways not being the same as ours—*or worse*."

Mrs. Welsted quivered at this last. "We can only hope you were wrong, Mrs. Skinner, but with what they say is painted on the wall at Summerset Cottage—"

"But it wasn't them!" cried Mrs. Skinner, determined to deliver her punch line now that enough tension had been cranked up. "It was the police—and they wasn't dancing, oh no." Her eyes gleamed. "Digging, that's what they were doing. Digging in the Kettle Wedge!"

"I said it was police cars I saw," crowed Margery.

"Why should they sound like castanets?" said her mother.

"That was Ned Potter with a great metal sieve, shaking fit to bust—and that Foxon lad from Ashford walking about with headphones and a giant vacuum cleaner or similar—"

The door opened, the bell pinged, Mrs. Henderson came in. She spotted the skein of red wool on the counter beside Mrs. Skinner, and bristled. Mrs. Henderson was another who had chosen to depict the incendiary events of 1380.

"—and the other lad with a spade, digging…"

Mrs. Henderson's voice was louder than Mrs. Skinner's. "Did you know there's police over there digging in the churchyard?"

"We were just saying," began Mrs. Welsted. Mrs. Skinner prepared to repeat her story. Mrs. Henderson gave her no time.

"You know why, don't you? Acting like they're looking for summat with one of them new-fangled metal detectors, but that'll be just a bluff. Mr. Treeves wouldn't let them go treasure-hunting among the graves. Not respectful to the dead, is it?"

"No," said Mrs. Welsted, "it isn't," but Mrs. Henderson rushed on before the organist could say more.

"But if it was a grave they were digging, or rather, *digging up*…"

Even Mrs. Skinner had to share the delighted shudder that filled the little shop. All four women looked at each other with a bright, speculative gaze. Mrs. Henderson nodded.

"The vicar would let them dig, all right, if it was police business and an exhumation…"

It was the most exciting news in the village for years.

Plummergen revels in excitement. It is any villager's unspoken duty to fan the smallest ember of gossip and surmise into heart-warming flame for the benefit of the curious. Forgotten by Mrs. Skinner and Mrs. Henderson alike were the long-dead flames fanned by the raiding French in 1380, and their place in the Plummergen Quilt. Mrs. Skinner paid for her wool and hurried off towards the post office. Mrs. Henderson told Mrs. Welsted she'd forgotten her shopping list and would be back later. She went in hot pursuit of her rival and caught up with her. They entered the post office together.

Tongues wagged. Theories were concocted, exchanged, shot down.

"…wrong part of the churchyard for really historical graves…"

"…most recent burial old Griselda…"

"…could be one of her sisters, buried beside 'em…"

"…all three, maybe—or the old colonel…"

"…they *said* it was a stroke, but you never can tell…"

"…wicked temper—one of 'em could have slipped summat in his food…"

"…anyone could have slipped summat to any of 'em…"

"…whole family poisoned, and Griselda the last…"

"…servants disappeared—gone back to London to hide…"

Only now did Miss Nuttel and Mrs. Blaine, eager listeners but for once unable to break into the swift, shrill, speculative flow, find their chance to throw cold water on at least one of the theories.

"We saw the Brattles the other day," said Mrs. Blaine. "In Brettenden. If I'd poisoned my employers I wouldn't be so foolish as to move just a few miles away, where anyone might see me. It can't have been them who did it—if anyone did at all," she added. Wholesale, undetected slaughter in a small village over several decades seemed less and less likely the more she thought the matter over.

"Might of come back for a visit," someone said, but was ignored.

"Odd pair," said Miss Nuttel. "Talking to Miss Seeton. Not like them."

"Never talked much to anyone when they lived here, that's true," conceded Mrs. Spice.

230

"Perhaps Griselda didn't want 'em to," said Mrs. Skinner. "Or allow them. Who pays the piper calls the tune, and them Saxons piped for years, the colonel and his girls."

"Perhaps they were asking Miss Seeton for a job," said Mrs. Henderson.

"Everyone knows she's got Martha Bloomer," countered Mrs. Skinner.

"The Brattles might not know." A point to Mrs. Henderson. Never exactly mixed, that pair from London, had they? At least, not enough to hear things about people in the village, and who they worked for. Martha Bloomer, a very different sort of Londoner and married to a local, had adapted much better than the Brattles to life in Plummergen, obliging for several other ladies as well as Miss Seeton. Those who paid Martha paid her well, and kept her services. Bribery (as some had found to their cost) did not work. Hadn't she been with old Mrs. Bannet for years before Miss Seeton? And she'd been almost as long with the Colvedens...

Everyone realised at the same time the possibilities in what had just been said—and in what was not being said. Voices hushed. Eyes glittered. Brains were busy.

"They do like their privacy at Rytham Hall," someone said at last. That long-ago lady lumberjack who had retreated with a telescope to Dungeness was not forgotten. Nor was the family's reluctance to exhibit the wedding presents anywhere but in the village hall.

"With Louise a foreigner," said Mrs. Henderson, brooding on 1380, "you can understand they might not want her right there in the house with them."

"Griselda could of lived for years," said Mrs. Skinner, likewise thoughtful.

"Lady Colveden used to visit every week," said someone.

"Kept her on the doorstep, though, didn't they? Shows they never trusted her inside."

"More than one door to any house. Can't be everywhere at once…"

"…easy enough for summat to be slipped in a cup of tea…"

"…pillow or cushion over her face…"

"…never heard official what she really died of, did we…"

"What a time for young Nigel to come back!"

And everyone thrilled to the dreadful shock the young couple were about to receive once Nigel's mother had been arrested on suspicion of doing away with old Miss Saxon in order to provide her son and his bride with a home of their own in a conveniently empty Summerset Cottage.

On the desk of Superintendent Brinton in Ashford, the telephone rang. "Potter? Still having fun with your bucket and spade? Found anything?" The receiver quacked excitedly in the superintendent's ear. "Stopped? For pity's sake, why?" More quacks, and more excited. "They're saying *what?*"

He listened in dismay to the explanation, and could only shake his head. He began to feel giddy. He took a deep breath and looked across to the desk of his sidekick, ready to tell him to pick up his extension, but Foxon was in Plummergen, with a metal detector he had, according to PC Potter, dropped when Mabel Potter came hurrying down Nowhere Lane to tell the three policemen the latest gossip she'd heard while out shopping, and what did they think ought to be done about it. All Brinton could do was tear his hair, and groan periodically until the story came to its apologetic end.

"No, I don't see what else you could have done, especially if…No, not your fault, mine. I should never have listened to the Oracle. I should have thought how it might look to those scandal-mongering fools in your blasted neck of the woods…Yes, and a long shot anyway, as the detector bloke said from the start. Thirty years under the ground and the whole lot could be rusted away to nothing…Yes, tell 'em to pack up and forget the whole damned business. You can drop in on the vicar and explain, although—" Brinton knew the Reverend Arthur "—perhaps you'd best report to his sister at the same time. She's got a head on her shoulders. A few words from Miss Treeves should stop the worst of it…"

It was as well for Brinton's peace of mind that he did not know, and PC Potter did not remember, that Molly Treeves was locked away with the rest of the Quilt Committee, busy with layouts in the village hall.

Foxon came with exaggerated care through the office door, rubbing his back. "Worse than digging my gran's garden, sir." He perched daintily on the corner of his desk, grinning at his superior. "I won't sit down just yet, if you don't mind. Ned Potter's as much of a slave-driver as you could ever be—or Gran Biddle."

Brinton glowered. "You survived the ordeal, I see, even though you've cost us a pretty penny smashing up the equipment and—"

"No, sir!" Foxon seldom interrupted without good cause, so Brinton let it pass. "It just slipped from my hands and one of the dials got knocked off the setting. A few twiddles and it was fine again. We dropped it off at the shop before reporting back here, sir, and he said in the interests of public relations he wouldn't charge us for the whole day."

"Very generous, but then, I suppose it's the man's livelihood."

"How he can make money at it I've no idea, sir. Why anyone should think it's fun to trudge up and down through a load of weeds and brambles with headphones beeping in your

233

ears all the time I can't imagine. We should have thought to take a scythe. I'm all for Women's Lib after this morning, sir, believe me. Now I know how they feel when they have to hoover the carpets."

"I hate women," said Brinton. "Especially the gossiping sort."

Foxon, filling in the gaps, was sobered at once. "We couldn't believe it when Mabel told us what they were saying in the village, sir. An exhumation is daft enough—don't they realise how long it takes to arrange something like that?—but to go around saying Nigel's mother poisoned half the Saxon family because Sir George wanted a tenant who could pay more money…"

Brinton sat up. "I thought it was only Griselda she poisoned, because she was the last one left in the house and the newlyweds wanted to move in."

Foxon sighed. "Ned thought it might be a good idea if we had a cup of tea and a bun at the bakery tea-rooms, sir, on account of all the thirsty work we'd been doing looking for a set of Second World War buttons *and nothing else*—and not finding them, anyway."

"A good man, Potter. It ought to have worked, but I take it that by the time you went in they'd thought of something else?"

"Oh, they had. The latest is that both of 'em, Sir George as well as her ladyship, were in cahoots with the servants to help Griselda on her way, and that's why the Brattles went off in such a hurry after the funeral, sir. In case awkward questions were asked by the authorities—probably meaning the police, but with us there they didn't spell it out."

Brinton clutched his hair, and brooded. "We can only hope some new turn of events occupies their pestilential little minds before too long. But maybe there could be something in what they're saying—oh, I don't mean the Colvedens," as Foxon let out a protesting yelp, "but you can't deny it's odd the way the Brattles vanished without even hanging around to see if they'd been left a keepsake or two in the old girl's will."

"They haven't exactly vanished, sir. I forgot to tell you, someone saw them the other day in Brettenden." Foxon paused. "They were, uh, chatting with Miss Seeton, sir."

The explosion did not come. "It needed only that. Do tell me. What do they think about this…this brief encounter?"

"They don't, sir." Brinton blinked at him. "Honest. For once, she's out of it."

"She won't be for long. She can't help it. It'll just happen, and we poor sinners will have to put up with it and try to make the best of it." Then he brightened. "That bank-box sketch of hers—I wonder if it could tell us their address? I think we need to have a word with them, if only to set my mind at rest." He was reaching for the telephone when Foxon stopped him.

"I've had a thought about that, sir. They're retired, aren't they, so even if the Saxons left them nothing they'll still have the state pension to live on." Brinton's hand fell back. Maybe a call to the Oracle might not be needed after all. "We could check at the main post office first, sir, and if there's no joy we can ask around the banks in case it's paid direct to their account."

"Almost, Foxon, you can be intelligent. Why didn't I think of that?"

"Because we weren't exactly concentrating on the Brattles at the time, sir. You'd have thought of it soon enough if you felt it was important."

"Well, my feeling now is that it may be. Call it a process of elimination. Well done, laddie. I'll leave it all to you for the moment."

Foxon slipped off the desk, and stretched himself. "The post office won't believe me over the phone, so it's got to be face-to-face and I'll show my warrant card. I'll go over to Brettenden right now, sir. Fancy a change of scene?"

Again Brinton paused in the act of reaching for the telephone. "I've better things to do than leave my office on what may prove to be another wild goose chase. Come back for me if you find the golden egg this time around, and we can hatch it together."

Foxon, halfway out of the door, looked back. "Say hello to Bob Ranger for me, sir." And was gone, grinning, before the superintendent could find anything to throw at him.

Nor could Brinton find anyone at Scotland Yard, or at least no one who would have understood his state of mind. The switchboard reported that both Chief Superintendent Delphick and Detective Sergeant Ranger were taking a few days' leave. Was Superintendent Brinton's call urgent? Would he like to talk to Commander Gosslin? The superintendent declined the offer and rang off. Commander Gosslin, the Oracle's boss, of course knew of Miss Seeton as Plummergen's most important (from the official viewpoint) inhabitant, but he didn't know Plummergen the way Delphick did. Life was far too short to explain to the high-ups why the gossip brought back by Foxon made Superintendent Brinton uneasy.

He took a gloomy peppermint from the packet in his desk. As he savoured its extra-strength fumes and the sugar boost to his brain, he brooded on the lull before the storm, the war movies when *It's quiet out there—too damned quiet* heralded imminent mayhem. But that was for ordinary people, ordinary circumstances. You couldn't call Plummergen ordinary. Ever since Miss Seeton had come to live in the village things were very rarely *too damned quiet* and even if they were, they got worse than anyone could reasonably expect before they got better. And too much had been going on there in recent weeks. Potter, good man, kept him fully up to date on the place with regular reports as per Standing Orders, even if there could be times when he didn't report anything untoward for weeks at a time. Now the place was seething with foreign fascists and rumours of Nazi spies and murderous servants and death-dealing aristocrats and, heaven help him, buried treasure too...

And all since Miss Seeton came back from her holiday.

He took another mint, and did his best to look on the bright side. Perhaps he was over-reacting. In "a few" days—which could mean anything from two or three to a week—things might have calmed down, and he'd feel a fool for having rung a bloke of higher rank, friend or not, just to say he had an uncomfortable idea the mulligatawny might be about to boil over when maybe, after all, it wasn't. But the Oracle and his sidekick were on leave. They knew nothing about his problems. He'd have to cope, if any coping was needed, without the acknowledged experts. You couldn't deny that Plummergen did things, saw things, differently. The whole blasted village was simmering, according to Foxon, and that sort of mood in that sort of place usually led to trouble sooner or later...

No wonder, he told himself as he crunched a third peppermint, that his wife and his doctor kept warning him about his blood pressure.

Chapter Eighteen

Half a packet of peppermints later, Foxon reappeared. Brinton was still at his desk, trying to distract himself by catching up on paperwork. "Good grief, sir! Your in-tray—it's almost empty!"

"You could at least shut the door before you start shouting your mouth off. Now the whole ruddy station knows. They'll collect up every bit of bumf for miles and bring it to me because they think I've nothing better to do—"

"But you have, sir. I've found the Brattles—not through the post office, I tracked them down through the third bank I went to. They weren't keen to tell me the address at first, though after some prodding they confirmed the name. They did a *very* close check of my ID and agreed I might be me, but to make absolutely sure they telephoned Sergeant Mutford…"

"Who complimented them on their trustworthiness and recited a verse of scripture."

Foxon grinned. Desk Sergeant Mutford, who considered himself the mainstay of Ashford police station, belonged to the Holdfast Brethren, a teetotal, vegetarian sect of the Christian church whose tenets included the strictest possible adherence to the law. If banks were supposed, by law, to keep client confidentiality, Mutford was duty bound to be delighted that this particular bank was keeping it.

"He asked them for a full description, sir." Foxon's eyes danced. "Lucky my gran made me this tank top. There's nothing like it anywhere else in Kent."

"Thank heaven." Brinton rose to his feet. "But I admit a Fair Isle pattern wouldn't have been as good, for identification purposes. Just don't let her knit you another." They headed out to the car. "I must say, I'm pleased to know it takes a bit of arm-twisting for a bank to let someone, even a copper, waltz in and ask where I live, and be told. Everyone's entitled to some privacy."

The ten-mile journey to Brettenden took longer than Brinton would like, but slow tractors pulling heavy trailers can be safely overtaken only when the road ahead is visible for several hundred yards. Young Foxon, for all his daft ways, was serious about his job. Good driver, too. Brinton wondered again about letting him try for sergeant. He didn't want to stand in the lad's way, but he wondered how hard it would be to find someone else if the high-ups decided promotion meant relocation. They might send him back to Maidstone, where he'd started on the beat before plain-clothesing his way across to Ashford. There was a bit more life in Maidstone, he supposed. He couldn't blame the lad for getting itchy feet...

"And here we are," said Foxon. Brinton blinked. "Everything okay, sir?"

He'd spent longer brooding on Foxon's career prospects than he'd realised. Well, it had taken his mind off his other worries. He pulled himself together.

"Good. Let's hope they're home, not out chatting to Miss Seeton again."

"Nice little house." Foxon lived in lodgings. "Not quite roses round the door, but I wouldn't say no if you were thinking of my next birthday."

"The plumbing and mod cons must be an improvement on where they were before, from what I've heard."

Sam Brattle opened the door. Brinton recognised him from Miss Seeton's Bluebells-on-the-Bank-Box sketch, though he'd seen it only the once. No doubt about it, the old girl was sometimes bang on the money with her scribbles.

Mr. Brattle eyed the two policemen thoughtfully, hardly glanced at their identification, and ushered them into an armchaired room at the front of the house.

"I'll fetch Agnes," he said, before Brinton had properly begun to explain. They heard his feet thud up the stairs.

"Almost as if they were expecting us," murmured Foxon.

"He didn't seem all that surprised," agreed Brinton. "Guilty conscience?"

"You don't think it might really be true about—"

"No, I don't!" burst from the superintendent as voices and footsteps overhead showed that whatever Mrs. Brattle had been doing upstairs she was about to stop and come down to join them.

She and her husband manifested themselves quietly at the door, and as quietly came into the room. Agnes Brattle studied their identification rather more closely that had her husband, but like him she did not seem unduly surprised at the visit. She settled herself on the edge of a chintz sofa, while he sat beside her.

"We'd just like to ask a few questions, and we hope not to keep you too long," said Brinton. "We understand that you lived until recently in Plummergen, working for Miss Griselda Saxon."

Both Brattles exchanged a quick glance, then nodded.

"And when she died, you came here. You're not from these parts originally?"

"London born and bred," said Sam. "The pair of us." Agnes nodded again.

"You weren't tempted to go back home when the chance came?"

"We've been a long time in Kent," said Sam. "Came down with the colonel before the war. There'd be nobody left in the Smoke that we'd recognise, or them us, even if we wanted them to."

"Which we wouldn't," said Agnes. "Besides, there've been so many changes, with the bombing and clearance and rebuilding, it wouldn't feel like home any more."

"Then why not stay in Plummergen? After forty years that must have felt like home."

Once more the Brattles exchanged glances. "Gossip," said Sam. "Tongues wagging, nosiness, no real privacy. We've always preferred to keep ourselves to ourselves—a polite nod in passing, not the Spanish Inquisition every time you leave the house. The Saxons were a good family for that. They didn't go out much, especially after the colonel was took sick, and they didn't encourage visitors. Minded their own business and left us to mind ours, which was looking after them and nothing more."

"Shopping in Brettenden to avoid the wagging tongues, of course. But now you're living here…"

"We still don't have to talk to the neighbours beyond Good Morning," said Agnes.

It was Sam's turn to nod. "A quick chat in the street with a stranger we'll never see again is one thing, but much more than a hello where you live, and next door will be round every five minutes to borrow sugar, or the lawn mower, and then just happen to drop by at the right time for afternoon tea. We wouldn't care for that."

Agnes murmured her agreement. The two detectives knew there was no law that said you couldn't try for absolute privacy in your life, if that was what you wanted. Brinton thought of the bank. He wondered how the Brattles would react if they knew how Foxon had tracked them down. He thought of what he himself had said about arm-twisting privacy...

"Interesting you should mention chatting to strangers in the street. Did you have any particular stranger in mind?"

"The umbrella," said Sam Brattle promptly. "We wondered if it might be that—we both recognised your name, you see. A lady dropped it, and we picked up her stuff and she told us you'd given it to her, and we admired it—very nice, nothing vulgar—and we chatted a bit about gold not tarnishing and needing polish the way silver does, and she said there was some Roman stuff in the museum. And that was about it."

"That's right, Mr. Brinton. A quick chat, as you might in a shop when buying something, but a minute or two at most, and it wasn't as if she fell and hurt herself. She just dropped everything when she bumped into us, and we helped her collect it all back into her basket."

Brinton couldn't prevent a smile, while Foxon, taking discreet notes, kept his head low to conceal his grin. Dropped everything? Umbrella included? To be picked up by witnesses nobody at the time knew might be important? He regarded that sort of thing as pretty much par for the course with Miss Seeton.

"I hope she's not saying now there was any more to it than that," said Sam. "Because if she is—"

Brinton raised an imperative hand. "Nothing to worry about there, Mr. Brattle. That's not why we'd like to talk to you both. It's about Miss Saxon."

After a brief hesitation, Sam Brattle asked, "Oh? What about her?"

"She left you nothing in her will, which is unusual for an employer whose employees have been with her a long time."

"She'd got nothing to leave, Mr. Brinton. If you've talked to her man of business, and you must have done to know about her will, then breach of confidence as it is I'd have thought he'd tell you that."

"I'd have expected a pension of some sort. Even a small one."

"She didn't have anything to leave." Again, Agnes was her husband's echo. "She had next to nothing to live on, by the end."

"And you stayed to the end. Highly commendable. A model employer, evidently, even if she didn't pay well."

The Brattles exchanged looks. Sam shrugged. "She wasn't the sort who'd thank you for liking her, nor any of the family—but we'd been with them from first marrying and it suited us to stay. We did a good job, and they respected us for it and didn't interfere, nor us with them. Of course, as they dropped off the twig one by one things was bound to change, but the proper distance was always kept on both sides."

"A purely business arrangement, then." Both Brattles nodded.

"By the time it was only Miss Griselda," said Agnes, "her health wasn't so good, and of course the house didn't help. I did my best with that range, but you need to keep warm and out of draughts as well as eat proper. It was hardly our place to ask Lady Colveden for help when Griselda had her rules, and she never was one to mingle. She began to lose interest in pretty much everything that last year or so—just ticking over, was what it boiled down to. We really looked forward to our shopping trips because we could be sure of a decent meal once a week, and somebody else to cook it on a proper stove."

243

Sam nodded. "We're glad to be in a place of our own like this. Central heating and hot water and not having to chop wood."

"No draughts or damp patches," Agnes added, "and a lovely fitted kitchen."

"It must have cost you a pretty penny," interjected an envious Foxon, without thinking. Immediately, he and Brinton sensed both Brattles grow wary.

"And you say there's no pension?" asked Brinton, silently daring Foxon to say more.

"Our old age pensions," said Sam.

"And we've saved, over the years," said Agnes. "Nobody could call us extravagant."

"Could they call you honest?" Brinton remembered the Bank-Box sketch, and hadn't entirely forgotten the blackmail theory. Either would explain how the Brattles could afford to buy a modern house while Griselda, last of the Saxons, faded slowly towards an impoverished death.

He expected indignation. They'd been quick enough to protest at the idea they might have harmed Miss Seeton in some way, but they said nothing. He had the feeling, from the way they stiffened, that they were trying not to look at each other. He didn't seriously think they'd had a hand in Griselda's death any more than he suspected Lady Colveden—the old girl had been investigated thoroughly at her post-mortem—but it did seem there was something. Thanks to Foxon, and Miss Seeton, they'd got on a trail without realising where it led.

"We didn't help ourselves to the housekeeping," said Agnes at last, "if that's what you're suggesting. More like us helping Griselda out, towards the end, with just her pension to keep her going, but in the early days they'd paid us well—"

"Reasonably well," interjected Sam. "Not generous, though."

"Paid us reasonably well," amended Agnes, "only they didn't allow for such a thing as inflation. Expected it all to stay the same from before the war. But like I said, we'd put a bit by over the years, so I suppose you could call it turn and turn about when we had to help the old girl. But it wasn't much, and it wasn't for long."

"Ah, the war." Brinton spoke almost casually. "Did you share their Nazi sympathies?"

There was a sudden release of tension in the room.

"We didn't know if you knew," said Sam. "It isn't right to speak ill of the dead, and she's not been gone five minutes. And we didn't talk politics with any of them. Like I told you, we respected each other's privacy—and of course it isn't a servant's place to presume in any way, which politics would have been."

"Not that we held with their carrying-on," said Agnes. "Some of the friends they made in London! Some of the things my husband heard them say! Had to bite your tongue more than once, didn't you, Sam?"

"I did. But it's not a servant's place to disapprove of his employers." He smiled at his wife. "It's 'for better, for worse' once you've took their wages. And for a servant what matters is not so much what your employers think, it's the way they behave. How they treat you. And by their lights they treated us well enough, at least in the early days."

"Before the money got tight," said Brinton.

"We could have left when the war broke out," said Agnes. "But we didn't. Everyone else upped and went the minute they could, but we wanted to stay together, and found ourselves war work locally. Sam helped on the farm at Rytham Hall, and I got took on for the domestic. The place was full of the military, only don't ask why because to this day I don't know. None of my business to know, beyond there were men in uniform everywhere. And even hush-hush men want meals and laundry and mending done, just like anyone else."

"What did the Saxons do during the war?"

"Looked pleased when it seemed as if he might come, then you could say they sulked when it seemed he wasn't going to." Sam Brattle frowned. "They had a few chickens, but as to sharing a pig or keeping rabbits there was nothing of that sort. It would have meant mixing with the common folk, and they never held with that."

"Did you know about the wireless?"

The Brattles looked at each other. There was a long silence. "We were never sure," said Sam, "not until after the war, but as for *during*…well, from things they sometimes said, though they didn't talk much in front of the likes of us…but we did have to wonder, servants not being as daft or deaf as some people like to think."

"And after the war? How did you find out?" He doubted if they'd been told the secret of the priest's hole. "Surely nobody after the war would ever have admitted to a thing like that in the house!"

"Spotted the aerial one day in the roof," said Sam, "once we were allowed to put things up there again, the risk of bombs and fire being gone. Running under the ridge and down through the rafters, though how you got inside to use it I dunno. But I built myself a cat's-whisker set as a boy. I guessed what it was all right—and neither of us can say we were really surprised."

"A good chance to ask for an increase in wages," Brinton suggested lightly.

Once more there was a pause, uneasy and thoughtful.

246

Agnes stirred at last. "Might as well tell him, Sam. He'll keep on until you do, and we've had a good run for the money."

"You know I never asked for a penny!" he protested. "But years after, with the colonel and the two oldest Misses gone, money did seem to be getting tight. They'd have used up what he made from selling Rytham Hall, and no more to come beyond the old age pension. Griselda decided she had to trust us, sort of. You could see she hated having to do it. Told a pack of lies about family inheritance and her grandfather not thinking banks were safe—which is why we knew it for lies. We'd never heard before about the colonel's father being a prospector. Never the sort to chatter to the servants, and then suddenly she did."

"She was getting old," said Agnes.

"Aren't we all? So one day she asked, when we came back from shopping, if next time we went into Brettenden I would change some old gold coins into proper money for her."

"At the bank?" Brinton would have supposed a British bank would have been curious, to say the least, at the sudden appearance of—"Not German coins, then."

"Gold sovereigns from South Africa," said Sam. "They'd been hid somewhere in the house—full of nooks and crannies, that old place. Every now and then, on a day when we'd been out, she'd hand me a dozen. Next week I'd take 'em to a bank, or an antique dealer, sometimes even a pawnshop— though I never told her when I pawned them, knowing she'd be shocked at having to deal with Uncle—but always careful, like she asked. Even went as far as Ashford, sometimes. And...well, she never took a daily paper, to check up on me. The whole family'd been just waiting for their chance to be bosses again under the Nazis..."

"Collaborators," snapped Agnes. "We're no Nazis, never were. There's a big difference between grumbling about the way things are and wishing they were better, and plotting to hand over your country to a man who looks like Charlie Chaplin in jackboots and all he'll make better is for him and his cronies, treading everybody else underfoot."

Light dawned on the superintendent. "So you decided to take agent's commission for each transaction? Because she couldn't look in the paper for the exchange rate. Clever. What did you consider a fair rate?"

"Started at ten," admitted Sam Brattle, "but when she didn't notice I upped it to fifteen, then twenty—but no further. Wouldn't have been right." Brinton said nothing about this quaint notion of rectitude. "Like Agnes said, she was getting old. So long as she had money to live on we didn't see why she should have all the benefit of what was traitors' gold in the first place. Contaminated, you might say."

"With your rising percentage helping to decontaminate the rest. There's logic in that argument—of a sort—but what about the Inland Revenue? Death duties?"

"But it wasn't honest money," Sam objected. "It was never hers, it was from the Nazis for after the invasion. And there's no Nazis left these days, or not a government with legal rights, just a few wicked old men in South America and places…"

"And he's probably right," grumbled Brinton as he and Foxon drove away. "I'm no legal eagle, but I'd say the most we could do the Brattles for is fraud, maybe embezzlement. And was it even Griselda's money in the first place? No, laddie, the only people to see any point in sending them for trial would be the lawyers."

"And Griselda's dead and the dosh has probably all gone anyway," said Foxon. "Or it's still where she kept it, and nobody knows where. You bet if the Brattles had known they'd have helped themselves to the last percentage before they pushed off, and they certainly gave the impression they didn't."

Brinton was silent.

"Or they could," persisted Foxon, "be good liars. Perhaps they did help themselves to what's left, and they've got it hidden until the legal position's been sorted out. Which could take yonks." Envisaging these long, tedious years of legal argument, he tooted loudly at a cock pheasant strolling across the road. It took no notice. He tooted again. There was little difference in the bird's waddle rate. Foxon braked, and sighed.

"This time of year they're really stupid, aren't they? Shame it wasn't a lucky black cat crossing our path." As the pheasant finally reached the safety of the verge he put his foot down, and then laughed.

"What's so funny?" Foxon's almost relentless bright-side-seeing sometimes pushed Brinton's forbearance to the limit.

Foxon subsided. "Sorry, sir, it just popped into my head. The man who broke the bank at Monte Carlo. We've been talking about money, and banks, and lucky black cats, and I had this sudden vision of that bird's hands in its pockets as it walked along the Bois Boolong with an independent air."

Brinton muttered under his breath, and then sat up. "Foxon, turn round."

Foxon slowed the car. "But I didn't hit it, sir, and in any case—"

"Pheasant for dinner be blowed! Turn the car round. We're not going back to Ashford. Visions? The very word. We're going to Plummergen to call on your artistic lady-friend who has more visions than you or I can ever understand."

Foxon checked the road, then achieved a neat three-point turn into a farm gateway and out again. "She might be shopping or something, sir. Should we radio ahead and ask Ned Potter to find her and let her know we're on the way?"

Now he'd voiced the suggestion, Brinton was no longer sure it was such a good idea. The Oracle was the real expert at making sense of Miss Seeton's sketches, and the Oracle was on leave. If he involved anyone else besides himself and young Foxon he'd be committed, good and proper—and official. They'd know at Ashford nick. They'd know in Plummergen. Potter wouldn't let anything slip, but if she didn't answer her phone they'd see him looking for her…And he'd look as stupid as that pheasant when she did one of her doodles and it made no sense and he'd have wasted her time, and the Yard's retainer fee…

"Or shall we just take pot luck?" Foxon understood his chief rather better, sometimes, than Brinton realised. "See that couple of magpies? One for sorrow, two for joy. They're a good omen, sir!" And he continued to drive Plummergen-wards, grinning broadly.

Chapter Nineteen

Brinton was about to knock on Miss Seeton's front door when it opened. Bob Ranger loomed before them.

"Hello, Mr. Brinton, hello, Tim. Come in. Miss Seeton's making a fresh pot of tea and Anne's cutting more gingerbread. I thought I recognised the car."

Brinton hesitated. "Wouldn't like to interrupt a family party." He hadn't expected any audience other than Foxon when he asked Miss Seeton for help.

Foxon understood his reluctance, but Bob misread the signs. The proud father laughed. "Don't worry, sir, we didn't bring the sprog—he's fast asleep being doted on back at the Knights'. It seemed a shame to disturb him, so it's just me and Anne. Do come in and help stop the cakes going stale. Martha had a change from sewing yesterday and cooked for an army. Aunt Em can't possibly eat it all."

Well, if he couldn't have the Oracle, his young giant might be a fair substitute. Brinton followed Bob through to the sitting room and Foxon closed the door.

Miss Seeton was delighted to welcome the newcomers. For a while the conversation was general as tea was drunk, sandwiches were nibbled, cake was devoured. It was Anne who introduced the topic over which Brinton was clearly dithering, even as he sighed, licked his lips, and patted a satisfied stomach.

"Now the inner man is satisfied, would you like me and Bob to go away, Superintendent? It's obvious you didn't turn up here simply to pass the time of day."

Again Brinton hesitated. Bob started to rise from his chair. Brinton made up his mind, and waved him to sit down again. "I know you can keep your mouths shut, and local knowledge might come in handy. I suppose you've heard all the rumours."

Miss Seeton, who hadn't, showed nothing but polite interest. Anne looked annoyed and Bob, resigned. "About Summerset Cottage and the Saxon family," added Brinton quickly. "Nothing to do with anything or anyone else."

Anne was relieved. Miss Seeton was fond of the Colvedens. It would have upset her to learn what village gossip was implying. "The Saxons," Anne echoed cheerfully. "Well, they do seem to have been a strange family." It would be breaking no professional confidence, when it was for the police; and in any case, Griselda was dead. "Dad was called in by the Brattles when old Griselda was so poorly they got frightened, and that was the first time he'd ever seen her. He sent at once for an ambulance to take her to hospital, and it was the last time he ever saw her, too."

"The Brattles—yes." Right to the heart of it without him even hinting. "We've had a word with them. They seem to think the old lady might have had a hiding-place where she kept…a hoard of gold coins." Brinton glanced at his hostess. "They're the people you bumped into the other day in Brettenden, Miss Seeton, and sketched so well that I knew them as soon as I saw them."

Miss Seeton murmured something. Anne exchanged a quick look with Bob, and they both looked at Foxon.

"Metal detectors," said Bob. "Of course."

"Everyone's been talking about it," said Anne. "I wouldn't have thought it was very practical, myself. I still think it was poachers Jacob Chickney saw. Even in the middle of the night someone could have seen them digging their hole, and waited till they'd gone back to the house and dug it up again."

"I'd have buried it in the garden," said Bob. "More privacy."

"More risk of being seen by the servants," said Anne, "and we talked before about the risk of blackmail, didn't we, burning the uniforms in the kitchen range?"

Miss Seeton sighed. "It is a sad thought that the whole family, as I understand, supported the Nazi cause. Dr. Braxted's discovery of the priest's hole and the wireless would seem to be proof positive. Foolish thought it may be, one cannot help but wonder if the…the influence of that unpleasant fresco of Henry VIII might have had something to do with it."

"You always like to see the best in people, Aunt Em," said Anne gently.

Brinton took this for the warning she intended. He modified the remark he'd been about to make. "I'm afraid there's little doubt they felt that way some time before the war, Miss Seeton, when they still lived at Rytham Hall. Quite a few of our upper class did, secretly—or not so secretly. Look at the Mitford girls and Oswald Mosley, for starters."

Miss Seeton, sighing again, nodded. "There were doubts about the Duke of Windsor, as I recall. One would expect a former king to remain loyal to his country under all circumstances, and of course nothing was proved, but he was a sad disappointment generally and people found the stories easy to believe, even though I cannot believe that he would have taken Nazi gold the way it has been suggested the Saxon family did."

Brinton stared. She smiled. "As dear Anne pointed out, everyone has been talking about it, and Martha talks as well as anyone I know. And I do remember the war, Superintendent, and how rumours could start from the least little incident."

And, thought Brinton, you've done your best to ignore any rumours ever since peace was declared. And managed it, most of the time. Lucky you.

"The Brattles," he said, "somehow gave the impression that the gold, supposing there was any gold, was hidden inside the house rather than out of doors."

"Dr. Braxted," said Miss Seeton, on whom Euphemia had paid a follow-up call for further enthusing, "has told me a little about priest's holes." Euphemia had in fact told her a great deal, in a flurry of words and gesticulation that left her bemused, able to take in only part of what she was saying. "She explained how sometimes they would have a second, smaller place of concealment hidden within the first, so that should the secret be betrayed the priest had, in theory, time to slip into an even safer place."

"And you think the gold might be there?"

"But, sir," said Foxon, "Potter told me about that priest's hole. He's been inside. She was an elderly lady, in poor health. She wouldn't want to go scrambling about up and down ladders for her money. She'd want it the easy way."

Bob nodded. "Dr. Braxted wouldn't even let me try, because the space was so tight. She said that after the ladder she had to balance across the rafters and worry all the time about falling through the ceiling, and then swing on a roof beam to open the hidden door. An old lady couldn't do anything like that..."

He broke off. Miss Seeton couldn't be called old, though she was no spring chicken. And he'd bet that she would, if asked, tackle rafter-balancing and swinging on beams without turning a hair. Years of yoga had turned his adopted aunt one of the most sprightly pensioners in the country.

From the suppressed chortle that drew Brinton's glare, Bob could tell that Foxon had shared the same thought. Probably old Brimmers as well, and only glaring because he'd been caught out. Bob grinned, saw Anne's quick frown, and sobered.

"So if it's in the house at all," he finished, "it's somewhere…handy."

Brinton took a deep breath. "And that's why I've come to you, Miss Seeton. To see if you might have an idea for this handy hidey-hole, if it exists."

"But why ask me, Mr. Brinton? Dr. Braxted and her students have undertaken the most thorough research, which is how they discovered the priest's hole—measuring every room and comparing the proportions. When these didn't match, they found it. You would do far better to ask them if they have found any others that don't match for I assure you, I am no expert."

"Maybe not on priest's holes, but you have other talents, Miss Seeton. What I hoped was that if you just sat and thought about it for a while, seeing as you've been inside the house and picked up the atmosphere, you might be able to sketch a general idea of the sort of place the gold might have been hidden."

She was still puzzled. "But they have measured all the rooms, Mr. Brinton. Dr. Braxted told me so. I believe they even used squared paper, as an additional means of checking." She thought of the Plummergen Quilt, and would have smiled, until she saw his disappointment. One didn't mean to be unhelpful, but…

"But in any case," she added, "I would have thought that to build more than one priest's hole, in so modest a house, would be most unusual, though Dr. Braxted would be able to explain this to you far better than I."

"Sliding panels," suggested Brinton, inspired. "I take it this place has panelled walls?"

"Yes, the hall is panelled in oak, as well as the parlour, but they tapped all the panelling as well as measuring the walls, so Dr. Braxted said. Had there been anywhere that sounded hollow, I feel sure it would have been investigated before the search moved to the upper floor, and thence into the attic."

"But once they found it, they stopped looking." Brinton still had hopes for his theory. "In all the excitement they might have missed anything else."

Miss Seeton looked doubtful. She knew her Euphemia. "Dr. Braxted is a most thorough researcher. It seems unlikely…but if you ask, I feel sure she would be prepared to give you every assistance."

"Provided you swear an oath of secrecy," Bob warned him. "She's worried about rival academics stealing a march on her. When I turned up looking for the Oracle—Mr. Delphick— she shouted at me to go away until he told her who I was. She did the same to him, as well, before she had a good look at his warrant card."

Miss Seeton smiled. "Dr. Braxted is, understandably, jealous of her reputation as a historian, but I believe, Mr. Brinton, that once she is assured of your bona fides she will co-operate with you to the best of her ability."

Like Delphick on a previous occasion, Brinton realised that Miss Seeton wanted to have as few direct dealings with Summerset Cottage as possible. "I wouldn't ask you to go there to sketch it," he said, as the penny dropped. "Just to dig out your gear and sit quietly and think about hiding-places, while we old pals chatter among ourselves. Young Foxon and I will be shown thousands of baby snaps—" he winked at Anne "—and, if you can oblige, you could rough me out an idea of the sort of place someone might have built in Tudor times to hide something they didn't want anyone else to see."

"I know where Miss Seeton keeps her sketching things." Anne jumped to her feet and went to the bureau. "As this sounds like an official request, Aunt Em, I promise we'll chatter very quietly and not disturb you."

"And if we had any photos of his lordship with us we'd make you look at them all to keep you quiet," said the proud father, "but we haven't. We'll just have to chat."

So they did, trying to ignore Miss Seeton as she leafed through her sketchbook for a blank sheet. She paused when she came to the Three Weird Sisters, and frowned before turning the page. Mr. Delphick had seemed interested in that one. She hadn't then known why, but now she could guess. No wonder the women wore the same clothes, and what must be jackboots. A most unpleasant and distressing idea, that the family had been in thrall to the Nazis...

Bob had the best view, sitting at an angle to a painting in its frame above the fireplace. He smiled as he watched her in the reflection. Years ago, after their first encounter, she had drawn a swift cartoon likeness of himself as the footballer she didn't then know he was, that she later gave to Anne. In similar fashion she had produced a watercolour of a bleak, windswept heath that was somehow a realistic impression of the then Superintendent Delphick, seen by Miss Seeton as a Grey Day and which, in the course of a later adventure, had been made more wintry still by the application of pastel chalks and given a new name: *Ilkley Moor on a December Day*.

Now it was having its third incarnation, as a looking glass. He watched her study a blank page, fiddling with her pencil. She flipped back to glance at some previous sketch, seemed about to close the book, then suddenly her fingers twitched, she seized the pencil, and began dashing its point across the paper. Good for MissEss. That quick, instinctive drawing was what old Brimstone had wanted—and she was coming up with the goods before his very eyes.

"…didn't find a sausage," Foxon was saying, as Bob returned to the muted chat and left Miss Seeton to work in private. "The super told me I'd be getting fresh air and exercise, but all I got was backache."

"You should help in your gran's garden a bit more," said Brinton, whose potatoes sometimes won prizes at local shows. "You're getting soft. A fine way to thank her for your birthday present, wouldn't you say?" he asked of the Rangers.

"Mr. Brinton would have preferred a Fair Isle pattern." Foxon indicated his stripes. "I'd never dare tell my gran that, though…"

Bob tuned out again. In the glass, Miss Seeton now sat without moving, gazing down at her sketchpad. He glanced across at Brinton, rolled his eyes, and tilted his head to one side. Brinton at once looked in the same direction.

"All done, Miss Seeton? That's splendid. May I see?"

"It's not particularly helpful, I'm afraid. I seem to have muddled it with something I drew earlier." She passed the sketchbook to the superintendent, who grinned.

"Three old biddies climbing the stairs." Miss Seeton turned pink.

"They…they were coming down them, before. At first I thought of the Fates, or the Weird Sisters in *Macbeth* because Nigel Colveden said that was what he and Julia used to call them, when they were children—the Saxons, that is."

Brinton's head jerked up. "You mean these are your idea of the three Miss Saxons? Show me the one you think you muddled it with."

He handed the sketchbook back, and she leafed obediently through until she found what he wanted. He gazed at it, with Foxon peering over his shoulder, Bob and Anne as interested spectators. "Coming down the stairs," said Brinton. "And going up them."

"I believe they are wearing jackboots," said Miss Seeton. "At the time, of course, I had no idea, but Martha has told me, and so has Lady Colveden, a little…"

"If you think the stairs are important, Miss Seeton, so do I." Brinton hesitated, then returned the sketchbook and rose to his feet. "Come on, Foxon. Let's hope your horrible clothes don't panic the lady into raising the alarm. We're going round to this cottage we've heard so much about to ask Dr. Braxted if we can come in to look for a hidden panel on the stairs. And I'll lay you odds we find one!"

Bob looked at Anne. She smiled and nodded permission as he, too, rose with alacrity to his feet. "You could be right about those stripes, sir. They're enough to terrify anyone out of her wits—sorry, Tim." Foxon grimaced as Miss Seeton emitted a discreet little chuckle and Anne giggled. They could all see that Detective Sergeant Ranger, on leave or not, was eager for any excuse to be back in action. "If I come with you, well, Dr. Braxted's met me, and I can vouch for both of you." He turned to Miss Seeton. "May I leave Anne here with you? You could show her your sewing, if it wouldn't be giving away too many secrets. With luck we won't be long…"

The three men tried not to hurry as they made for Nowhere Lane. "Let's just hope," growled Brinton, "nobody starts spouting more rubbish about exhumations."

As expected, Euphemia Braxted appeared at a window the instant their feet sounded on the path. She took one look, immediately recognised Bob, and flung the casement wide.

"You grow no smaller, Sergeant Ranger! You still won't fit—but your friend the psychedelic Tigger would, if he wanted. I'll come and unlock the door."

Bob waved thanks, and she vanished as Brinton began to laugh. "I warned you about those stripes, young Tigger. Psychedelic—the very word!"

Foxon joined in the laughter. "I notice she didn't offer to let you, sir, climb the ladder and scamper about on the rafters. Perhaps she thought you'd be as out of place as Sergeant Ranger?"

Whatever Brinton might have wanted to reply, he didn't. Euphemia was at the open door, with a nod and a smile to usher all three policemen inside. Bob made the introductions, then left Brinton to explain why they were there.

"Panels on the stairs? Hmm. Felix! Madeline!" Feet clattered above, and Mr. Graham appeared from one direction while Miss Staveley came from the other. Both carried notebooks; Felix had a camera slung around his neck, Madeline held a flat leather cylinder in her other hand.

"They're not interested in my fresco, they don't want to see our priest's hole," Euphemia said after further introductions. "Probably a wise decision," she added, calculating the chances of a safe ascent, balancing act and descent on the part of Superintendent Brinton, potato fancier, and not liking the result. Foxon chortled quietly; Bob hid a grin. Felix and Madeline were courtesy-to-strangers personified. "They'd like you to check your measurements for the stair panelling."

Consultation in notebooks, discussion, shaking of heads. "There's no difference between the wainscoting and any of the rooms alongside," said Felix. "Everything fits."

"There's an alcove by the chimney breast in one room," said Madeline, "and we had our doubts about that, but Felix is right. It's deceptive, but it does all work."

Euphemia flung out her arms. "Have you ever met researchers as thorough as these two? If they say it's impossible, then it is. Every day I pat myself on the back for having persuaded them to come and help."

Brinton sighed. In the absence of the Oracle, Bob Ranger or no Bob Ranger, his inexpert interpretation of Miss Seeton's special sketches must be wrong. Just as he'd been afraid.

Foxon was less easily quenched. "But you were looking for somewhere big enough to hide a man?" The three historians agreed. "Would you have bothered checking the measurements of the stairs themselves? The width of the treads, the height of the individual steps?"

"The vertical part," said Dr. Braxted, in lecturer mode, "is the riser." But she, like the others, looked taken slightly aback. "Not in detail, no. Once we found the secret room it didn't seem necessary to check elsewhere—the stairs are too far from the attic, and much too public, for a bolt-hole."

So where, thought Brinton, might someone agile have hidden a stash of gold coins in days past. He'd have to send young Foxon up in the roof after all…No, he wouldn't. The old lady was producing South African sovereigns for Sam Brattle to change into English pounds not long before her death. And she'd been declining for several years. Foxon had said she'd have wanted them within easy reach. And Miss Seeton had suggested…

"Could you measure the stairs now, please? For any discrepancy that might show there's a smaller than man-sized hiding place there?"

He felt obliged, now, to explain to the historian and her colleagues why he wanted to know, though he kept the details brief. *I saw three old biddies going up and down the stairs in a drawing* was pretty weak, as an explanation. *We have reason to believe* would have to do: he could hardly say *acting on information received*, given the sort of information it was.

He hoped the other two who'd been there would keep quiet about it all.

They did. They stood with him and watched as Felix and Madeline, whose flat leather cylinder was a tape measure, went painstakingly up the stairs, measuring each step at a time, tapping the wainscoting for good measure.

At the second step from the top, they stopped. "Sounds a little different," said Felix.

Madeline checked the measurements. "It's the same size as all the others." She peered along the whole width of the stair. "Far too big to slide sideways into the wall—it would stick out several feet into the next room, and I can't see a join for only part of it to move." Her fingers ran lightly from one end of the riser to the other. "I can't feel any join, either."

"But it's at ceiling height," said Felix. "Suppose there's a beam directly opposite on the other side of the wall, and it's not structural but hollow?"

"Well done, Felix!" Dr. Braxted shot a triumphant look at Brinton. "The riser could slide sideways into the beam, and nobody would see it." She looked at Bob Ranger, six foot seven in his stockinged feet. His shoes would add another inch. His arms were in proportion to his frame…

"You may not be able to investigate the priest's hole, young Goliath, but for people in a hurry you're an excellent substitute for a stepladder." She beckoned him to follow her into the neighbouring room. Felix and Madeline double-checked their measurements. Brinton and Foxon exchanged glances, and hurried after Bob. The room had leaded windows and what looked like the original beams, massive and black.

"Splendid, aren't they?" said Euphemia. "But," she added, after some stretching on Bob's part and further checking of measurements, "there isn't one in the right place. A great pity. It was such a good idea."

"Too good, perhaps," suggested Brinton. "I don't mean clever-clever," he corrected as she bristled on behalf of her protégé, "but too obvious, maybe. For something supposed to be hidden. If it's there at all," he finished. Yes, he needed the Oracle. Talk about a wild goose chase.

There came a shriek from the stairs. Everyone rushed back out to the hall. They saw Madeline, left behind when Felix took the tape measure in to the others, with her hand on one of the uppermost balusters.

And they saw, as they hurried up the stairs, a dark, narrow crack at the base of the riser that hadn't been there before.

"I heard you talking, and guessed it was no go. I was a bit fed up, and tried to push it sideways anyway, and grabbed at the baluster to keep my balance, and—I felt it move! Only a little, but I twisted it some more, and—look!"

With a slight effort she repeated the manoeuvre. There was a faint squeak of oak on oak, and the narrow crack widened as the riser tilted back on an unseen hinge. Everyone crowded round to watch. Eyes were bright, breath was held. Madeline, encouraged by Euphemia, twisted some more. Further back went the riser—darker and more secret grew the cavity now revealed.

"Good girl," said Brinton. His grin was as wide as any of Foxon's. "Well done, young Madeline!"

"Here's a torch." Euphemia tugged a small flashlight from her cardigan pocket. "You're not afraid of spiders, of course..."

Then congratulations became loud and general as Miss Staveley put her hand into the hiding-place and rummaged about, before withdrawing a grey canvas bag.

It clinked.

Chapter Twenty

Foxon drove back to Ashford. Brinton glowed with satisfaction deeper even than when his potatoes took First Prize. Who'd thought of asking MissEss to sketch? Who'd made sense of what she drew? Who needed Chief Superintendent Delphick? Or perhaps that was going too far. But the Oracle was on leave, his Goliath sidekick officially wasn't there either…

"It'll have to be reported to the coroner," he said aloud.

"Surely not exhumation after all, sir!" Foxon knew his duty as feed.

"Treasure trove, laddie. Valuables found in a place of deliberate concealment. The legal bods are going to have a high old time deciding if it counts as part of Griselda's estate. The Brattles can testify she was spending that lovely golden oodle almost to the end—until she grew too frail to turn the baluster, I suppose, which is why the Brattles thought the money had run out—but does it count as hers in the first place?"

"The sovereigns were minted in South Africa, sir. The old colonel's father really might have brought them back from his prospecting days. We can't prove they're anything to do with the Nazis—"

"So it's just coincidence the shoulder-flashes and buttons were in the other bag."

"A safe hiding-place is a safe hiding-place, sir." Foxon grinned. "The way backache is backache. The hours we trudged up and down with that metal detector—"

"You might have enjoyed it. Plenty do. A new hobby, the chance to apply your detecting skills in a different way."

"Not my idea of fun, sir—though some of the rougher elements have been in the shop asking how much the things cost. I'm surprised they took the trouble to ask. Knowing the Choppers and their pals, a brick through the window and help yourself is more their style."

"They'd have to know how it worked. Even if they had the sense to think of swiping one at the same time—which they haven't—I doubt if the Choppers could read their own names on a charge sheet, let alone an instruction manual."

Foxon was thoughtful. "I wonder how the foreigners managed. From what he said, it could have been the Costaguanans who bought a detector the other day. Their English is pretty basic, according to Ned Potter."

"It was probably them prowling round the village after the gold that started the rumours in the first place. Exhumations be damned!" Brinton sighed. "Dr. Braxted may swear everyone to silence about that painting, but by *not* swearing her or those youngsters to silence, with luck the word will get around that there's nothing for anyone to find, and it will all calm down again."

"With Plummergen, sir, you never can tell." A strange logic prompted Foxon's next remark. "MissEss was pleased, wasn't she?"

"All nice and officially receipted, with a cheque in due course." Again Brinton savoured his—Miss Seeton's—triumph. She had been delighted that her sketches had helped, and showed great interest in the sovereigns, though her distaste for the Nazi buttons, buckles, and insignia was clear. She had, she reminded him, lived through the Blitz.

And she had been quick to change the subject. "Her sewing's pretty good too, isn't it, sir? Her work looks just like her cottage—and no need to swear any oath. The map's not what they're all in such a tizz about, it's the quilt. Everyone in the village who can sew seems to have joined a secret society. They're worried Murreystone will try to steal a march on them."

"I thought all this rigmarole was in aid of that writer bloke's centenary for being born in Plummergen. Unless the chap was really born in Murreystone and moved when he was a kid, how could they possibly steal a march—or even take a stroll?"

Foxon lamented his superior's short memory. "You know they've been squabbling for a thousand years, sir. If Murreystone can outdo Plummergen, they will. Remember the cricket match—how they got that horse drunk on fermented apples and took it to the smith for shoeing? Dan Eggleden is Plummergen's best bowler, and they nobbled him good and proper. And what about the Best Kept Village competition and the—"

"Shuttup, Foxon. Dammit, of course I remember. And I don't see how Manville Henty can be anything to do with Murreystone—or why it has to be kept so secret."

Foxon, having spent a morning metal-detecting up and down the Kettle Wedge with PC Potter, had the all facts. "It's because the quilt is depicting local legends and history, sir. Anyone can make a map of their own village, but Murreystone isn't so far across the marsh—"

Brinton guffawed. "So both sides might have a claim on the same stories?"

"Yes, sir, and Plummergen wants to get in first. As anyone would after the Brown Wilt, and the moles, and everything."

During the Best Kept Village competition, Murreystone had outdone itself in skulduggery. Plummergen's unloved and unlovely mole catcher, Jacob Chickney, was bribed by the across-the-marsh rival to supply living moles rather than dead, to be released to do their worst in Plummergen gardens—which gardens were also attacked in the night by Murreystone with flasks of boiling water, scalding prize plants to withered brown stems, and spoiling the green of velvety lawns with ugly, burned blotches.

"And everything," echoed Brinton. "Oh, yes, I get it now. Murreystone'll probably find an old house with *two* priest's holes and a smugglers' tunnel to boot, and make a quilt twice the size into the bargain."

"Yes, if they could." Foxon half believed it. "Hence the need for secrecy."

"Not one word more from you, then." And Brinton settled back to resume his quiet gloating on secret panels, treasure troves, and final proof of Nazi sympathies, if a two-way radio hidden in a priest's hole wasn't enough. Buttons, buckles and flashes were more than enough. The de-buttoned uniforms would have been buried, of course, as they couldn't be easily burned. Natural fibres—no nylon, in those days. Somebody once told him that if you left a book, all paper and glue and cloth binding, in the open air it would disappear within a twelvemonth. The churchyard soil, so close to the canal, must be pretty moist all year round. After thirty years…He was going to enjoy writing up his report. The Imperial War Museum could argue with Brettenden and Dr. Braxted over who got to keep the radio once the security bods had taken a look. He rather thought he'd back Euphemia to win that argument…

Superintendent Brinton, Miss Seeton's sketches neatly folded in his pocket, two canvas bags safe in the boot of the police car, was almost entirely content.

There was one small niggle of unease, right at the back of his mind. He ignored it.

In the post office Mrs. Blaine shuddered, her hand to her head. "That noise—it's too dreadful. Why must motorbikes have such loud engines?"

"That Wayne and his pals," said Mrs. Henderson, "did really oughter be stopped, racketing about for hours and not the first time, neither." She looked round in case Mabel Potter was there. She wasn't. "What I'd like to know is, what's Ned Potter doing about it?"

"You can't rightly call it *hours*," said Mrs. Skinner. "Two or three times at most, today."

"Much too fast," said Mrs. Blaine. "They might run someone over. Those people at Mrs. Venning's nearly killed Bert, remember. You're right, Mrs. Henderson, the police should be doing something about it. I've half a mind to report him."

"But you can't be sure it's Wayne." To Mrs. Stillman, as to most of female Plummergen, one motorbike looked much like another. "And they all look the same in their helmets, don't they? It wouldn't be fair to blame the boy when nobody saw his face. Was there anything else, Mrs. Blaine?"

"Oranges, Bunny," prompted Miss Nuttel.

"Thank you, Eric—that new recipe. I was going to make a fool." Mrs. Stillman thought Mrs. Blaine would have made a fool of herself if she'd gone complaining to PC Potter; but it didn't do to upset the customers.

"How many would you like, Mrs. Blaine?"

"Six, please, and a tin of cornflour—oh, and a bottle of olive oil. As you know, we never touch animal products, but there are so many substitutes…"

The omnivores present shuddered at the very idea of using olive oil as a substitute for honest milk and cream. Them noisy bikes must've turned her brain.

"Reminds me of the mock cream we had during the war," someone said.

"And you can't say worse than that," said someone else.

"Oh, I dunno. What about mock duck?"

There was laughter from all save the vegetarian duo at this reference to the strange sausagemeat-and-breadcrumbs concoction of the 1940s. Mrs. Blaine, headache forgotten, looked affronted and might have snapped at the mockers had the shop-door bell not just then heralded the entrance of Mrs. Potter.

"Or Woolton Pie." A quick-thinking pacifist. "Hello, Mabel."

PC Potter's wife seized her chance. "Talking of the war, have you heard they've found the gold that Hitler paid the Saxons, hidden in Summerset Cottage?" She gave details. "… back to Ashford with him," she concluded. "So there's nothing left in the place now but that picture on the wall." And, having bought stamps she didn't really need, she went back to the police house feeling she had done what Mr. Brinton wanted. The word would soon be round the village that the gold had been not only found, but taken into safekeeping by the authorities. Poison and exhumation were simple misunderstandings. The rumour of buried uniforms, long gone, had been proved true by the bag of metal notions. The wilder gossip could now die down, leaving Plummergen to meet its deadline for the centenary commemorations.

But the rumours had spread farther than Brinton realised…

As Foxon had half-wondered, the Costaguanan purchase of a metal detector did not go unremarked in Ashford. The broken speech and accent of the purchasers, their dark hair and black eyes, their clothes, had been too exotic to be ignored. Word soon spread, and was magnified. A hoard of Spanish gold—a chest, two chests, treasure uncountable from the Spanish Main—buried not many miles away, and these foreigners trying to take it from the trusty English soil that had concealed it for centuries. The cheek!

The Choppers thought it more than cheek. Buried treasure? And them English born, and local! But why do the searching and digging when someone else would do it for them? Burglary, petty theft, even robbery with violence—they didn't mind violence when they were on the winning side—yielded small pickings when set against treasure beyond their wildest dreams. Sacks of gold and silver, ropes of pearls, jewelled necklaces, bracelets, brooches. Find, take, fence—easy money, and theirs for the making. A handful of foreigners against the Ashford Choppers? No contest.

They had only to find out where the foreigners were based.

It took some days, travelling to nearby towns, keeping eyes and ears open. Someone in Brettenden spilled the beans. Spanish folk in Plummergen, he thought. Seen 'em once or twice, shopping. In a small town a Bentley stands out, or perhaps it was a Rolls, not the usual sort of car, anyway. Not that Plummergen was the usual sort of place. Never had been, and now even worse than usual. Some kind of secret everyone was keeping—heard 'em muttering, seen 'em following each other from the bus all over town. No idea why. He never went there, too much talk of ghosts and witches. Inbred lot they were, on the edge of the Marsh.

The Choppers, based miles from the Marsh, didn't believe in witches. Ghosts were another matter, but only on Halloween, or at midnight in a churchyard—the Choppers went to all the X-rated films, and knew about horrors. A grave made a handy place to hide chests of treasure. How deep did metal-detectors reach? They sent a further deputation to ask for more advice at the Ashford shop.

Another group of bikers visited Plummergen in search of evidence to support metal-detecting, or digging, or foreigners.

On their first visit they found nothing of interest, but while they roared up and down The Street a second time and gave Mrs. Blaine a headache, they saw great activity at the village hall—bunting being hung, and a large banner proclaiming the Grand Opening the next day of the Manville Henty Centenary Display. Those of the community up ladders refused to speak when questioned, those on the ground shook their heads about what it all meant, and said the entrance fee was destined for local good causes and they'd have to pay like everyone else.

The tallest of the bikers slipped round the back of the hall. The blinds were down on every window, every window was locked—like the main door of the hall once the banner-hangers had disappeared inside. Baffled, the Choppers roared off on their bikes. They passed a black Bentley rolling majestically down into Plummergen, and guessed they were on the right track. They brooded all the way to Ashford…

As always, Remendado escorted Mercedes into the shop and stood with the phrase-book ready. The maid smiled shyly as she handed her list to Emmy Putts. "Please," she said, and Emmy nodded as she always did.

Mrs. Stillman came forward as Emmy went to fetch a cardboard box. "A lovely day," she smiled to Mercedes and her chaperon. Both smiled back.

"Fine weather for a drive," probed Mrs. Skinner.

"Shopping," said Remendado. "Cooking. Today, very busy—as also, you." He waved vaguely towards the northern end of The Street. "*Las banderas*—" a fluttering motion with his fingers—"for fiesta."

"Oh, the bunting—the little flags," said Mrs. Stillman, the past weeks having shown that hand gestures were almost as good as words. "Yes, that's for tomorrow. Grand opening at ten o'clock, everyone invited, and all the money is for the church."

Mercedes recognised *church* at least, and she smiled, saying something to Remendado, who nodded, then looked thoughtful. Emmy returned with the box, and he watched as Mercedes selected items from the shelves and passed them to Emmy for ringing up on the till before packing them. The total was announced, the money handed across; change was given. Mercedes bobbed a quick curtsey and picked up the box. Remendado bowed, and Emmy Putts blushed and simpered until Mrs. Stillman frowned at her. The doorbell jingled as the two foreigners finally departed.

It was the middle of the night. Every house was dark. Except when roistering, Plummergen tends not to keep late hours. The moon had yet to rise, but patches of stars spangled a half-cloudy sky. Amelia Potter's Tibs, the police house tabby for whom the gardens of the lampless Street were as the jungle to a prowling tiger, saw movement in the grass. She pounced. A sudden squeak, then blood ran red as feline jaws bit and crunched.

Tibs, whiskers a-twitch, prowled north from Lilikot. She had left the corpse on the back doorstep: some cats have a sense of humour, and the squeals of outraged vegetarians were always music to carnivorous ears. An owl hooted—whether sharing the joke or complaining of theft, impossible to tell.

Tibs, nearing home, saw movement through the grass. She stiffened. Lights, dancing across the ground. Her ears flicked. Voices, low and muted. She did not know them.

The Choppers loved their bikes, but had to admit that riding them close to the village would be a bad idea. They switched off the engines as they passed the nursing home, and coasted as far as they could before having to dismount near the fork in the road and push their bikes the rest of the way. Even in the council houses, crowded with small children and elderly grandparents, no light shone. Everyone was asleep.

The motorbikes were wheeled into the sewage farm access lane and left on the wide grass verge facing the recreation ground, itself almost directly opposite the village hall and the police house—where, too, there were no signs of life. The Ashford roughs slouched across The Street, bearing muffled torches and various tools useful in burglary.

A Bentley's engine is as quiet as that of a Rolls Royce. Round the back of the village hall, busy with jemmies and wrenches, none of the Choppers heard the arrival of four Costaguanan men coming in search of the gold for which they had searched so long and so hard, hampered by language difficulties and the need to be unobserved, warned by post office chat that the money, only just discovered, was now in the village hall and would eventually be donated to the church. Money that could fund another revolution…

Each carried a torch; El Dancairo in addition had a jar of honey, wrapped in a stout dishcloth. Remendado held an adjustable spanner, a chisel, and a screwdriver, Zuniga a selection of knives in a canvas bag, Lillas Pastia a paintbrush and two more bags. They had no idea how much money, how many coins, there would be. At the side of the hall, beneath an overhanging tree, they set to work. If the window could not be forced it must be broken. They could not be sure which would be quieter.

Tibs, curious as only a cat can be, came closer. Men laboured over sturdy window-frames and catches. There was cursing. A sweet, sickly smell, a sticky sloshing sound, a strange noise, a body boosted upwards to dislodge sharp splinters.

Tibs skittered back as glass was tossed to the ground. Boosted again, a body squirmed through. There was a thump as feet landed awkwardly on the floor.

There came a yell—several yells—from inside, and sounds of skirmishing.

"Others are within!" cried El Dancairo. "Pastia must be supported! Round the back to find how they entered!" He guessed that whoever was in the hall must, like his own small group, be there for no legitimate purpose and had used an equally illicit means to get in. "Zuniga, that way—Remendado, with me!" He might not have the military mind of his supplanter, but El Dancairo knew the value of a pincer movement.

He did not, until too late, know that the dark shape into which he blundered was a large and ill-tempered cat.

Tibs let out a screech to curdle the blood. As the Costaguanans rounded the hall and met at the jemmied emergency exit, a light came on in the police house. Amelia Potter could tell her pet's every mood from her voice. This was no yowl of triumph—this was pain.

Amelia jumped out of bed and rummaged for her shoes. Her mother, waking, went to expostulate with her offspring…

Uproar was heard in the village hall. Mabel called to her husband, who flung open the bedroom window and listened.

"More than one," he said. "Too many for me on my own— while I get dressed you call Brettenden, then Sir George and Mr. Jessyp."

Some years ago, an upsurge in the Murreystone feud had resulted in the Night Watch Men, a muscular and protective company established by Sir George Colveden and Martin C. Jessyp. The Watch was revived from time to time as necessity dictated, and what remained all year round was covered by what Mr. Jessyp called the Double Spiderweb Alert. In an emergency, the first two people on his list would be alerted by the villager who spotted the trouble. Each would alert a designated two more, and the resultant four would telephone, in turn, a further eight. Lines would never be blocked by everyone trying to raise the alarm with everyone else at the same time.

Within minutes, as battle raged inside the hall, Plummergen's men rushed to join the uniformed Potter outside. Boots thundered up The Street from cottages and farms, down from the council houses. Torches flashed, weapons were brandished.

"Them bikers from Ashford…"

"Parked on the grass down Sewage Lane…"

"That Bentley from Mrs. Venning's outside the Rec…"

Sir George appeared with Nigel, asking the official representative of law and order what was required of the troops. PC Potter said Brettenden was sending a car, maybe two, but if they could sort out that rumpus as soon as possible it did ought to stop what sounded to him like a massacre.

"If it's them foreigners from Mrs. Venning's place fighting with the Choppers," he explained, "far as we know it's just four of them against a dozen or more."

"And the Choppers are dirty fighters," Nigel said, a cricket bat in one hand and a heavy flashlight in the other.

"But them Spaniards might use knives," said Potter. "We can't have bloody murder on our hands."

"Quite right," said Sir George, champing at the bit. "In the dark, what's more. Someone to turn on the lights, that's the ticket. Potter, got your whistle?" He himself clutched an ancient football rattle and a starting pistol filled with blanks. They'd been used before, and in similar circumstances. "Detail men to back and front—catch 'em as they come out, Potter?"

PC Potter said that was what he'd thought, once reinforcements had arrived, there being only one of him and knowing the Choppers of old. "And Brettenden won't be long," he added hopefully.

Sir George having deployed his men—Len Hosigg with orders to find the main switch and defend it at all costs—the Night Watch began a slow, circular sweep towards the front and back doors of the village hall. "Watch out for windows, too," warned Sir George.

In the distance blue lights flashed, coming nearer, coming fast. Sir George was tempted to halt the advance, but shouts and yells from within were now augmented by screams. Knives? Bad show. As Potter said, risk of death. "Forward!"

The circle closed, awaiting the signal. As the first of the Brettenden vehicles swept into the driveway PC Potter blew a shrill blast on his whistle. The Night Watch Men, helped by headlights, charged. Car doors were flung open, more men in silver-buttoned blue joined the attack. The hall lights went on. The combatants, dazzled, yelled defiance. The Night Watch, roused from sleep and angry, thumped indiscriminately at every unknown hand holding a weapon. Sir George, football rattle twirling, barged through the melee, climbed up on the stage and counted heads. At least twelve. He raised his voice to deliver what he could recall of the Riot Act while below, adrenaline exhausted, Choppers and Costaguanans alike began to succumb to the power of the righteous.

"Like herding sheep," gasped Nigel as Len abandoned his post at the main switch and joined the mopping-up operation.

"S'right," agreed young Mr. Hosigg, one eye closing and a bruise on his forehead.

"Bastards," swore Kevin Scillicough. "Look what they've done!"

"If they've torn it—" groaned Trevor Newport. The brothers-in-law, like every Plummergen male with a seamstress in the family, knew how much hard work had gone into the Mural Map, and how long it had taken to arrange it to best effect for the Commemoration.

"What did they want it for?"

"Tie the others up?" it was suggested, as handcuffs were produced.

But the truth was not disclosed until late the following day.

Miss Seeton, passing Lilikot, heard a shriek. Miss Nuttel had found the corpse. A clatter of sudden wings as a wood pigeon blundered in alarm from the garden. Miss Seeton raised her umbrella. The pigeon missed her—and only then did it begin to rain.

The post office might have taken this coincidence as further proof of uncanny powers, but nobody noticed. Husbands, brothers, sons had been involved in last night's engagement, and there was much point-scoring as to courage shown and damage inflicted. Miss Seeton, shaking her head for human folly, collected her pension and went home again.

Martha came to tell her all about it. What nonsense! Everyone chasing after gold that wasn't even there any longer but safe in Ashford, and now Stan limping with a hacked shin, Nigel's arm in a sling, Len Hosigg with a lump on his forehead and a real shiner, poor boy, not to mention the rest of the village menfolk.

Miss Seeton sighed, and proposed raw beefsteak, or a cold poultice, for the swelling—Cousin Flora's mother's *Enquire Within* suggested oatmeal, linseed, or bread.

"At least you can eat the steak afterwards," said Martha, thinking of waste.

"The hens could eat the poultice," supposed Miss Seeton.

"A pack of frozen peas, more like." Martha was irritable. "If only the dratted men would sit still long enough to give it time to work, which of course they never do."

Farmers. Always so busy. Miss Seeton, alone once more, savoured the peaceful view from her French window. Sparrows pecked busily at stray grain by the henhouse at the bottom of the garden. Wings clattered: a wood pigeon, swooping to displace them. So much larger than the sparrows—no doubt they feared it a bird of prey, though not for long: they flew back, a perky brown hubbub darting about stately grey, each ignoring the others as they pecked and bobbed together. Miss Seeton thought of children frolicking round an elderly headmaster, stiff white collar, pale plum waistcoat, formal dress without the top hat. *Dignity and Impudence* with birds, not dogs. And the other way round, of course.

She wandered to the bureau—collected her sketching materials…

How curious. No sparrows, just the one bobbing pigeon wearing—good gracious—a pearl necklace over its double-breasted waistcoat. The buttons were pearl, too. She really should concentrate—it had seemed so amusing an image when first she considered it…

Her second attempt far more resembled Landseer's skilful parody of the Dutch school, only, of course, the other way round. A most pleasing contrast. One might say, definitely amusing, and perhaps worth developing from a mere crayon sketch. Rather than the large brown dignity of the bloodhound, there was the plump grey pomposity of the pigeon. The impudent white terrier was a cheeky black-eyed sparrow, perched beside the pigeon on the window sill. Miss Seeton smiled.

Superintendent Brinton asked if Sir George could spare the time to pop across to Ashford for a discussion of the previous night's events. Sir George demurred. His son and his young foreman had been in the fight, and were unable to work at full throttle today. He was needed to make up numbers.

Brinton said in that case, so long as they didn't expect him to join in anything laborious, he'd drive across at some time convenient to the General.

"All of 'em bandaged, some in plaster, a few in hospital," he summarised, as the two men walked a field boundary and Sir George brooded over inactivity. "And all of 'em been charged—Choppers and foreigners alike."

"Ah, yes." Sir George stroked his moustache. "The, ah, Spanish chaps." He coughed. "Odd thing to do, trying to pinch our mural. What's it to them? If they want a memento of their visit, Welsted's has postcards."

"Ah, yes." Brinton glanced at Sir George. "The Spaniards."

Sir George cleared his throat. "Had a phone call from Delphick a while back. Thought I should know who they really were, just in case. Politics, you see. Assassins, and so forth. Watching brief."

Brinton sighed. "The Oracle might have let me know—two heads being better than one—but anyway, they'll all be deported after last night's little upset, I imagine. Political asylum! They should be grateful we let them in the country at all, and they should keep quiet, not smash the place to bits the first chance they get. Two of my men were quite badly hurt."

"Our own countrymen were involved, too." A magistrate must be fair-minded.

"Oh, we're throwing the book at them as well, but we're stuck with our home-grown Choppers and we aren't with the rest. Breaking and entering, causing an affray, grievous bodily harm, attempted robbery—we don't need that sort of thing here. They can go back to Costaguana, or try their luck in Switzerland, or chuck themselves over a cliff, for all I care."

"Robbery," Sir George repeated. "As I said—odd."

"Not the way they tell it," said Brinton. "Boiling it down, there's quite a few old Nazis in Latin America, boasting how one day they'll be back and there are still folk who sympathise with the cause and are biding their time. For some reason El Dancairo latched on to Plummergen as the most convenient place to try. Young Foxon thought they might be after Armada silver to pay a bunch of mercenaries to reinstate him, and that was near enough. But they couldn't get a handle on just where the oodle was hidden, hence all the midnight metal-detecting and torches and the rumours about—" he paused "—raising Hitler's ghost," he said quickly. "So when they came up against your tapestry project, everyone sworn to secrecy about what they were doing and talking about maps—and with their English not so good, and seeing the same few people in and out of the village hall locking the doors and planning a celebration, they decided it was a map of where the gold was hidden." Sir George snorted. "Full of clues for a treasure-hunt."

Sir George spluttered. Brinton sighed. "And I'm afraid your Mrs. Duncan didn't really help," he went on. "Quite by accident, of course, but that tenant of hers..." Mrs. Duncan, foreseeing rather more interest in Quill Cottage than she would like in the immediate future, had rented a bungalow in Hove for three months, letting her own home to an American historian keen to research Smugglers and Spying in Napoleonic Times. Professor Fehrenbach had turned out to be as skilled with a needle as with a pen. A second likeness of Manville Henty's birthplace had been offered to the Quilt Committee, complete with the missing blue plaque that the whole village felt sure must not be long in being awarded. Should authority prove reluctant, then Plummergen would design and attach its own plaque...

"And the fools decided it was a clue, so they thought they'd better grab it before anyone else saw it and worked it out."

"Mad," said Sir George. "We're lucky they didn't take it into their heads Meg and the rest knew about the blasted gold and go in for a spot of kidnapping. Hot-blooded types. Might have turned nasty."

"The Choppers thought there was buried treasure in the hall, the celebration being because someone had found it, and they were going to pinch it before the exhibition opened. Just as mad, in its own way. One lot hasn't got the lingo, the other lot hasn't got the brains. And between 'em both lots have caused us a lot of bother…"

He did not mention the plaint of El Dancairo, accusing his men of cowardice in the matter of giving him time to pull the mural from the wall while they held off the Choppers. From what the Choppers had said before their legal advisers advised them to keep quiet, thwarted of treasure, with nothing but "an old curtain and a load of scruffy books" to be seen, their frustration was such that only violence could relieve their feelings. The foreign trespassers had got all they deserved. The Choppers wished it had been more. Brinton charged them all and left Desk Sergeant Mutford to book them.

Sir George was thoughtful. "Good thing Miss Seeton helped find that hidden panel when she did. Nigel and Louise are going to live there, sooner or later. Not a good start to married life, burglars and treasure-hunters forever breaking into the place. Not as if it was worth that much, from what you say, but people do exaggerate. The children would never know a moment's peace."

"The word will get around. I'll see to that."

"Offer it to the museum once the legal people have decided, perhaps—like that ghastly Devil Henry painting. Not at all the sort of thing I'd care to live with."

"Dr. Braxted will be thrilled."

"Articles in academic journals, she says. The Roman hoard was a good start, but the priest's hole and the rest will put her and the museum right on the map."

"It was the map that caused all the trouble." Then Brinton laughed. "Talking of trouble—do you realise, Sir George, there's something odd about what happened last night?"

"The whole business has been dashed odd," said Sir George.

Brinton shook his head, and laughed again. "Trouble, did I say? That was unfair. Oh, Miss Seeton was in it from the start—drawing her sketches, finding the painting, and the gold, and the buttons and buckles—but she wasn't there last night! She stayed fast asleep right through, just like anyone else..."

And the superintendent laughed so heartily that Sir George, fond of Miss Seeton as he was, found that he, too, was laughing.

Back from their hard-earned leave, Chief Superintendent Delphick and Sergeant Ranger thankfully resumed regular detective service. During their absence the office had been purged of every single security file. They could, at last, talk to each other without having to stretch over, or peer round, teetering piles of paper.

"I suppose we'll never find out who murdered Gabriel Crassweller," said Bob, with a hint of regret. "Or what happens to the traitor—whoever it might be..."

In Plummergen, Miss Seeton caught the Brettenden bus, taking her latest watercolour, that amusing avian *Dignity and Impudence*, to be framed.

Preview

Miss Seeton Flies High

Lucky Miss Seeton! A modest Premium Bond win means a whole week in magical Glastonbury. She can draw and drink in the surroundings, just what she needs for her scene-painting role in the village production of 'Camelot'.

By coincidence, the kidnapped Heir to an industrial family may be hidden around there and Chief Superintendent Delphick has asked the ex-art teacher to create some of her famous, insightful sketches. Even he is nonplussed by the resulting images of capering sheep in straitjackets, flashing false teeth!

But the Heir is in danger, a murderer is lurking, and the first victim may not be the last. Then fortune favors Miss S again, her raffle ticket winning her a hot air balloon flight, and well, it's just amazing what you can see from above …

The new Miss Seeton mystery

COMING SOON!

About the Miss Seeton series

Retired art teacher Miss Seeton steps in where Scotland Yard stumbles. Armed with only her sketch pad and umbrella, she is every inch an eccentric English spinster and at every turn the most lovable and unlikely master of detection.

Further titles in the series—

Picture Miss Seeton
A night at the opera strikes a chord of danger when Miss Seeton witnesses a murder . . . and paints a portrait of the killer.

Miss Seeton Draws the Line
Miss Seeton is enlisted by Scotland Yard when her paintings of a little girl turn the young subject into a model for murder.

Witch Miss Seeton
Double, double, toil and trouble sweep through the village when Miss Seeton goes undercover . . . to investigate a local witches' coven!

Miss Seeton Sings
Miss Seeton boards the wrong plane and lands amidst a gang of European counterfeiters. One false note, and her new destination is deadly indeed.

Odds on Miss Seeton
Miss Seeton in diamonds and furs at the roulette table? It's all a clever disguise for the high-rolling spinster . . . but the game of money and murder is all too real.

Miss Seeton, By Appointment
Miss Seeton is off to Buckingham Palace on a secret mission—but to foil a jewel heist, she must risk losing the Queen's head . . . and her own neck!

Starring Miss Seeton
Miss Seeton's playing a backstage role in the village's annual Christmas pantomime. But the real drama is behind the scenes . . . when the next act turns out to be murder!

Miss Seeton Undercover
The village is abuzz, as a TV crew searches for a rare apple, the Plummergen Peculier—while police hunt a murderous thief . . . and with Miss Seeton at the centre of it all.

Miss Seeton Rules
Royalty comes to Plummergen, and the villagers are plotting a grand impression. But when Princess Georgina goes missing, Miss Seeton herself has questions to answer.

Sold to Miss Seeton
Miss Seeton accidentally buys a mysterious antique box at auction . . . and finds herself crossing paths with some very dangerous characters!

Sweet Miss Seeton
Miss Seeton is stalked by a confectionary sculptor, just as a spate of suspicious deaths among the village's elderly residents calls for her attention.

Bonjour, Miss Seeton
After a trip to explore the French countryside, a case of murder awaits Miss Seeton back in the village . . . and a shocking revelation.

Miss Seeton's Finest Hour
War-time England, and a young Miss Emily Seeton's suspicious sketches call her loyalty into question—until she is recruited to uncover a case of sabotage.

Miss Seeton Quilts the Village
Miss Seeton lends her talents to the village scheme to create a giant quilted tapestry. But her intuitive sketches reveal a startlingly different perspective, involving murder.

About Heron Carvic
and Hamilton Crane

The Miss Seeton series was created by Heron Carvic; and continued after his death first by Peter Martin writing as Hampton Charles, and later by Sarah J. Mason under the pseudonym Hamilton Crane.

Heron Carvic was an actor and writer, most recognisable today for his voice portrayal of the character Gandalf in the first BBC Radio broadcast version of *The Hobbit*, and appearances in several television productions, including early series of *The Avengers* and *Dr Who*.

Born Geoffrey Richard William Harris in 1913, he held several early jobs including as an interior designer and florist, before developing a successful dramatic career and his public persona of Heron Carvic. He only started writing the Miss Seeton novels in the 1960s, after using her in a short story. Heron Carvic died in a car accident in Kent in 1980.

Hamilton Crane is the pseudonym used by Sarah J. Mason when writing 13 sequels and one prequel to the Miss Seeton series. She has also written detective fiction under her own name, but should not be confused with the Sarah Mason (no middle initial) who writes a rather different kind of book.

After half a century in Hertfordshire (if we ignore four years in Scotland and one in New Zealand), Sarah J. Mason now lives in Somerset—within easy reach of the beautiful city of Wells, and just far enough from Glastonbury to avoid the annual traffic jams.

Note from the Publisher

While he was alive, series creator Heron Carvic had tremendous fun imagining Emily Seeton and the supporting cast of characters.

In an enjoyable 1977 essay Carvic recalled how, after having first used her in three short stories, "Miss Seeton upped and demanded a book"—and that if "she wanted to satirize detective novels in general and elderly lady detectives in particular, he would let her have her head ..."

You can now **read one of those first Miss Seeton short stories** and **Heron Carvic's essay in full**, as well as receive updates on further releases in the series, by signing up at farragobooks.com/miss-seeton-signup